W·CLARK
PUBLISHING
A STATEMENT IN LITERATURE

LICKIN' LICENSE II

More Sex, More Saga
A Tale of Street Erotica
by
Intelligent Allah

Wahida Clark Presents Publishing, LLC
60 Evergreen Place
Suite 904
East Orange, New Jersey 07018
973-678-9982
www.wclarkpublishing.com

ISBN 13-digit 978-0981854571
ISBN 10-digit 0-9818545-7-5

Library of Congress Catalog Number 2012902891
    1. Urban, Lesbian, Erotica, New York, Atlanta, African-American, Street Lit – Fiction

Cover design and layout by Oddball Design
Book interior design by Nuance Art.*.
Contributing Editors: JazzyPen Communications

Printed in United States
Green & Company Printing, LLC
www.greenandcompany.biz

Book Reviews and Author Praise
For
Lickin' License 1 & 2

"This incarcerated author, who has a great ear for trash talk and urban slang, also writes with a true feel for the streets... The lesbian sex scenes are hot, hot, hot. Heck, so are the hetero scenes...Fans on high-octane sexual street lit will love it."
-libraryjournal.com

***

"Turning obvious fiction into something plausible is a true sign of a talented author and Intelligent Allah easily does so within the pages of Lickin' License II making for an entertaining read."
-theubs.com

***

"'Lickin' License' is a gritty, in-your-face looking at what jealousy and envy will do to friendships. Just as the title suggests, this novel contains steamy sex scenes... I recommend this story to readers of urban lit."

Acknowledgements

All praise is due to the Father Allah and The Nation of Gods and Earths for nurturing my introspection and ability to see things for what they are and not what they often appear to be. Much love to my mother for supporting me in every way imaginable. And my physical brother Merciful Uneeke, the Twitter King (Lol).

To Wahida Clark, thanks for staying real and staying focused. Props to everyone at WCP. Ne Ne Capri (The Pussy Trap), unfortunately my predicament can be a hindrance, but I respect your contribution of something official to the industry---maybe next time. Joan Burke Stanford (Jazzy Pen), thanks for another thorough job. LC (LC-Devine and FlippinFlint2First), you remain an inspiration. Thanks for making Lickinlicense.com a reality. Zenola Watkins, you embody the word friend. To Nut, Hasan, Kahlil and Angel aka Henry from Wagner. Good lookin' on the feedback on my first draft.

Big up to Don Diva for rating Lickin' License a #1 bestseller in your magazine. To the book reviewers like Lashonda, Delonya Conyers, Rollie Welch and the customers like Margo Horn, Cutelady113 and anyone else who posted reader reviews online. To Barnes & Noble, the Mom and Pops, libraries, street vendors and everyone else who got Lickin' License in the hands of readers.

To my manager Holladay (Harsh Reality), Whyz Ruler (IBI) and everyone else who promoted Lickin' license and supported the movement. Victorious (East Medina), Be Born, Ib and Rasheen. Papoose, good lookin' on the promo flick. My man Groove, thanks for coppin' the book and having a landline all these years to help me keep my ears open to the world that matters.

My heads in the pen who copped Lickin' License or who help keep me stay focused and often inspire me by just maintaining your authenticity in a world of frauds. LA, I'll be following you soon. Rell, Dakim, Divine G, Casino Mike, Bar, S.P. aka Seto Kiva, Cincere, Jullian, Cub, J.O, Ish, Trini Don, Tee, Ty, Dre, Renny, Salih, Juice, Papooch, Gysia, Shakim, Frans, VJ, Jah Gunz. My peeps who exited this cipher of incarceration with their sanity and ambition intact: Dashiem, Sha-Rize, Johnson, Ray, Starmel and Natural. There's a million more comrades in this struggle, but space is limited.

To every Professor, incarcerated person and volunteer who taught a writing class I took, I owe you. To those who I'll be learning from in the future, I'm hungry for your knowledge. Every person who shed some light on the publishing/writing world in person or through the countless books I've read— thanks. For everybody about to read the latest installment of Lickin' License, I'm lookin' forward to your posts. (Lickinlicense.com, Facebook/IntelligentAllah, Intelligent Allah, #95A4315, WoodBourne Corr. Facility, Box 1000, Woodbourne, NY 12788.)

Thanks for the support and motivation!

Peace.

CHAPTER ONE
CANDY

P ut it in my mouth," Candy begged as she dropped to her knees and reached for Rich's dick.

Rich cradled her head in his palm, steering her toward his dick as Vanessa juggled his balls in her mouth. He tilted his head back and gazed at the sky from the 21-story balcony of the MGM Grand Hotel in Las Vegas.

Candy twirled her tongue around the head of his 10-inch anaconda, then gripped it with both of her hands. She closed her eyes and savored the juices remaining from the past twenty minutes when he had sexed Vanessa against the sliding glass door of the balcony. Candy removed her hands and took in almost all Rich had to offer. She could feel the blood circulating in his veins as it pulsated his erection. She pulled Vanessa's head until they both were working Rich's shaft.

"Damn," Rich mumbled. "Shit."

2

Candy's eyes rolled up to his dark, chiseled chest, then to Vanessa's bushy 'fro and flawless, light skin. For over two years the trio had been experiencing an unconditional love that had snatched Candy from a world of lesbianism and introduced the curvaceous beauty to her bisexual identity. It didn't matter that she had sexed some of the most notorious hustlers in Harlem before she ventured into the world of girls. She was done with men until Vanessa convinced her to have a threesome.

"Yeah, work that shit," Rich mumbled.

Candy watched the dark skin of Rich's six pack illuminate under the sunlight as he gripped her head tighter. She knew it was a sign that he was about to cum. She worked her tongue more and swallowed deeper. Her lips touched Vanessa's as they both pleasured Rich's thick shaft.

"That's it," Rich grunted before his knees buckled.

Candy closed her eyes and swallowed every drop of cream that spurted from Rich's chocolate rod.

"Damn, y'all ain't nothin' to fuck with," he said as he regained his composure.

Candy turned to Vanessa and they began kissing passionately. In seconds, Candy's amazon figure was entangled with Vanessa's petite frame. The two lovers pleased each other on the air mattress beneath the sky. Vanessa's head was clenched between Candy's thick thighs while Candy's tongue stimulated Vanessa's clit.

Rich leaned against the door, watching the women

engaged in sixty-nine.

"Ahh, ahh," Candy moaned. The redbone with the face of a model palmed both of Vanessa's small buttcheeks, slipped her tongue inside of Vanessa, then back and forth to her clit.

"Yes, God," Vanessa muttered as her body began to shake uncontrollably into a climax.

Candy slurped Vanessa's juices, probing the slippery folds of her jittery frame until she was still. When they separated, Candy stared into Vanessa's blinking eyes. Candy always enjoyed the expressions of satisfaction she gave Vanessa.

Rich grinned and stepped off the hotel balcony into their suite.

Candy gently smacked Vanessa's butt. "Shower time."

The two women headed inside, showered and dressed. Candy was sitting on the king-sized bed, tying the straps of her Roberto Cavalli heels around her ankles when she got a glimpse of Vanessa that caused her to contemplate. Vanessa stood in front of a mirror applying cocoa butter to her face. The Bohemian beauty was dressed in a paisley dress, Howard University T-shirt and short blue blazer. Beside her clutch on a nearby chair was a small .380-caliber Grendell.

Vanessa turned around. "What's up? I can see you watching me through the mirror." "Nothing." Candy smiled.

"You never was a good liar and you know I don't enjoy people pissing in my ear."

Candy huffed. "I was just thinking about all we been through. How the hell somebody like me, with the hottest salon in Harlem and a line of hair care products, end up hiding out in Vegas?"

"Hiding implies that you're scared of someone. And scared people don't empty a full clip into someone's face at point-blank range like you did to Chase."

Candy watched Vanessa walk toward her. Vanessa put her hands on Candy's shoulders and gently massaged her. Candy placed her hands on Vanessa's waist, then palmed her butt. "What's funny is I've been on the streets of Harlem with hustlers and thugs damn near all my life," said Candy. "And you're the one who seems to be holding up better than me. Vanessa Denay, the college student raised in a Park Avenue condo. How did you, me, Rich . . . how did we end up here?"

A glassy look was developing in Vanessa's eyes. An image caused by emotionally painful droplets slowly released from her tear ducts. Vanessa's eyes began watering. She gently rubbed her hands over Candy's face. "Those bitches destroyed everything we were building. That's how we got here. And that's why every last one of them has to die."

The seriousness in Vanessa's eyes evoked all the memories and anger that Candy had been trying to suppress since she and Vanessa killed Chase. But Candy knew he deserved it. Rich had forced him to reveal who had helped him kidnap, torture, and molest Candy and then beat Rich's baby from her womb. Virtually everyone who was someone to the threesome was involved. Candy's former salon employees, Chanel, Meisha and Leah. Candy's ex-lover Vera and her twin brothers. Vanessa's former friend Mimi.

The more Candy thought of the guilty culprits, the angrier she became. The vindictiveness that circulated through Vanessa's veins pumped through Candy's blood as well. But it was Rich's constant reminder of the seriousness of their circumstances that had continuously worried Candy. Was it possible to murder seven people and get away with it? Was it worth the risk of losing the relationship and wealth they had worked hard to build? Rich answered no and Vanessa yes. Candy shifted back and forth on both sides of the coin.

"Feel this," said Vanessa, placing Candy's hand on her stomach.

Candy's head dropped and she closed her eyes as she felt where Rich's seed was once cultivated. Vanessa had gone through with an abortion, against Candy and Rich's wishes. It was a rebellious act Vanessa rationalized as a show of camaraderie since she and Candy were set to give birth around the same time until Candy's kidnapping ended that.

"I could never bring a child into this world until we take the people out of this world that took our child from your womb," Vanessa stated.

Her words reinvigorated Candy. They were the boost she needed but feared the flame to ignite her desire for revenge. She grabbed her iPhone off the bed and called Domingo. The mature young man was her link to the streets of New York City, the key to executing everyone on her hit list. He lived in Brooklyn's Red Hook Houses as did Vera and her brothers. He knew the other women involved through Candy's Shop. Domingo was a priceless asset. But Candy knew he was a hustler whose loyalty was to old white men with names like Benjamin Franklin and Ulysses Grant. It was for that reason Rich was always warning her not to trust Domingo.

"Mamita, you ready to have my baby or what?" Domingo answered the phone with his flirtatious Spanish accent.

Candy stared at the small screen on her phone, watching the young Latino sporting a fitted hat with his hometown of Brooklyn etched on it. "There's enough babies having babies in this world," she responded.

"Babies don't fill out a Magnum and pop Viagra like I do."

"Okay, enough of the *Comic View.* Let's get down to business."

"You talkin' my lingo, Mamita."

7

"What's new on Vera?"

"I wish I could say a hairdo, 'cause her wig piece is crazy, ya heard?"

Candy giggled.

"Real talk, though. She gonna be in the East with the whole cre—"

Candy stood up and cut Domingo's statement short. "The East as in East New York? Crew meaning Mimi, Chanel, Leah, and Meisha?"

"Everybody except the Twins," Domingo said.

"And I gotta call to find this out? When you was planning on tellin' me this?"

"When you drop Rich and pick me up."

"Comedy is cool, but time is precious, so don't waste mine."

"I got you, Mamita. You got some weeks before this go down. That's why I ain't tell you nothin' yet."

"Date, time? I need specifics."

"June nineteenth, all day."

"Father's Day," Candy said, nodding.

"Exactly. The Father's Day Tournament at Seventy-two Park in the East." Domingo explained that Vera and the other women would be at the annual Father's Day Basketball Tournament held in the park of P.S. 72. It was an East New York festivity that attracted hustlers and cheddar-chasing chicks like Chanel each year.

"So this should be simple," Candy said.

8

Domingo shook his head. "East New York, Brooklyn ain't the Upper East Side of Manhattan. We talkin' about the Murder Capital of New York City. The place where they started bustin' shots in Cypress Projects when the mayor was speaking about stopping gun violence. Don't think you just gonna come through, shoot shit up and bounce. If you don't come correct, don't come at all."

CHAPTER TWO
VANESSA

V anessa and Candy were discussing everything Domingo had just said. Although Vanessa had grown up in a wealthy, virtually crime-free neighborhood, she was not ignorant to East New York. Between the news coverage of the neighborhood being violent and Chanel's war stories of drama she saw being raised in the neighborhood, Vanessa knew that pulling off a multiple homicide would not be easy. A couple of years earlier, when Vanessa was simply a straight-A college student with an apartment in Greenwich Village and a fear of violence, she would have not even considered the task at hand. But her love for Rich and Candy, coupled with the drama that the trio had experienced, had transformed Vanessa into a woman who had killed in cold blood and knew more about guns than many men.

10

"We gotta plan this out right," Candy said.

Vanessa nodded. "On another note, you need to let Domingo know that flirting with you is disrespectful. I told him about that already."

"Girl, you know how he is. Been like that since I met him."

Vanessa shook her head. "That doesn't change the fact that it's disrespectful to me and Rich."

"It's not that serious."

Rich walked in the room, preceded by the scent of his cologne as he adjusted his striped tie on top of his Egyptian cotton shirt. "What's good?"

Vanessa looked at Candy, then Rich.

"Nothing." She flashed a cheesy smile.

Rich walked over to the bed, eyeing each woman. "The more y'all look all nervous the more I start to speculate." He plopped down on the bed. "So who gonna tell me something first?"

Candy looked at Rich and then reached for her iPhone on the bed.

"You gotta be quicker than that," Rich said as he snatched it up.

"A former drug dealer is tapping my phone," Candy said, sucking her teeth. "Guess I'm good enough to have sex with, but not good enough to trust, huh?"

Rich pressed redial.

Oh God, Vanessa thought, peeping the nervousness plastered on Candy's face. Vanessa could still envision when Rich chastised her and Candy days earlier after he discovered they were still in contact with Domingo. This was after they had conceived their plot. But Rich instructed them to forget the idea and to never contact Domingo again.

Rich stressed not only Domingo's untrustworthiness, but also that it was important that their contact with people in New York be limited. Vanessa had maintained contact with her father and her literary agent. Candy stayed in contact with the manager who oversaw the employees of her hair care line. Rich spent a limited amount of time at the exotic car rental service he co-owned with his uncle. Rich stressed that the trio's presence in New York City should be minimal, because there was speculation that they had killed Chase. Although two years had passed since Chase took his last breath, they had to be careful because murder had no statute of limitations.

Rich let out a deep breath when he saw Domingo's face pop up on Candy's iPhone. He hung up immediately, then turned to Candy. "Why it's so hard for you to listen to me?" He turned to Vanessa. "I taught you to use a gun. I'm the one that was duckin' bullets in the streets and puttin' in work. I seen grimey dudes like Domingo pull snake moves on a regular. I'm puttin' you on to shit because I lived it." He tossed Candy's phone on the bed.

"You ain't the only one that was in the streets," Candy

said.

Rich grinned. "It's a big difference between fuckin' gangsters and living the life of a G."

"Gangsters don't leave beef unresolved," said Candy.

Rich laughed and shook his head. "Candy, you're a beautician not an expert on gangsters and beef."

"Fuck you, Rich!" Candy barked.

"All right, all right, all right." Vanessa stepped in front of them. "We're not actors and this is not some television drama. There's no way I'm going to sit here and allow Chanel and the rest of these hos to damage our relationship anymore than they have already."

Candy looked at Rich. "You know I love you and Vanessa more than life itself."

"Then give me the benefit of the doubt on my assessment of this situation. We got nothing to gain."

"Peace of mind, Rich. That's what we stand to gain," Candy said.

"She's right," Vanessa agreed. "We haven't been the same since this situation happened." She recapped how their relationship had been reduced to a war that pitted Rich against her and Candy. Rich had managed to retire from the streets that he had run on since a preteen. He knew all that the streets entailed and was adamant about staying away from them. On the opposite side of Rich's argument was Vanessa's and Candy's newfound thirst for gunplay and their relentless hunger for revenge.

"I can't rest until they're dead," Candy said.

13

"Me, either," Vanessa added. "We've been holding back because of you, but it's time to finish what they started."

"Pardon me," said Candy as she answered her phone and smirked at Rich. "You sure you need me?" Candy huffed. "Okay, Okay." She dropped her phone and shook her head.

"Who the fuck was that?" Rich demanded to know. "Better not had been Domingo again."

"I gotta go to New York City."

Rich shook his head.

A million things were running through Vanessa's mind. New York City was off limits. It was a zone that could place them in jeopardy of prison.

"What's up?" Vanessa asked Candy.

"The business." She explained that the executive team she oversaw needed her physical presence at an important meeting.

"You know the rules." Rich shook his head.

"Cash Rules," Candy said. "You make things a lot easier for me, but I never depended on a man for money. My ship is sinking and they need the captain."

Rich stood up and looked at both of his women. "I guess this is Fuck Rich Day."

Candy frowned. "That's the fuckin' problem. It ain't about you, Rich. The world don't revolve around Rich."

"A reckless mouth ain't gonna do none of us no good, so

turn down the volume and swallow the venom."

Candy reached under the mattress and pulled out a .22-caliber Walther PPK, then tucked the small handgun in her Prada bag. She turned to Vanessa. "I got better shit to do than listen to this, and I know you do."

Vanessa kissed Rich on the cheek. "I love you, Rich." She paused. "But if we wanna save our relationship, we have to get rid of the people causing us problems." Vanessa walked out of the door with Candy.

* * *

Vanessa rode with Candy down the crowded elevator in silence. They exited at ground level and strolled through the hotel lobby toward the front door.

"Where are we going?" Vanessa asked. "New York?"

"Not yet, just where our feet take us."

"That's real definitive."

"Was I wrong?" Candy asked.

"Huh?"

"Rich. How I handled him. Was I wrong?"

"You were truthful, and that's all that matters."

"We're in Vegas and you still can't call a spade a spade." Candy chuckled.

"It's Sin City, I'm entitled to a lie or two every now and then. But I think you handled Rich fine. It's a harsh reality that I know he understands."

"Hope so."

Vanessa and Candy walked in silence down the

congested Las Vegas strip filled with bright lights and what seemed like every sound imaginable. They had been there for over a year, but Vanessa hardly enjoyed the lively setting. The ancient Egyptian-styled architecture. The limousines coasting. The rowdy college kids. The classy couples draped in diamonds and custom clothing. Vegas had a life just as vibrant as its gamblers. Vanessa wanted to enjoy it, but she couldn't. Her days were filled with thoughts of revenge or arguments with Rich over those thoughts. And beyond that, Vanessa was homesick. She removed her iPad from her handbag and began rereading some of her diary. She had planned to turn it into a novel since her agent was stressing her to meet the deadline for her second book.

Kelly Roland's "Motivation" sounded and Candy pulled out her smartphone at the tune of the ringtone. It was Domingo on a face time call.

"What's good, Mamita?"

"You tell me," Candy said, looking at Domingo's face on the small screen.

"Figured it was something since your man Rich playing phone games with me."

Candy thought of Rich snatching her phone earlier. "That's a long story you don't need to read."

Vanessa inched close beside Candy. "Hey, Domingo." She put her iPad away.

"What's up my soul sister?"

16

"Listen, Domingo. I know you might not mean any harm by it, but like I said before, I would appreciate it if you toned down the flirting with Candy."

"I ain't even know you was serious about that, ya heard?"

"Yes, I was," Vanessa said.

"What, you mad I ain't givin' you no rhythm, my soul sister? You fly, but I like them big booty girls with them tig old bitties like Candy."

Vanessa sucked her teeth and rolled her eyes.

"This is what I'm talking about. Show me some respect."

"Anyway—"

"No, it's not *anyway*. You're not going to keep disrespecting me, Domingo, and that's that!" Vanessa raised her voice.

"Calm down, Vanessa." Candy looked at Domingo. "Try to curb your tongue."

"All right, all right, all right. Anyway, like I was saying before Vanessa caught a titty attack. I just got a e-vite from Leah inviting me to her baby shower. She was tellin' me about it before, but she just sent the invite at the last minute."

"Really? Leah?" Candy responded, clearly anxious to hear about her former employee.

"You got a big ass, but I wouldn't blow smoke up it."

"Where is the shower gonna be at?" Candy watched Domingo's head turn away from the screen.

"Yo, Ma, let me holler at you," he said, then paused. "Oh, it's like that, Ma?"

"Domingo!" Candy barked into the phone.

He turned back to her. "Mamita, it's bad enough you ain't ready to let me taste that and see why they call you Candy, but now you cock blockin' too."

"I'm payin' you to handle business. You can get your dick wet on your own time."

"All right." Domingo turned back away from the phone, then faced it again. "I gotta go get this little broad, so I'm hangin' up. But I'm a send you that evite Leah hit me with, ya heard? One."

Candy turned and hung up her phone. "His little ass is too much."

Vanessa rolled her eyes. "Tell me something I don't know."

Minutes later, the women were reading the invitation. The location of the baby shower was in the Brooklyn neighborhood of DUMBO. The date was weeks away.

"This is it," said Candy.

"You wanna shoot up a baby shower?" Vanessa inquired, her eyebrows elevated.

Candy looked into her eyes. "They didn't care about my baby when they beat him out of me."

Vanessa knew she was right. The rules had been broken a long time ago and Leah was the mastermind behind the plot that changed everything. She had destroyed the life Candy was bearing. Someone had to pay. Whether in broad daylight on the doorstep of a church, or at night as the culprits slept in the privacy of their bedrooms, wherever they were and whoever was at fault, they would suffer.

CHAPTER THREE

RICH

A fter Candy and Vanessa left Rich in the suite, he found his way to the craps table downstairs. He blew $12,000 before taking a seat at the bar. Over shots of Ciroc, he reflected on his surroundings and how his life had spiraled out of control. It was a twist of irony for a thirty-seven-year-old whose discipline and intellect had allowed him to dominate countless women and regulate a large portion of the drug trade in New York City.

Now, after escaping death on the streets and having little value for women, he was faced with two women he loved who were bringing him back into a world of murder and mayhem. He felt guilty. Guilty because he had created a monster the moment he placed a .380-caliber Llama in Vanessa's hands and taught her to shoot. Although Vanessa would not hesitate to squeeze a trigger, Rich knew that it took more than an index finger

20

to survive and handle beef effectively. Quick thinking and a calm demeanor were necessary to survive shootouts and evade police.

Rich downed his third shot of Ciroc and stepped off from the bar.

He stopped and looked at the text message from Free, an employee and associate of the luxury car rental company Rich co-owned. Free reminded Rich that profits were down for the fourth month straight. Rich shook his head and continued walking.

As he navigated through the loud casino, weaving in between crowds, his ears pulled his eyes to a familiar voice at a nearby poker table. He grinned at the sight of King Justice Allah. King was a goon from the Brownsville section of Brooklyn. He and Rich had met in a gambling spot in Harlem and had done a lot of business together. King specialized in squeezing drug dealers until there was no more money left in their pockets, and Rich had pointed out a number of competitors in the drug game to King. Rich had not seen King since he disappeared about five years earlier following a shootout involving King that left a Dominican kingpin in a wheelchair.

He don't look much different. Rich gazed at the man who shared the same dark chocolate complexion with himself. But while Rich's athletic frame was that of a middleweight boxer, King could pass for a Chicago Bears linebacker. A thin black diamond chain hung from his neck to the white T-shirt that fell just below his waistline, above the pockets of his crisp Red Monkey jeans.

Just as Rich neared King, the Brooklynite turned to him. His deep baritone voiced, "You know I don't let nobody creep up on me. A king knows every square inch of his cipher." He stood and hugged Rich.

"What's good, King?" The duo parted and Rich stared at King's sneaky grin. "Been a long time."

"Actual fact. Had to spread my wings so I could fly." King told Rich he had moved to Atlanta and opened a modeling agency.

"So you got tired of putting your hands in the pockets of hustlers?"

"It's hard to get tired of easy money." King chuckled. "But change is inevitable."

"As a man that retired from the game, I can feel you."

"Retired from the game?" King's round face scrunched up. "What that mean? You got a 401K from your connect?"

"Still got jokes."

"And you still gotta be hustlin'. Dude like you been in the street before you could spell street. And what's up with Chase?"

Rich was thrown off by the mentioning of Chase's name. King was the first person Rich had crossed paths with from the streets who knew Chase. "I left the game, Chase stayed. That's where we parted."

22

"Parted? The same Chase that did five years for you? You can't separate the sun from its light."

"A lot of things changed since you broke out. If a notorious extortionist can become the owner of a modeling agency, anything is possible."

King nodded and grinned. "Change is inevitable, but a wise man changes for the better."

As they talked, Rich noticed a slender cocoa-toned woman in her mid-twenties gliding his way. Her slanted eyes met his, conveying her interest in him without a word. Her full lips that were coated with lipstick which matched the burgundy dress clenching her curvaceous body. She drew the attention of every man that she stepped past in her open-toe heels. She smiled as she stopped beside King, her eyes still on Rich.

King put his hand on her shoulder and said, "This is—"

"Zora," she reached out and shook Rich's hand. "Zora Phillips."

"Rich."

"My personal assistant," said King. "We're out here on business."

Zora sized up Rich, eyeing his navy blue Armani suit and diamond cufflinks. "You here on business also?"

"If it don't make money, it don't make sense."

"True hustler," King said, turning to Zora. "Rich used to switch up his cars like Nicki Minaj switch up wigs."

King and Rich began reminiscing about their heyday

on the streets. Rich could see Zora becoming more intrigued with each word she heard about him. He fueled her interest by recounting tales of him buying out the bar at nightclubs and making it rain big faces at strip clubs. He even tossed in the stories of him purchasing his first condo at age twenty-one and him hosting a Y2K Theme New Year's Eve bash in the Hamptons.

"So, you here all alone?" she asked. "No Mrs. Rich?" Rich thought about Vanessa and Candy as he caught a glimpse of Zora's hips shift. Before he had met Vanessa and Candy, he would not have hesitated to answer Zora's question with a negative. Back then, his BlackBerry was overflowing with women's phone numbers. The word faithful was something that never entered his mind, nor exited his lips. He looked at Zora. "I rarely travel alone."

She smiled. "You seemed kind of apprehensive about that response."

"That's a matter of perception."

"Pardon self," King interjected. "A brother gotta use the bathroom." He grinned at Rich, clearly indicating he was giving Rich and Zora some space. King stepped off.

Rich wanted to be faithful, no matter how angry he was with Vanessa and Candy, so he tried to change the subject. "Where you from?"

"It's not about where *I'm from*. It's about where *we're* going."

"Can't accuse you of being indirect."

"You look like you can appreciate a woman who knows what she wants and is not afraid to go after it."

"So drive this bus and just tell me the destination."

"My hotel room, if the traffic is clear and we don't get pulled over for speeding."

Staring at Zora's luscious lips, Rich couldn't help but imagine them wrapped around his dick. He began to rationalize cheating on Vanessa and Candy by pointing to the drama he had been through with them earlier. They were flirting with death in total disregard for him, so he was not obligated to honor their relationship.

Zora looked at her watch, then pulled out the keycard to her room.

Rich stared directly into her sexy eyes. "You really want it, but I hope you can handle it."

"My suite is upstairs."

Rich led the way toward the elevator, but he stopped alongside Zora at the bar where she bought a bottle of Moet. They sped to the elevator and Rich stood behind her. His eyes were stuck on her ass like the triangle logo on a pair of Guess jeans. He could tell she was either wearing a thong or nothing underneath her sheer silk dress.

The elevator doors opened and several people stepped out before Zora and Rich stepped inside. Zora pressed the button of her floor, then stepped back as the doors closed. "I knew the moment our eyes met if there was a Mrs. Rich, she wasn't a problem."

"There's actually two misses. And since they're probably somewhere pleasing each other, it's only right I have some fun."

Zora's eyebrows arched. "Pleasing each other? So one woman ain't enough?"

"Why else would we be headed to your hotel room?"

Zora laughed. But her smiles were cut short when the elevator came to an abrupt halt, flinging her into Rich's arms.

"You okay?" Rich asked, inhaling her perfume as he cradled her in his arms. "I'm okay, but I think we're stuck."

Rich stepped over and pressed a few buttons. The elevator didn't move. He opened the emergency box and tried to place a call on the phone. "The line is down."

"I'll use my cell," Zora said, pulling out her Sidekick. She called the hotel lobby and was told there was a problem with all of the elevators and they were being worked on. "Thirty minutes?" She shook her head, then hung up and looked at Rich. "Get comfortable, because they said a half-hour, which really means an hour."

"Damn. I think this AC went down too." Rich removed his tie and took off his blazer.

Zora held up the bottle of champagne. "This should cool you off," she said as Rich removed his shirt and tank top. "Nice six pack." Zora pressed the cold bottle of Moet against Rich's stomach.

He inched back and took the bottle.

26

"I'm starting to sweat already," Zora said, her bracelets jingling as she fanned her face with her hand.

"You need to lose that dress."

"You just wanna see my goodies." Zora giggled.

"When you got a sweet tooth like mine and you're hungry, you do more than look at goodies."

Zora stripped down to her thong and bra. She began unbuckling Rich's belt and helping him step out of his pants. He stood with nothing on but his Polo boxer briefs and dress socks. Zora's eyes were stuck on his underwear as she stepped back.

"Time to celebrate," Rich declared. "I'm trapped in an elevator with a beautiful woman that's half naked." Rich licked his lips and began shaking the champagne bottle. "What more could a man ask for?" He popped the cork of the bottle and doused Zora with suds.

"Stop." She giggled, covering her face with her hands.

Rich watched the champagne drip down her cleavage over her smooth brown skin to her navel. Beneath her thong. In between her legs. His dick grew hard at the sight of the champagne glistening off her chocolate flesh. The wetness of her thong highlighted the mound between her legs. Rich drank from the bottle, then passed it to Zora.

She took a swig and poured some on Rich, screaming playfully.

Rich wrestled the bottle from Zora and pinned her against the elevator wall, removing her breast from her bra. Slipping his tongue in her mouth, he kissed her passionately before he drifted to her neck. He licked the trail of Moet that led down her soft skin.

"Umph...ahh," she moaned as Rich circled one of her nipples with his tongue.

He massaged the champagne into her other B-cup. Her nipple hardened in his hand before he took it in his mouth. His hand slipped into her thong, causing her to whimper as he worked one breast, then the other.

"Please," Zora moaned. Her back arched, breasts pushing forward, deeper into Rich's mouth as she put her hand over his. They applied the perfect amount of pressure to her clit.

Rich stepped back and dripped some more Moet on her chest and followed it down her chest with his tongue. In one swift motion he removed her thong and placed his tongue against her clit.

"Oh shit," Zora blurted. She instinctively hoisted one of her legs over Rich's shoulder.

Rich could feel her body twitch as he jabbed her clit with his tongue. The taste of the champagne mixed with the juices of her shaven pussy was surreal. He could feel her manicured nails digging into his scalp through his 360 waves.

"Eat me. God. Eat me."

Rich palmed her soft buttcheeks. He lifted her from the elevator floor while swiping his tongue back and forth from her clit to inside the warm flesh between her pussy lips.

Zora gripped his head tighter. "Come on. I'm about to cum. Make me cum, Daddy."

Rich felt her legs lock around his head as she reached a climax. Her body continued to twitch as he let her down from the wall. He took a step back, her sweet nectar dripping from his lips. He dropped his underwear. After Zora was only stable on her feet for a minute, she kneeled and took Rich into her mouth. The sensation of her tongue glazing the shaft of his dick was overpowering him. He let out a quick grunt as she wrapped her lips around the head of his dick. Rich closed his eyes, pulling her back with him as he leaned against the elevator door.

Zora cupped Rich's balls. She rubbed them gently and applied more suction to the head of his dick as she worked her way up and down it.

Rich looked down at the straight hair trailing from her head to the small of her back. He grabbed a handful and pulled Zora to her feet with the perfect balance of care and aggression. He looked into her eyes as she rose.

"How you want it?" she asked.

Rich spun her, until she was facing the wall. He leaned behind her and moved her shiny mane to the side, kissing on her neck. He could feel her body tense up within his hands. Rich ran one of his strong hands between the crack of her ass before sliding his thick rod in between with the other hand.

"Urgh," Zora grunted as she balled her fist against the

wall while Rich stretched the tunnel between her legs.

"Damn, girl." He let out a deep breath, then worked up a slow place. There was a gentle clapping sound from his force against her behind. As Zora moaned louder, Rich stroked harder.

"Come on. Make me cum again," she begged.

Rich reached around to her breasts. Her hardened nipples were between his fingers. His solid frame engulfed her slender body. Champagne and sweat dripped from them in the elevator, which seemed to be hotter than a sauna. His body slid against hers, friction producing heat almost as intense as her tight pussy.

"Come on. Do me!" Zora screamed.

Rich rammed harder each time, deeper with each stroke. As what seemed like hours passed, Rich unhanded Zora. She faced him. Sweat trickled down her high cheekbones. Stepping forward, Rich inserted himself inside of her.

Zora blurted out a moan as she grabbed Rich's back and wrapped her legs around him.

"Yeah," Rich said. He cradled her rear and pumped into her, causing her sweat-soaked back to slide up and down the elevator wall. Rich leaned down, taking one of her erect nipples into his mouth.

"That feels so good. Suck it. Fuck me, Daddy."

Rich nearly dropped Zora as the elevator jolted. He could hear gears shifting and the motor at work. In seconds the elevator began quickly dropping. "Oh shit."

Rich looked around.

"Fuck me. Forget the elevator. Finish fucking me," Zora pulled Rich closer as her voice rose. "Come on, Daddy."

Rich sped up his pace, while peeking at the numbers on the elevator panel, which illuminated as it descended. They were on the eighth floor. Rich stroked harder and quicker.

"I'm about to cum!" Zora screamed. Her eyes rolled in the back of her head and her lips quivered.

Suddenly, the elevator sped up. It dropped to the ground floor in seconds. Rich and Zora fell to the floor with Zora on top of him, riding his dick as he held her close to protect her from the fall.

As the door opened, Zora slammed her pussy against Rich twice and screamed, "Ahhhh, I'm cumming."

Rich looked up and spotted several medics and firemen backed by a crowd of people who were waiting to get on the elevator.

Rich and Zora scurried to gather their clothes and dress as people laughed.

"What the fuck!" Candy said, peering at Rich with vengeance in her eyes as she stepped from behind the crowd with Vanessa in tow.

"That ho is dead!" Vanessa declared, gripping her clutch that Rich knew held her gun.

He quickly zipped up his pants and put on his shoes. He looked at Candy and Vanessa. "Things ain't always what they seem. Let me explain."

31

CHAPTER FOUR
DOMINGO

G reen eyes, dark brown hair and an inviting smile usually attracted older women to the stylish teen. His confidence, designer clothes and specs gave him a swagger that added to his magnetic personality. The slick-talking Puerto Rican named Domingo was seated at Vera's dining room table breaking apart an ounce of PR 80 weed he had recently picked up in Los Angeles. He began packing his blunt with the weed. He looked around the small Brooklyn apartment, thinking of the irony of Vera having no knowledge that it was him who let Candy into her abode and helped her trash it. That was several years ago when Candy was trying to sniff out the sex tape of her turning Vanessa out. It was that video, in large part that contributed to Candy and Vanessa now being on a mission to kill Vera. Now Domingo was sitting in Vera's home and she had no idea

32

the young hustler and Candy were plotting her downfall.

Vera walked into the dining room, her long black and brown dreads running down her back. Domingo ran his hand through his hair as he eyed the thick, dark-skinned woman with the oversized ass. He dropped a wad of money on the table. A crispy stack of hundreds he had gotten from moving bogus credit cards and gift cards. Plastic money was his primary hustle.

"You gonna start giving me a break on this plastic or what?" Vera flashed the American Express Card Domingo had just sold to her.

"A break for a break, ya heard?" Domingo said.

Vera propped her hand against her thin waist. "What's that supposed to mean?"

Domingo pointed at her butt. "You break me off, I give you a break."

"Domingo, you know I got my lickin' license."

"So

. We both eat pussy." Domingo sparked his blunt. "And you thought we ain't have nothin' in common."

"Come on, Domingo. You know I don't do men."

He exhaled a cloud of smoke. His head became light and Vera's pretty face and figure looked better by the second. "I ain't gonna lie, you makin' my dick hard, Ma." Domingo grabbed his dick through his Polo jeans. "But it don't matter if you don't do men, ya heard? You like gettin' that chocha ate and I'm hungry. If that ain't a perfect match, I don't know what is."

Vera pursed her lips. "You're high right now."

"High and horny. Good combination."

Vera shook her head and began walking past Domingo and into the kitchen.

Domingo grabbed her hand. "So you ain't gon' let me taste that?" He took another pull of his blunt.

Vera looked down at Domingo, his face inches from her pussy. "Unless you got a slit and a soft touch, you can forget this."

Exhaling smoke, Domingo grinned. He reached in his pocket with his free hand and pulled out an American Express Black Card. "It's enough paper on this plastic to refurnish your whole apartment, plus get you a couple of outfits." His eyes rolled from hers to between her legs. "You can close your eyes and pretend I got D-cups and a weave, ya heard? All I wanna do is please you with this." He ran his tongue over his lips.

Domingo could tell Vera was in deep thought by the way her eyes probed him and kept coming back to the card in his hand. He knew women well. He had seen and done more than most nineteen-year-olds during his fast-paced life where he ran with hustlers twice his age. He didn't have to be psychic to know that Vera was trying to balance the benefits of receiving oral sex from a man served on a platter with a lengthy line of credit as a side dish, versus a wet tongue from a woman. *It's a no-brainer.* Domingo knew that she was sitting on a stack of overdue bills, buried in debt from college loans as she struggled to make it through St. John's University on the few bucks she had left over each week after Uncle Sam took his cut from the checks dispensed by her boss at a popular clothing boutique.

Vera took a deep breath and sighed.

Domingo set his blunt in an ashtray. He slipped the American Express Black Card in her back pocket, then rubbed his hand over her ass. He looked into her eyes and began unzipping her pants. He glanced at the befuddled look on her face. She was clearly on the verge of doing something she didn't want to, but Domingo was determined to alter her fears.

"Please." Vera grabbed his hand and shook her head. "I can't do this."

"Ma, you can do anything you want to."

"I never been with a man."

"What about Vince and Dee?" Domingo inquired about the only two men he had ever seen Vera in a relationship with."

"We never had sex." Vera explained that the men she dated were merely smokescreens designed to cloud the fact that she had a lickin' license. She said the men eventually ended their relationships after they realized they could not break Vera's claim of celibacy. "For real, Domingo. I never been with a man."

"But you been with a tongue all your life. This ain't about you being with a man. It's about you having a tongue pressed against your clit with just the right amount of pressure." Domingo continued unzipping her pants. "It's about a tongue gently sliding between the lips of your pussy as you close your eyes and your toes curl until you nut. It's not about who's making you cum. It's about the fact you know it feels so good to cum."

Vera closed her eyes and removed her hand from Domingo's as he put his blunt in the ashtray. She let out a deep breath.

Domingo slowly pulled her pants down. He stared at the thin layer of hair surrounding her pussy lips. *This freak-ass broad ain't even got on no panties.* He sat her on the glass table.

Vera laid back as Domingo gently spread her legs apart. She moaned softly when his hands touched her.

Looking at her pussy and thick thighs was making it hard for Domingo not to slide his dick in the pussy he knew had never been touched by a man. He gently rubbed her thighs, from the outside to her inner thighs. Her jittery body told him the foreign feeling of a man's touch was disturbing her or exciting her. That made him more determined to please her. Making her cum was not about Vera. It was about Domingo's ability to conquer. Being the first man whose tongue graced the flesh between her legs was an ego booster. Beyond that was the potential for her to eventually allow Domingo to transcend oral sex to traditional sex.

"Ahhhh," Vera cried and inched back as Domingo's

tongue swiped across her inner thigh. Domingo paused. He allowed her to calm down. Then he slid his tongue across her other thigh, drawing a similar response as the first one, but not as intense. He inched closer, staring at the fat lips of her pussy before touching them with his tongue.

"No!" Vera grabbed his head and leaned forward with a dim look that verged on crying, minus tears. "Please, we're not supposed to be doing this."

Domingo put his index finger on her lips. "Shhh. Close your eyes and think about the baddest chick that comes to your mind."

"No." She shook her head.

"Yes." Domingo delicately placed his hand on her face and closed her eyes. He shifted back down, then repositioned himself between her legs. He swiped his tongue over her pussy once more, drawing almost no response. He slowly inched his tongue inside.

"Whoaaa," Vera blurted.

The intensity of her moan convinced Domingo that he had gained control of her. He applied more suction to her clit.

"Eat me, Mimi," Vera begged.

Mimi? Domingo tried to stay focused, but it was hard to as he thought of Vanessa's ex-friend Mimi. Either Mimi and Vera were undercover lovers or Vera had long been fantasizing about Mimi. Making the matter more serious, Mimi had been having a relationship with Vera's brother Jahiem for years. It was part of the reason she had sided with Vera and the others when they flipped on Candy.

Within seconds, Vera was pulling Domingo closer to her, clawing into his scalp and neck as beads of sweat dripped from her palms and between her thighs. "Mimi. No, Mimi. Yes. Eat me," her voice rose. "Ahhhh, yesss," Vera screamed as she came. Her body convulsed while Domingo sucked her dry. "Huhhh." She released Domingo from her clutches.

He lifted his head, gazing down at her biting her bottom lip, eyes closed, savoring the moment. Domingo could see the twenty-two-year-old's nipples standing at attention through her white blouse. He had successfully subdued Vera, claiming his stake on land that had been uncharted by man. This was more than a sexual exploit. Domingo knew he now wielded a degree of power over her. But he had to ascertain how much power he wielded and how he could turn that into dollars. No matter how intimate the relationship Domingo had with someone, the underlying premise was how it could serve him financially. His hustler's ambition was what enabled him to survive on the streets since age twelve.

When Vera opened her eyes, it was clear to Domingo the reality of what had just transpired was setting in her mind. The pair stared at each other in silence for a moment, before Vera jumped to her feet and pulled up her pants. "You have to leave," she said.

"After you tell me how it felt."

She sighed and shook her head.

Domingo smiled. "After two people lay down together, they're never the same when they get up."

"As far as I'm concerned this never happened."

"And Mimi never happened either, huh?"

Vera froze. Her mouth opened as if she had just discovered she was busted.

Domingo could tell she had been so engrossed with his tongue she did not know she had called Mimi's name. He sparked his blunt and stood. "Don't worry. We'll discuss that later, ya heard?"

Vera grabbed his arm. "Please," she begged. "What happened has to stay between us and us only."

"I'll see you later."

"Leah, Chanel, Meisha—they can't find out about this. And definitely not Jahiem."

Domingo snickered.

"I'm serious."

"Don't worry. You let me eat. I ain't gonna bite the hand that feeds me."

"Thank you." Vera wiped her forehead and exhaled.

"Just remember that I got a hella appetite, ya heard?" Domingo stepped out of the door.

CHAPTER FIVE
CANDY

G et the fuck over here!" Candy barked as she grabbed Zora by the neck. She had Zora cornered next to the hotel bar not far from the elevator.

Rich was nearby, calming Vanessa. He had managed to keep Zora alive for the ten minutes after Candy and Vanessa found them on the elevator.

"I'm sorry," Zora mumbled, tears falling from her eyes as she stared at Candy's imposing body.

Candy pinned her against the wall, choking her. Zora tried to pry Candy's arm away to no avail.

As Zora twisted her head back and forth, the butt of a gun crashed down on her face, nearly breaking her nose. "What are you doing?" she screamed, gazing at Vanessa, who had struggled free from Rich.

Rich snatched Vanessa. He grabbed her gun and tucked

40

it inside his blazer. "You got an appointment with the county jail or something? This is the MGM Grand, not no side block in Harlem." He looked at Vanessa like she was insane. He quickly scanned the area, but found no witnesses or surveillance cameras viewing them in a distant corner.

Zora took off running before Rich finished his statement. He turned to Candy and Vanessa. "I would ask what the hell is on y'all minds, but you gotta have a mind for something to be on it. And this little performance y'all just put on got me questioning that."

"You got some nerve!" Candy declared. "Fuckin' some ho in the elevator and—"

"Hold up, hold up, hold up," Rich interrupted her. "This is about—"

"You and your bullshit. That's what it's about," Vanessa said. "Don't try to flip this on us."

"Baby, I ain't Denzel and this ain't *The Great Debaters*, so ain't no competition about who can outtalk who." Rich looked around, then back to the women. "As a matter of fact, I'm outta here."

Candy watched Rich walk off and get on the elevator. "You see this shit?" Vanessa shook her head. We can't let him get away with this."

"Come on." Candy led Vanessa toward the elevator.

* * *

Candy and Vanessa burst through the hotel door in search of Rich. They found him naked, stepping into the

41

marble Jacuzzi. Candy looked at his dick hanging almost halfway down his thigh. She took in the sight of his well-defined frame. It was not just his body, but how he worked it that helped her discover she was comfortable with men and women. But as she thought of Rich sexing Zora, everything changed. Some unknown woman had been privy to the intimacy reserved only for her and Vanessa. Rich had given away something only she and Vanessa deserved. The exclusiveness of his sex and their love had been tampered with. "How you gonna disrespect us like that, Rich?"

Rich huffed. "You can't name a time I set out to disrespect either one of y'all. What player gonna go at his team?" He sat in the bubbling water of the Jacuzzi.

Candy was silent, reflecting on Rich's words. No matter how deep she dug, she could not find a single time Rich had done anything to intentionally hurt her or Vanessa. In fact, he had gone to great lengths to bring them pleasure on so many levels and to protect them. But this was not about intention. It was about actions and outcomes.

"Your track record might be good, but fucking some broad in the elevator of the same hotel you're in with us . . . What, you were taking her to our room before the elevator went out?" Candy asked.

Anger and pain forced tears from Vanessa's eyes. "Fuck you, Rich! She wiped her eyes. Rich got out of the Jacuzzi and walked over to Vanessa.

42

"Go find your elevator, ho," she said. She and Candy turned and walked away.

Rich ran over and grabbed both of them by their arms. They turned around, pulling loose from him. They looked on in silence.

"So where we going with this?" Rich asked.

Candy rolled her eyes and turned away. Rich grabbed her arm and she tried to slap him with her free hand. He blocked her swing by grabbing her other arm. "Get the fuck off me!"

"Or what?" Rich asked.

Vanessa pulled on his arms and he pushed her.

Candy grabbed his neck, choking him. Before Rich knew it, Candy and Vanessa were rolling around with him on the carpeted floor. He pinned Candy's arms to the floor. "Now calm the fuck down."

Vanessa jumped on Rich's back. He flung her small body off of him and pinned her to the floor beside Candy.

Candy looked into the eyes of the man she loved and would do anything for. She watched his face descend before his lips puckered. She turned away. But the softness of his lips met her neck. All the pain and anger began to subside. Suddenly, she heard a loud slap and felt Rich move from her.

"Fuck!" Rich blurted as he grabbed Vanessa's hand and pulled her. They were face-to-face, both kneeling. She struggled but managed to get one hand loose and swung at Rich again. He grabbed her and pinned her to the floor with her hands behind her back like she was a perp being arrested by a cop.

"Let her go, Rich," Candy pled as she now stood over them.

Vanessa's small body squirmed beneath Rich's 210 pounds of muscle. He clamped both of his palms on the back of her hands and forced them on the carpet.

"Get the fuck off me!" she barked.

Rich leaned down and began kissing her neck and giving her a hickey. Vanessa's screams turned to heavy panting. "I love you," he said in between planting kisses on her neck.

Candy watched Rich's naked frame, still wet from the Jacuzzi. Her juices began to flow as Rich pulled off Vanessa's clothes and her small round butt popped out.

"This what you want, right?" he asked.

"Yes," Vanessa whispered while Rich entered her. Her head twisted from side-to-side, brushing against Rich's head.

Candy's hand slipped between her legs. She fingered herself while stimulating her clit as she stared at Rich ravishing Vanessa. Her body was overheating and her fingers soaked with wetness as her eyes shifted to Rich's ass. She took her slippery fingers and rubbed her nipples, Her lush internal fluids began trailing down her leg.

Vanessa screamed, "Fuck me!"

Candy could no longer fight the throbbing feeling between her legs. She dropped to her knees and crawled on top of Rich. She parted his cheeks and dove face-first between them. Holding one, Candy tried to stop Rich from fighting. With her other hand, she toyed with her clit, grinding against her hand.

"Oooooh, shit," Rich howled. "That's enough." He reached back, moving Candy.

"Come here. Let me taste you." Candy said, pulling Vanessa onto her face as she laid back. Candy was still playing with her pussy as Vanessa began riding her face. She felt her legs part and lift off the floor, then Rich's stiffness enter her fiery flesh. She wanted to scream with joy, but a mouthful of Vanessa's pussy rendered her mute.

"Candy!" Vanessa screamed. Her climactic moisture seeped into Candy's mouth and dripped down her face.

The light in the ceiling shattered Candy's vision as Vanessa stood. Candy could feel Rich's thrusts against her pelvis. His pubic hairs stimulated her clit as he grinded himself inside of her with a rhythmic swerve. She cocked her legs wider, allowing deeper penetration. "Right there. Hit it right there," she begged.

Vanessa leaned down and began sucking one of Candy's large breasts while fondling the other.

Candy screamed joyfully, pulling Vanessa closer. Vanessa's delicate touch and Rich's forceful strokes and firm grip on her waist took her over the top. "Huh, huh, huh, huhhhhhhh," Candy let out an extended moan as she and Rich came simultaneously.

Rich collapsed beside her, his body outstretched on the floor, a leg entangled with hers.

Candy looked at Vanessa's smile, then into Rich's eyes as he faced toward her. He gently ran his hands over her face. She loved Rich and cherished his sexual skills. But it would take more than a stiff dick and soft tongue to remove from her mind the image of Zora riding him in the elevator.

"I love you," Rich whispered.

Candy smirked. "I guess you figured fucking that broad on the elevator was the perfect way to prove that."

"You should get a Grammy for acting like everything is cool, then fuckin' up the mood," Rich snapped.

"I hope the mood is all right when you wake up in a cold bed." Candy rose and began dressing. "Guess you can call up ol' girl and tell her y'all don't need to use the elevator no more." She turned to Vanessa, who was also getting dressed. "Come on."

Rich looked on in awe as Candy began walking away.

Candy knew she had to take a stance. A position that hurt her as much as Rich. A statement through actions that spoke louder than words of discontent. It pained every fabric of her being to walk away from the only man she had been intimate with since she began dealing with women. The man who had somehow managed to successfully balance his love for two women equally. Although she had no idea if her walking away from Rich was the start of a temporary departure or a permanent separation, she knew the gap widening between them with each of her steps was necessary.

"Candy, we can work this out," said Vanessa.

"You don't need no unfaithful man when you got a faithful woman," Candy said. She grabbed her Coach bag.

"So now y'all on some female bonding, girl power, gender unity shit?" Rich jumped up, still naked.

"It's about you bonding with broads in elevators because your gender has no self-control."

Rich walked over to Vanessa and softly placed her hand between his. "Baby, we done been through situations far worse than this. When the world was against us, we didn't start running away from problems." He stared at Candy, who responded by rolling her eyes.

Candy turned to Vanessa. "I said come on," she emphasized through clenched teeth. The first of several tears fell from Candy's eyes as she headed for the door. Turning the knob, she looked back at Vanessa who reluctantly pulled her hand from an awestruck Rich. Candy knew things were taking a twist for the worse. What she had no idea of was just how bad things would become for the trio.

CHAPTER SIX

VANESSA

A mixture of guilt and grief was weighing Vanessa down as she picked up her clutch and walked away from Rich. She felt Rich deserved a chance. Yet, like Candy, his actions tormented her. The pain in Candy's watery eyes caused the strain on Vanessa's heart to grow. She paused as Candy turned the doorknob and exited the hotel room.

"We been through too much together," Rich said.

Vanessa closed her eyes, thinking of the truth in his statement. His words that followed faded to an inaudible level as Vanessa reminisced how Rich had bypassed countless women in Candy's Shop for her. He had introduced Vanessa to a life of love she had thought was reserved only for fashion savvy fly girls like Candy. Vanessa was an eclectic outcast who cool kids shunned as a child and most men walked by in her adult years. But she became a star when one of Harlem's most powerful hustlers, a known womanizer, made Vanessa his only woman. Rich had been all the man she wanted.

Even after Candy became an intimate part of their life, her feelings remained for Rich.

"If you walk outta that door, ain't no guarantee I'm gonna be here when you come back," Rich said.

Vanessa took a deep breath, then turned and left the hotel suite. She burst into tears when she saw Candy sitting on the floor, her back against the wall near the door. Candy's mascara and tears were a muddy mess. Vanessa bent down and wiped her tears.

"We don't deserve this," Candy said in between sniffles.

"Don't worry." Vanessa helped Candy to her feet. "It's gonna be all right. She kissed her on the cheeks and lips, then embraced her.

After their extended hug, they left the hotel and went to The Ming Terrace, a popular Chinese restaurant in Las Vegas. They sat at a corner table in a dimly lit area. Vanessa ate half of her stir-fried vegetables, but Candy had not touched the shrimp fried rice, her favorite dish on the menu.

"I usually give you my vegan spiel and try to convince you not to eat animals," Vanessa said, gazing at a huge shrimp on Candy's plate, "but now I hate to see you not eating meat."

Candy flashed a partial smile. "I put my heart in a man's hand and he throws it on the ground and stomps it out." Candy sighed. "The word trust is not in their vocabulary. It's part of the reason I stopped dealing with them after Dez died," she said, referencing the notorious Harlem hustler she used to date.

"Sometimes things just happen."

Candy glared at her. "Either you're gonna be my lover or Rich's lawyer."

Vanessa shrugged her shoulders. "I'm just saying. We both invested a lot in our relationship with Rich."

"And he took our investment and did what he wanted. Like Bernie Madoff did with all them people's money. Our relationship was a ponzi scheme." Candy laughed for the first time since Vanessa found her on the floor crying.

"But I guarantee you Bernie Madoff can't make you cum like Rich can." Candy paused.

"What you thinking?" Vanessa asked.

Candy grinned. "I'm still in love with him. If I wasn't, it wouldn't hurt so much."

"Me too. It hurt like hell for me to walk out that door and leave him in that hotel. You should've saw the look in his eyes after you left."

"I know he loves us, but how could he—" Candy stopped in midsentence. "How could he cheat on us? He's got two beautiful women that love him."

"He picked a good one, though," Vanessa said. "She was sexy."

"True that." Candy pulled out her phone after it began vibrating. She flashed it toward Vanessa.

"Domingo on face time," Vanessa said.

"Yup." Candy answered the iPhone.

"What's poppin', Mamita?"

"Tell me something good or don't tell me nothin' at all."

"What's good is I'm giving you one more chance to have my baby."

"Sure can't call you a quitter."

"Question is, when you gonna let me win you over. But that's another story. I wanted to let you know I got something major in the works with Vera."

"Oh yeah?"

"Yeah, ya boy on his grind hard body, ya heard? I just can't go into no details yet."

"So you just called to tease me?"

"It's funny hearing a woman that like slinging them tig old bitties and that big old ass around me talkin' bout teasing."

Candy laughed.

"Serious, though, you ever hear anything about Mimi havin' her lickin' license?"

"No," a wide-eyed Candy said looking up. "How about you, Vanessa?"

"Oh shit, my soul sister with you? Let me holler at baby girl."

Candy handed Vanessa the phone and listened as Vanessa told Domingo about Mimi admitting she had a sexual encounter with a woman once and enjoyed it. "But she told me she wouldn't do it again."

Domingo laughed. "Shit, if pussy tastes as good as it do to women as it do to me, I know that bullshit she told you is G."

"It does taste good," Vanessa said with a giggle.

"You got me thinkin' 'bout some twat right now. Matter fact, put my future baby momma back on the jack."

Vanessa shook her head and gave the phone to Candy.

"What's up?"

"You gotta ditch Rich, that's what's up."

Candy laughed.

"This ain't no laughin' matter."

"Speak for yourself."

"You'll get rid of that lame eventually. But I think Mimi got her lickin' license and Vera breakin' her off. But I'll keep you posted." He hung up.

"So he thinks Vera and Mimi gettin' it on."

"Doubt it," Vanessa said, eating a forkful of vegetables.

Candy was silent, a grim look overcoming her face.

Vanessa reached across the table and touched her arm. "What's wrong?"

"Just hearing about Mimi and Vera reminded me that they're the reason we're in Las Vegas and going through all this drama with Rich."

Vanessa was silent as Candy recounted how their lives had been changed by the women. Her vengeful streak came to the surface. She knew Leah's baby shower was coming up, so it was time for her and Candy to prepare for the day that could determine if revenge would be the justice they needed to move on with their lives.

* * *

The following day, Candy found herself rising from her seat at the head of the table in her company's conference room. It had been a long meeting about the company's declining income. Candy had made the decision to lay off three of her 25 employees.

She looked around the room as the last member of her executive team cleared out. There were enlarged photos of a few celebrities that had endorsed the line. Candy felt awkward, because she knew that her company was suffering because her presence was missing. No amount of Skype video conferences could make up for her physical presence on a regular basis. That was something she knew the company never had.

The suffering was reciprocal. Profits were down because Candy was gone and Candy's life was going downhill because she was not fully committed to the company. The more she thought of her problems, the more she thought of the drama that was preventing her from solving them.

Candy stepped out of the conference room and made

her way to the elevator.

"It was nice seeing you, Ms. Johnson," a perky receptionist said.

Candy simply smiled, realizing she could not even remember the young woman's name.

Within minutes, Candy was in the elevator stepping out of the building afterwards. The sun bore down on the busy Manhattan strip. In her high heels, Candy squeezed through the crowd on her way to the curb to hail a cab.

"Candy, is that you?"

Candy spun around, spotting one of Leah's customers who used to frequent Candy's Shop.

"Girl, I ain't seen you in forever and a day."

Candy flashed a nervous smile. "I've been busy."

"How's Vanessa and Rich?"

Candy didn't know whether the question was genuine or some investigative inquiry to unearth information for Leah.

"Y'all just disappeared after all that drama," the woman continued.

"Rich, Vanessa, everybody's straight." Candy turned and flagged a cab, then turned back to the woman. "I'm sorry, I gotta go. It was good seeing you." She hopped inside of the cab, which pulled off as the woman said bye.

Candy leaned back in her seat and closed her eyes. Paranoia was crippling her. She began wondering whether the woman would tell Leah about her. Would the woman tell someone else she had seen Candy? Had anyone else recognize Candy from a distance, but simply remained silent? Was someone following her? *This is why Rich said to stay out of New York. Or am I just overacting?* Candy did not know the answers to the questions popping into her mind. But she was certain that telling Rich would result in a bunch of 'I-told-you-so's'. Mentioning the news to Vanessa was likely to only worry her. So Candy planned to keep her run-in with the woman to herself. Crossing paths with her was a reminder of how unmanageable her life had become and how much the people responsible for that had to pay. But with her plan to murder Leah, Candy wondered if being spotted in Manhattan would make her a suspect when Leah turned up dead?

***

A lot happened since Vanessa followed Candy out of their hotel suite and left Rich behind eight days earlier. The women had decided they needed some space from Rich, but he should endure the anxiety of not knowing what was on their minds. So his calls and text messages to them went unanswered. They had managed to sneak inside the hotel suite and retrieve their belongings before relocating to a hotel on Long Island. It was a location they used to plan their attack by easing in and out of New York City, assessing the place where Leah's baby shower was set to happen.

On the morning of the baby shower Vanessa was seated between Candy's legs inside of the hotel room

55

having her hair braided. Vanessa had been thinking about their plot all night, finding it hard to rest. She and Candy had debated about the strategic details of the attack. Vera and Mimi would not be attending the event, according to Domingo. Vanessa's plan was to kill the rest of the women who would be present: Leah, Chanel and Meisha—each of Candy's former employees who cultivated the atmosphere within her shop that birthed the drama which changed her life. Candy thought it would be safest to make their move on Leah as soon as she arrived at the baby shower, which would be before the guests showed up. Less guests meant less witnesses.

"We get Leah now," Candy said, applying some Carrot Oil between one of Vanessa's cornrows. "We got plenty of time to get the rest of them. The Father's Day Tournament is next week."

"Tomorrow's not promised. But if we move when they're together, we get this over in one shot."

Catching all of the women at once was the ideal plan. It was a way to reduce risk. Less shootings meant less chances for arrests. It was this rationale that had caused the women to pass over other opportunities.

"Vera and Mimi won't be there, but they'll be at the Father's Day Tournament, so we'll get 'em then," said Candy.

Vanessa knew that Candy would have liked nothing more than to murder everyone on their list as soon as possible. But Candy also had always been calculating.

Vanessa was the emotional opposition to Candy's rational thinking. Exacting revenge was going to be well thought-out. Vanessa was coming to terms with that, no matter how anxious she was to hand out justice.

Candy was silent for a moment. "Sometimes I just wonder where we would be had they not kidnapped me?" she said.

Vanessa had the same thoughts. Their drama and being forced to move had changed everything. They had spent most of their time at Rich's upstate cabin, before relocating to Las Vegas to spruce up the boredom that came with the adjustment to a locale unlike the fast pace of New York City. Before that, Rich was a retired drug dealer looking to expand his legal investments. He still maintained his portfolio, but spending less time in New York City slowed his pace. Candy had been managing her hair care product business from a distance. Her input was relegated to instructions to her manager by phone and e-mail along with sporadic trips to the office of the company. As a trio, Rich, Candy and Vanessa had attained semi-celebrity status because of the sex tape going viral online and becoming a common discussion topic for Wendy Williams. Then Vanessa's erotic novel added to their notoriety. But after Chase's murder, Vanessa's love of writing had been replaced with an infatuation with guns and getback. Keeping Vanessa and Candy out of revenge mode was a fulltime job for Rich.

"Them hos messed up everything for us," Candy

declared, as she finished the last braid on Vanessa's head.

The women got dressed. Jeans, sneakers, hoodies and skullies were the apparel—tools of death. Candy rummaged through a duffle bag full of guns taken from Rich's stash at his cabin. Candy chose a 9-mm Glock and Vanessa settled for the .380-caliber Grendell she kept in her clutch. They left the hotel room and hopped in a rented Mazda.

After steering through Long Island, Candy drove through Brooklyn into the DUMBO section. The acronym stood for Down Under the Manhattan Bridge Overpass, so the locale made for an easy getaway over the bridge into Manhattan.

Vanessa observed the well-kept neighborhood populated mostly by white people. The immaculate brownstones and tidy apartment buildings reminded Vanessa of her life as a Greenwich Village resident. There was an artsy feel, welcoming people who cherished creativity and spent time in places like museums and art galleries.

Candy parked the car on a block filled with tall trees, a couple of factories and the commercial space Leah had rented for the baby shower. Several street lights illuminated the area after the sun set. Candy looked at her watch. "Another hour before it officially starts, but she gotta be here early."

"Domingo said she was setting up in the morning and coming back about a half-hour before it starts."

Candy nodded. "Her husband is pushing a blue Yukon."

Vanessa was just reminded that Moses would be with his wife. Vanessa had no problem killing Leah. She had even worked herself up to disregard the fact that they would also be murdering her unborn child. But in the back of her mind there was still a soft spot in her heart for the collateral damage. While killing Leah's unborn child was unavoidable, Vanessa would let Leah's husband live, if possible. As a vegan who had a respect for the lives of animals that people ate, Vanessa was always having an internal debate over the fact she had become a killer.

"Is that them?" Candy asked anxiously, watching a Yukon steer toward them on the wide two-way street.

"I think so."

Candy turned on the car. The women pulled down their hats and put on their hoodies. The Yukon parked across the street from Candy and Vanessa, about four cars down.

"That's it," Vanessa said, rolling down her window as Leah exited the car from the passenger seat into the street.

Candy hit the gas and skidded to a halt beside Leah.

Vanessa reached out of the window and fired the first two shots into Leah's pregnant belly. As she dropped to the ground, Vanessa and Candy hopped out of the car.

"Noooo!" Moses screamed as he ran in the direction of his wife, his eyes locked on her stomach.

Candy fired the Glock, sending a 9-millimeter hollow point through his shoulder. As his torso twisted, Candy and Vanessa fired a barrage of bullets into his chest and back.

Vanessa looked at Leah. The sexy Latina was stretched out next to the tire of the Yukon. She was holding her bloody stomach, crimson fluid leaking between her fingers. Her eyes beamed directly at Vanessa.

Vanessa aimed her gun at Leah and fired three shots in her head.

"Oh shit," Candy blurted as police sirens sounded in the distance. "Come on."

They scurried to the Mazda and pulled off. They removed their hoods as they turned the corner. Vanessa kept looking behind them, but there was no sign of police. She was pumped up, adrenaline flowing through her veins. She thought about how she and Candy had gunned down Moses. It was reactionary. A reflex that would have never come into play had Vanessa been the innocent person of years past.

But things were different now. She felt elated, having completed the first part of her plan. *Now all we have to do is get the rest of them.*

CHAPTER SEVEN
RICH

R ich walked through the car lot of Exclusive Autos in Westchester County, New York. He admired the Lamborghinis, Maybachs, Bugattis and other high-end vehicles. He had driven virtually every model on the premises. That was one of the perks of having a substantial stake in the business. Rich stepped in front of a pearl white Bentley Brookland, thinking back to the night he had wheeled the ride to a black tie affair hosted by Vanessa's publisher. She had sat in front and Candy in back. That was a time when they were a unit, three people of one mind—the good old days.

"Please step away from the car, sir."

Rich smiled and turned around to where the familiar voice came from. He hugged Free, a squeaky clean pretty boy who worked for Exclusive Autos. Free had introduced Rich to most of the legal connections he had.

They were connections that helped wash Rich's dirty money and lay the foundation for his aspirations of legal wealth.

"So, you got the company email, I guess," Free said. "There has to be a good reason for you to pop up on the premises."

"I've been known to make my rounds on occasion." Rich smiled.

"Now we both happen to be around when the chips are down."

"Bad news will definitely do it," Rich responded, referring to the email indicating the company was downsizing its staff by twenty-five percent. Rich had received the news from his uncle weeks before the email went out, before his elevator catastrophe at the MGM.

Exclusive Autos was suffering due to the bad economy that was affecting other corporations Rich had stock in. Rich's uncle wanted Rich's help. He needed Rich to use the managerial skills he had cultivated by running a successful drug operation. Rich was always giving him ideas, so his uncle was sure that Rich's presence could benefit the company. But Rich couldn't make time for Exclusive Autos, and he was leery that the company could truly expand with or without his help. He also had little time because he was consumed by drama with Candy and Vanessa. Yet, he needed to make money. The best way he could do that was to find a new place to invest his dough. That mode of thinking and several conversations between Rich and King since they reconnected in Vegas had resulted in a potential business deal between both men.

"Things have been pretty tight around here, to say the least," Free told Rich. "Everyone's scrambling to save their jobs and there hasn't even been an announcement of exactly who's being let go." He put his hand on Rich's shoulder. "Anyway, how's life treating the man with two misses?"

"Could be better, could be worse."

"You guys kind of fell off the map since you left Harlem. I can't remember the last time I've seen a post from you on Facebook or Twitter. Definitely not a YouTube video."

"A little space out of the public eye can be a good thing sometimes." Rich smiled although he knew his retreat from the spotlight along with Candy and Vanessa was hurting them financially. Readers of Vanessa's bestselling novel wanted to see and hear from the woman who had invited them onto her fictional world. Candy's distance from New York City was hindering her ability to run her company in Manhattan. Rich's biggest distraction from making money was Candy and Vanessa's obsession with revenge.

"Did the police ever find out who killed Chase?"

"Not that I know of," Rich responded. He knew that Free's inquiry was genuine. Free had no ties to the streets, thus no knowledge of the speculation of Rich's guilt circulating through project halls and tenement staircases.

"Chase had issues in terms of that ghetto mentality you managed to overcome. But no man deserves to be murdered."

"You're always one foot away from death when you're in the Life. That's why I gave it up. Got tired of watching my step all the time."

"Just thank God you made it out. Unfortunately, Chase didn't."

Rich and Free walked off and continued talking, but Rich's mind was stuck on Chase. He and Rich had been so close. They had done so much together. He had never anticipated their friendship ending with him killing Chase. That incident was a reflection of just how volatile and unpredictable the streets were. Rich thought of King. I really need to connect with him.

* * *

Rich sat in the passenger seat of King's Mercedes G55 as the customized truck steered down Freedom Parkway in North Eastern, Atlanta. The people lounging in Freedom Park, the ambulances parked in front of Atlanta Medical Center—things had not changed much since Rich's last trip to the city several years earlier. His last journey to Atlanta was to attend a business convention. Now he was there on business again. Rich was destined for Queens Incorporated, the modeling agency King opened several years earlier on Martin Luther King Jr. Drive. King and Rich had been discussing the possibility of Rich investing some money in his company.

Close to three weeks had passed since Candy and Vanessa walked out of Rich's life and he talked to Free at Exclusive Autos. During that time, Rich and King had spent a lot of time together in Las Vegas. Rich was impressed to see that King had totally left the streets behind and had become a successful businessman in the legal world. King was living the life Rich had planned for himself and had struggled to introduce Chase to. The life Candy and Vanessa were preventing him from living.

Rich had also gotten close to Zora while in Vegas. But he still spent a good portion of his time stressed over Candy and Vanessa. Their absence helped him understand just how close they were and how much he depended on them. Rich had disclosed more about himself to them than any person alive. Aside from missing them, he feared what could happen if Candy and Vanessa went through with their plans for revenge. The last time something tragic happened to Candy, Rich found himself in a shootout that resulted in two of Chase's henchmen being murdered and Chase being tortured and murdered. Even with Rich being separated from Candy and Vanessa, he knew that if they were harmed, he could end up concocting a murderous plot not much unlike the one he had tried to prevent them from executing.

King made a left on Peachtree Street not far from Atlanta Underground and Georgia State University. He was soon pulling up in front of the modern building that housed his company. "This is where Young Jeezy and damn near every other rapper and singer in the A comes for their video chicks," King said.

"Modeling is the new hustle for chicks in the hood. And it's more than videos. You got book covers, magazines, calendars. You name it get 'em in it."

Rich watched a few models that King pointed out as they exited the building. "Guess you gotta be a single man to work here," Rich said.

"Discipline, brother. Self-control goes a long way." King turned off the ignition and reached in the back of his truck for his briefcase. "And it will keep Zora from killing you."

Rich smiled. "I've been killed by women before."

"She's good people," King said with a serious tone. "I know that ain't wifey, but don't do her dirty."

Rich and King stepped out of the Mercedes and entered the building. As they began making their way through the fourth floor, where Queens Incorporated was located, Rich watched as people greeted King with smiles, nods and kind words. The racially diverse contingent of fifty or so employees was so far removed from the streets Rich and King had run together. The fact that within the corporate atmosphere King was the only person sporting jeans and Air Force Ones further demonstrated how far removed from the streets King's staff was.

Rich took in the scenery. Above a row of cubicles to his right was a wall donning magazine covers and calendars showcasing models. Nearby was a collage of enlarged photographs of rappers and celebrities posing with models. The sunlight beamed through the huge windows, bringing life to the enormous space filled with desks, cubicles and entrances to rooms and offices. Everyone seemed happy, darting to and fro with smiles and cups of coffee. *I like the vibe.* Rich nodded.

As King led Rich past a cluster of employees at the water cooler, Rich noticed Zora's slim figure sauntering toward him in slacks along with a turquoise blouse and matching turquoise Gucci pumps. "Hey, baby." She kissed Rich and hugged him, before greeting King.

"It used to be a time the boss came first," King said with a laugh.

Zora smiled at King, then scrolled through her iPad. "I left the Def Jam proposal on your desk. Their rep should be here in twenty minutes, so I had a fresh bouquet of flowers placed in your office. At ten-thirty you're doing lunch with Benny Boom at Justin's. Your afternoon itinerary is on your desk."

"Did you speak to the lawyer at King magazine?"

"Left him a message as soon as I got in this morning."

King turned to Rich with a smile. "Most reliable

woman I know."

Zora blushed.

"I gotta meet with my executive team before this Def Jam meeting," King told Zora. "Show Rich around." He gave Rich a pound and walked off.

"I missed you," she told Rich.

"It's only been two days."

"The first forty-eight is crucial."

"If you're good, I'll make it up to you."

"Good girls finish last."

"That's only possible when there's a competition. Right now, you're the only player in the game."

Zora smiled, clutching her iPad to her chest. "Look around you, Rich. This is ATL. Women outnumber men ten-to-one and that's doubled when you work in a modeling agency. If there was no competition, King wouldn't need a personal assistant and you and I would've never met in Vegas. So, thank God for competition."

Rich scanned the area, realizing the truth in Zora's statement. Besides the models prancing around with butts bigger than Nicki Minaj and more designer clothes than Lil' Kim, King's staff was comprised predominantly of equally attractive women in business suits and heels. There was a mirror on nearly every cubicle and office wall. There were no makeup-deprived women flaunting their natural beauty like Vanessa. Every woman, from the Latina in the nearby cubicle to the two Asian women in the conference room, who Rich figured were executives, was primped to perfection. Rich could smell women. The air reminded him of the atmosphere surrounding a Macy's perfume counter.

"Enough looking around. Let me show you around like King instructed." Zora led Rich throughout the company headquarters, introducing him to people as King's business partner.

Rich watched how women eyed him. He was used to females flocking to him. But he could see Zora was nervous about the competition.

"This is Nia, head of marketing and promotion. Nia, this is Rich, a very close friend and business partner of King."

Rich smiled and shook the gold-toned woman's hand following Zora's introduction. "It's a pleasure."

Nia's eyes unabashedly roamed down Rich's tailored linen shirt to the bulge between his legs, then back to his eyes. "The pleasure is mine."

Rich maintained his cool, practically snatching his hand back, because Nia didn't let it go.

"Your accent, where are you from?" she asked.

"New York. Harlem actually."

"What brings you to Atlanta?"

"Business."

"Well, Rich from New York, Atlanta has a lot more to offer than money." Nia flashed a seductive smirk. "Don't let it pass you by."

Zora's eyes beamed at Rich as he watched Nia strut

off, her hips sashaying as her butt protruded from her pinstriped skirt. "Come on, Rich." Zora tugged on his hand. "I wanna show you the stock room."

Competition. Rich knew Zora had just encountered her first challenge. He followed her into the large windowless room filled with boxes and a copy machine. Rich ingested the scent of paper and the cardboard boxes that housed it.

Zora locked the door behind them. "Only a select few people are allowed in here," she said, stepping in front of Rich. "It's where we keep hard copies of the records most essential to the company."

Rich turned around, taking in the sight of cardboard boxes stacked neatly against the back wall. File cabinets lined the remaining walls. The fact that King's company had accumulated so many records was impressive. The atmosphere diverged so much from their past, that Rich could not help but think back to the days he had helped King develop schemes to extort street hustlers. Back then, the thought of Rich being escorted by King's personal assistant through a corporation owned by King was unimaginable.

"Check this out, Rich."

When Rich turned around to Zora, her hands were planted on a file cabinet, her slacks at her ankles. Rich gazed at her thong that vanished in the crack of her ass. He was momentarily startled, but he knew Zora was a spontaneous freak. Their sexual introduction in the elevator was proof of that. An episode they later had in a movie theater confirmed it. But sex in the stock room of her job was the kind of risk that could leave her unemployed and interfere with the bond and potential business Rich and King were working on. But Rich was a risk taker too. "So this is what goes on in a modeling agency?" he said.

"Competition, remember? Water cooler discussions in the company are like a gossip column in the Enquirer about who's fucking who. But I told you that few people come in here, and I locked the door for a reason.

Rich looked around, and then back to Zora's perfectly round ass. He peeled out of his blazer, dropping it on a shelf. Then he dropped his pants. He took one step forward and slipped his index finger under her thong and glided his hand over her rear as he removed the thong. His dick was a brick. It had burst through the slot of his boxers the second he saw Zora's ass swallow her thong.

"Come on, Rich. Nothing extravagant, just a quickie."

He grabbed Zora's ass with one hand and used the other to guide himself inside of her. "Ahh," she panted.

Her hot flesh tightened around his dick as he slammed into her. "Damn, girl. Shit," he mumbled.

"Go deeper," Zora uttered. She rocked her ass back into Rich's thrusts.

Rich gripped her waist tighter, entering her quicker.

"Yes, yes, ahh, yes." Zora's moans came out faster

as Rich increased his pace. He continued for minutes, before he turned Zora around and pulled her down. She squatted in her Gucci pumps, taking Rich into her mouth. She sucked the hot nectar from his stiffness.

"Yeah, like that, girl." Rich grabbed the top of the file cabinet for support.

Zora slid her tongue down the side of his dick until she took each of his balls into her mouth.

"Damn," he moaned.

She began jerking his dick, while slurping his balls.

Rich closed his eyes, gritting his teeth as a jubilant sensation resonated throughout his entire body.

Zora continued jerking and slurping, before wrapping her lips back around his dick and juggling Rich's balls in her hand. As she sucked, she circled the head of his dick with her tongue, drawing Rich to a climax.

"Shit, damn, wooooo," Rich was breathing heavy as Zora swallowed his load.

She stood up, wiping her lips. "Nia ain't gonna take care of you like that."

"Nia?"

"I got twenty-twenty vision and a one-twenty I.Q., so I saw how she was on you and I know her intent."

Rich secured his belt and dusted off his blazer. "We got a good thing going, but I don't remember walking down no aisle."

"There's a level of respect that accompanies even open relationships. And that entails you not creeping with people I have to see every day for eight hours and on holidays at company events."

Rich pulled Zora toward him as she adjusted her blouse. He kissed her. "I do a lot of dirt, but I got more sense than to dump it in front of your door."

Zora looked into his eyes. "I hope so."

Rich had previously sensed possessiveness in Zora. Her mouth said open relationship, but her actions spoke a loyalty shared by people who exchanged vows and engage in pillow talk until Alzheimer's set in and they were parted by a casket. Rich had been through more drama than he could remember because of possessive women. The type of drama he hoped Zora didn't reintroduce him to.

CHAPTER EIGHT

DOMINGO

Domingo was inside Vera's apartment the day after Leah was murdered. He was seated beside Vera on a couch in the living room. Mimi and Chanel were sitting across from them on a loveseat. Domingo had been listening as the women tried to make sense of Leah's death while they grieved. Domingo was still surprised that Candy and Vanessa actually killed Leah, her unborn child and her husband. He had underestimated their appetite for vengeance and willingness to go to the extreme of killing her child and husband. While Domingo knew Candy's kidnapping and torture could turn sweet women like her and Vanessa sour, the only image he had of them were the delicate, beautiful women who seemed harmless.

"Why?" Vera asked to no one in particular as she gazed at the ceiling fan. She leaned her head on

Domingo's shoulder.

He wrapped his arm around her. It amazed Domingo that none of the women had even speculated that their actions and Leah's had caused her demise. *It's been a couple of years, though. Guess they rocked these chicks to sleep for real.* A substantial amount of time had elapsed since Candy's kidnapping and torture and her name rarely entered conversations between the women. But Domingo still assumed the women were street savvy enough to at least speculate on the possibility of Candy, Vanessa or Rich being involved in the fatal shooting.

"She didn't deserve that shit, feel me?" Mimi wiped the tears from her slanted eyes. The Asian hood chick had seen a lot coming up in Queen's Baisley Projects. But witnessing her pregnant friend get gunned down was new to her. She was in the back seat of the truck, but had been engaged in an intense phone call so she had stayed inside while Leah exited. Mimi nearly peed her pants as shots were fired and she watched Leah and her husband get brutally gunned down. Fear had paralyzed her in shock, making it hard for her to see through the tinted windows at the faces of Candy and Vanessa. "I'll never forget seeing Leah and Moses get shot. All I remember is how their bodies dropped."

Chanel stood up in the center of the living room, strands of her long weave shifting beneath the ceiling fan. The sexy, chocolate beauty dressed head-to-toe in Chanel looked at Vera. "What if Rich did this shit?"

"That motherfucker been missing in action for a couple of years now. Him and his chicks," Mimi said.

"What that 'posed to mean?" Chanel asked, shrugging her shoulders.

Vera said, "The chances of him being involved in this are slim."

Chanel shook her head. "You don't know Rich."

Mimi nodded. "People get rocked to sleep in the hood on a regular, feel me?"

"All right, all right, all right," Domingo said. He stood beside Vera, facing Chanel and Mimi. He cared less about Rich getting fingered. It might actually be a good thing if there was no potential for hearsay leading to the truth. That truth could cause Domingo to lose out on the constant stream of money from Candy for him relaying them information. And his hope to get inside her panties would be undermined by something happening to her. "Ain't no use chasing ghosts," he said. "Rich, Vanessa, Candy—they probably was in Westbubblefuck somewhere having a ménage when them hot rocks hit Leah. You need to be thinking about Jennifer."

"Jennifer?" Chanel shrugged her shoulders after voicing the name of Moses' ex-girl who he had dumped for Leah.

"You know she ain't get along with Leah," Domingo said.

Chanel shook her head. "But I can't see her trying to kill Leah."

"What's good?" Meisha asked. The chunky Harlemite walked into the room while moving her curly hair behind her ear.

Domingo turned to the brown-skinned woman who he considered Chanel's flunky since the day he met them both in Candy's Shop. "Chanel was over here pulling a mixtape."

"Mixtape?" Meisha's eyebrows rose.

"Freestyling like she on a mixtape," Domingo grinned as he adjusted his Gucci specs.

Chanel said, "We was talkin' about Leah—"

"And you started freestyling about Rich killing her," Domingo cut Chanel short.

"Domingo thinks Jennifer might have did it," Vera said.

Meisha flopped down on the recliner beside the sound system in the far corner of the room. Suddenly there was a somber look on her round face that appeared to be rooted in something deeper than Leah's death.

"Meisha, holler at ya boy," said Domingo.

She broke down, crying.

Chanel rushed to her aid, placing her hands on Meisha's shoulders. "What's up?"

After a moment of silence, Meisha wiped her eyes and took a deep breath. "Domingo might be on the right track."

"What?" Mimi asked.

"I didn't think about it until y'all just said Jennifer."

"Think about what?" Chanel asked.

Meisha huffed while slowly shaking her head. "Leah had told me Moses owed some money to Jennifer's brother and he was some major cat in the Bronx."

Domingo shook his head. "Can't be playin' with people bread. Dudes want they gwap." He sat down and listened as the women speculated about this mysterious man from the Bronx. He reflected on the memories of Candy and Vanessa as friends of the women in front of him and he was amazed. He knew Candy and Vanessa had a vendetta, but he still experienced an awkward feeling from the reality of them killing Leah. Domingo had seen countless failed attempts to kill official thugs in the hood. He had also seen bullets separate friends. But the killers had always been known gun slingers or men with reputations that made killing a logical step up in their drama-filled lives. But Candy and Vanessa defied these odds. As Domingo looked at the women in the room with him, he felt slightly bad for them, because he knew they were ignorant to the fact they were targets in the sights of two gun-toting women who were now merciless killers.

* * *

Later that night Domingo blew out a cloud of weed smoke and poured his third shot of Patron from the bottle that circulated through the room. He passed the blunt to Vera, who sat beside him. It was one of two blunts making its rounds to Mimi, Chanel and Meisha. Domingo didn't know if it was the weed and liquor, but he could have sworn Mimi actually peeped up Vera's skirt for what appeared to be the third time in the last ten minutes. The thought of Vera moaning out Mimi's name when he was eating her out flashed in his mind. He had never seen a sign of Mimi being interested in women. But Vanessa had revealed Mimi having at least one female affair. *They gotta be messing around. Must be that piff and Patron. Mimi can't hold her liquor or handle weed.*

Vera leaned back and stretched out, her dreads dangling behind the couch and her breasts bulging from her shirt as her back arched. "This Patron is serious," she giggled.

Domingo felt his dick getting hard as his eyes beamed at her breasts and quickly drifted down to her thick thighs. He thought about how he had struggled to get his tongue inside of her. *Damn, I gotta get my dick in that tight-ass lesbo pussy.*

Vera leaned forward, making eye contact with Domingo. She smiled and shook her head, before standing up. She began strutting to the back of the apartment.

Domingo watched Mimi's eyes following Vera's butt switch from her high-heel stride. *Mimi definitely got her lickin' license.*

"Pass that bottle," Chanel said.

Domingo handed the Patron to Chanel and gazed down her cleavage as she reached for it. "You need to cover up those tig old bitties before I lose control up in here."

Chanel laughed. "You gotta be gettin' it like Bill Gates just to drink from these D-cups." She laughed as she poured a shot of liquor. "But if you got Warren Buffet money, I'll let you get a close-up."

"That's a lotta paper for some eye candy," said Domingo.

"The Chanel Legacy is for the rich and famous," Chanel responded.

Domingo reached underneath his shorts and pulled a 40-caliber Walther from his waist. "This is for the rich and famous." He chuckled. "They make it, I take it."

"Shit, the way you reach in your pants, I thought you had the heart to show me something else," Chanel said, before sipping some Patron.

Domingo grabbed his dick through his shorts. "I pull out this Bazooka, you gon' run for cover before it start spittin', ya heard?"

Chanel's chinky red eyes shut as she downed the last of her shot. When they opened, she pointed at Domingo. "I got you by ten years, so let me tell you a jewel. Sometimes you gotta spare the rod to spoil the girl. 'Cause I need a tongue to cum, and I'm not talking no lickin' license shit."

Domingo stood, his high hitting him on another level. He braced himself, grabbed his crotch, and then flashed a peace sign with his other hand. "Deuces. I gotta go empty out this Bazooka."

"You are crazy," Mimi said as he stepped off.

Domingo walked into the back of Vera's apartment toward the bathroom. Stepping through the narrow hall, he watched her saunter toward him, her hips swaying rhythmically. As they neared each other, he gently grabbed her hands and stared into her dilated pupils. "When you gon' let me hit that?"

She giggled, the scent of liquor oozing from her. "Stop playing."

"Games for kids and I'm a grown-ass man, ya heard? You let me eat it, now let's take this to the next level."

"When you start wearing skirts and bras, call me." Vera grinned and pulled her hand from Domingo. She began walking off.

"Skirts and bras like Mimi?"

Vera stopped. Her jaw dropped as she turned around. "Excuse me?"

Domingo stepped over and grabbed her hand again. "You was calling for Mimi when I was eatin' that pussy and Mimi's eyeballs was all between your legs earlier." Domingo placed her hand on his dick as it almost burst through his shorts. "Chanel and Meisha don't gotta know about us. And definitely not Jahiem."

"What?" Vera screamed and jumped back as if his dick was poison. "You tryin' to blackmail me?" She laughed. "I'm the one that blackmailed Vanessa, remember?"

"I'm just trying to keep this between us."

"Oh, you don't want nobody to know how you ate my pussy and I sent you on your way? If you love your life, you definitely don't want my brothers finding out."

"You need to calm down."

Vera shook her head quickly, her dreads swinging wildly from side to side. "Fuck that. You wanna talk about me and Mimi, so fuck it."

This chick is wildin'. I ain't trying to go to war with her brothers, Domingo thought as he trailed behind her and she stomped into the living room waving her hands helplessly.

"What's up?" Chanel asked as Vera took center stage beside the coffee table the women sat around.

Vera grabbed the Patron off the table and downed the mouthful left in the bottle. She faced Mimi, then Chanel and Meisha. "Me and Mimi got it on twice."

"Yeah, right," Meisha said.

"I'm dead ass." Vera retold the story of how Mimi had cried on her shoulders after an argument with Jahiem. Conversing led to a hug that led to Vera's lips and tongue relieving Mimi of her stress before they ended up naked in bed. Mimi admitted to having had an experience with a woman before. She and Vera admitted to having a second affair within the following week.

Domingo was silent.

"This shit is crazy," Chanel said. "It's Candy and Vanessa all over again."

"It happened and that was that," Vera said. "Shit happens."

"Yeah," Mimi confirmed.

82

Vera pointed at Domingo. "But this flirtin' motherfucker ate my pussy and tried to blackmail—"

"He what?" Chanel interjected. "A man ate you out?" She leaned up from the couch, struggling to keep her bloodshot eyes from closing.

"Yeah. He kept his dick in his pants and his tongue in my pussy." Vera lifted her skirt, revealing her black thong. She bit down on her lip. "And girl, he ate this pussy like his tongue was custom-made for me." She laughed and turned to Domingo. "Your fuck game must be trash, because you eat pussy like you makin' up for falling short in the dick department."

Domingo clapped his hands and laughed off Vera's rants. "You blowing ya cool and wasting everybody time all at once, 'cause you don't score no points for gettin' a self-proclaimed freak between the sheets to eat pussy. The only flavor my tongue can sense is pussy."

"This is *General Hospital* and *All My Children* in the hood," Meisha said.

Domingo sat in the recliner while Meisha rattled on. He noticed Chanel had trouble taking her eyes off of him. It was obvious that Vera's exposé had cultivated Chanel's interest in his tongue.

"I think it's time for you to go," Vera told Domingo. "Everybody, for that matter."

Domingo stood and put his hand on Vera's shoulder. "I still got love for you."

She removed his hand and shook her head. "Bye,

Domingo."

"This went far enough," he said.

She smirked. "You think I was actually gonna bring my brothers into my business about you or Mimi?"

Vera said her goodbyes to the women.

"Damn, you never know who got they lickin' license," said Meisha, shaking her head before walking out the front door.

Chanel attempted to follow her but stumbled, clearly overwhelmed by hours of liquor and weed.

"You can't drive home like this," Domingo said. He put his arm over her shoulder and helped her out the door.

She reached in her Chanel bag and handed Domingo the keys to her Escalade. "Drive me to East New York and I'll pay for a cab to bring you back here to Red Hook."

"I got you." Domingo wrapped his arm around her waist, certain that he would get a taste of the sweetness between Chanel's thighs. That's where he needed to be for both his personal pleasure and the financial security that would come from him setting her up for Candy and Vanessa to kill.

CHAPTER NINE
CANDY

C andy gazed out of the window of her hotel room. As she took in the glittering stars that ignited the night sky, she thought of Rich. She couldn't believe that he had not tried to contact her or Vanessa lately. His absence made her realize that her love for him was stronger than she thought. The more she tried to remove him from her mind, the more thoughts of him surfaced.

Candy closed her eyes as she felt Vanessa's arms embrace her from behind. In her moment of stress she needed the comfort Vanessa provided. But she also needed Rich. Candy and Vanessa had both admitted that during late nights as they cried on each other's shoulders. But they were too stubborn to make the first move and they had assumed he was gone and happy without them.

"I love you," Vanessa said.

85

Candy heard her, but remained silent.Vanessa eased in front of Candy, gazing at the tears welling in her eyes. "What's wrong, baby?"

"Look at us. We're a hot mess. Rich is gone, we're on Long Island where we don't know nobody, we just murdered a woman that was once like a sister to me, not to mention we killed her husband and unborn child." Candy paused. "And there's a list of other people we plan to kill that I would have once risked my life for."

Vanessa wiped the tears that fell from Candy's eyes. "We can't control what we confront in life, but we can control how we handle it."

"I know, but we deserve better."

"Well, Leah and the rest of those hos thought otherwise."

"I know, you're right."

"Of course I'm right. We didn't ask for this shit. They gave it to us. How do you think it felt for me to kill an unborn baby and its parents?"

Candy watched how Vanessa's eyes fluttered and her lips moved slowly as she spoke. There was a level of emotion reverberating from Vanessa that was foreign. Candy could see she was visibly upset as she rehashed taking two innocent lives. "But at this level, we all we got," Candy said.

Vanessa nodded and then hugged her.

"I love you," Candy declared. She felt Vanessa's hand caress her butt. In seconds, Candy's skirt was up and Vanessa's soft hands roamed underneath her thong and into her crack.

Vanessa slowly dropped to her knees. She planted tender kisses on Candy's legs, slowly working her way to her inner thighs. She shifted Candy until her back was against the window.

Candy gasped and closed her eyes as Vanessa inserted a finger in her ass and swiped her tongue over her pussy at the same time. She cocked one of her legs over Vanessa's shoulders and pulled her head with both hands. Her back arched each time she felt Vanessa's fingers go in and out of her asshole.

Vanessa found Candy's clit. She surrounded it with her lips and sucked while pushing the tip of her tongue into it rapidly.

Candy panted and cooed as chills ran through her body. "Vanessa," her high-pitched whisper sounded as her shoulders pressed against the window.

Vanessa ran her hand up Candy's leg and inserted two fingers inside of her throbbing pussy. She worked it simultaneously with the finger in her asshole while sucking her clit.

"Ah, ah, ah, ah, ahhhh, ahhhhhhh." Candy's legs fell from Vanessa's shoulders to the floor as she reached a climax. She unloosened her grip on Vanessa's head. Candy closed her eyes and exhaled.

Vanessa rose to her feet, slowly caressing Candy's body. She wiped her cum-soaked lips and puckered up.

Candy leaned down and locked lips with her lover. She worked her hands down to her butt, before she began kissing Vanessa's neck. She steered Vanessa back to the bed and undressed her. Candy towered over Vanessa's bare body, gazing at her small perky breasts down to the bald slit that shined with the glare of increasing wetness underneath the sunlight beaming through the window. Candy's lips watered as she descended on Vanessa.

"That feels so good," Vanessa mumbled as Candy's delicate hands caressed her breasts. Candy lapped her tongue on Vanessa's navel.

Vanessa cringed as Candy worked her hot spot. "Right there," she begged.

Candy continued downward as the heat from Vanessa's body invited her. Parting her thighs, Candy nudged Vanessa until she inched back on the bed. "I'm a fuck the shit outta you," Candy said in her most seductive tone. She sat on the bed and posted herself against the headboard.

Vanessa smiled and licked her lips while turning and inching toward Candy.

Candy lifted one of Vanessa's legs up to her shoulder as they maneuvered until their pussies touched. Her hands slid between Vanessa's legs and she pressed her body forward, pulling Vanessa toward her while she humped her pussy.

"Yes," Vanessa blurted. "Come on."

Candy closed her eyes. The lips of her pussy smothered Vanessa's clit. Each unification of their vaginas ignited an indescribable sensation that flowed throughout every part of Candy's body. She loved the sound of Vanessa's passionate cries that added to the euphoric realm Candy was in. Sweat soaked her brow as she worked up a sensual rhythm with the help of the slippery juices between their legs. "Ahh." Candy winced as she stretched her neck, her head titled back while her lower body shifted forward.

"Fuck me, Candy. Fuck me," Vanessa begged as if the beat of her heart depended on it. She pumped her small frame into Candy's grinding.

Candy could hear Vanessa's breaths increasing and could see her teeth clench in between sensual cries. Those signs coupled with Vanessa's flinching told Candy she was ready to explode. Candy quickly unloosened her grip on Vanessa and dove face-first between her legs.

Vanessa's legs locked around her neck as Candy sucked her into submission. "Candy, no, yes, please. Damn. God." Vanessa's body jolted as she reached her peak.

Candy lifted her head from between Vanessa's lap, and stared down at her as she regained her sense of normalcy. The look of bliss on Vanessa's face, her small sexy frame, her extra smooth skin—Candy loved everything about how she looked. Candy had never been so sexually compatible with another woman. The fact that Vanessa was a caring person with intellect and was comfortable with herself added to her physical beauty that made Candy crave her.

"You're too good to me," Vanessa said with a smile.

"You get what you deserve."

Vanessa smiled. "You deserve a sponge bath." She pointed to the Jacuzzi in the large room. "I prepared it before we got carried away."

Candy smiled and helped Vanessa from the bed, before trekking the carpeted floor to the large hot tub of bubbling water. Stepping inside the tub after Vanessa, Candy grabbed the issue of *The Daily News* on the stand beside the Jacuzzi. It was turned to the seventh page where an article about Leah's murder consumed an entire page.

"Still marveling at your work?" Vanessa said with a smile that turned to a frown as she spotted the bittersweet look on Candy's face.

Looking at the old picture of a smiling Leah for the third time, Candy's mind flashed back to the fear she saw in Leah's eyes before the young Latina lost her life. Killing Leah had done far less for Candy than she had anticipated. The painful memories of being kidnapped and tortured remained. While there was some relief knowing that she had finally followed through with the plan she and Vanessa plotted, there was still a hunger for more—a hunger that would likely never go away. She wasn't sure if it was the thirst she had for meting out justice to the others who violated her, or if it was part of the reality that no matter who was killed, she would still remain scarred by the memories of her unborn child dying and everything else that came with her kidnapping and torture.

"Candy?" Candy looked up from the newspaper as Vanessa waved her hand in front of it. "I called you twice."

Candy fully snapped back into reality. "Just thinking about all of this." She set the newspaper back on the stand.

"Please don't start this back up again," Vanessa said.

"What?"

"Caring about the people that ruined our lives. This love thy enemy stuff verges on Stockholm Syndrome." As Candy went to respond, Vanessa put her index finger over her lips. "That doesn't require opposition." Vanessa kissed Candy, then turned and slid her back into Candy's embrace.

Candy exhaled and wrapped her arms around Vanessa, then leaned her head back. She felt calm. Her senses were heightened. Candy could hear the bubbles in the Jacuzzi and she watched the intricate inscription in the chandelier above her. Even the scent of Vanessa's body seemed stronger. The missing link was Rich. "I wonder if Rich is thinking about us right now," Candy asked.

"It's hard to think about your ex-women when you're having sex with a new woman."

"So you think he's in another relationship already?"

Candy asked.

"A relationship and fucking some ho like that one that was in the elevator are two different things," said Vanessa. "You know more about Rich and more about women than me, anyway."

"He was good while he lasted. A man who came from a world where killing was normal is upset because we vowed to get the people that—" Candy paused, thinking of what happened to her. "It's just ironic."

"I miss him, too. But we have to be strong for each other now."

"Would you accept him if he comes back?"

"I'm pissed with him, but I love him," said Vanessa. "I want him back as much as you do."

"I knew it."

"But he's the one that was wrong and if he still loves us—"

"You know he does," Candy interjected.

"Then he'll find us."

"But we disappeared to Long Island."

"Our phone numbers are the same." Vanessa turned around and faced Candy. "We can't go running behind him, Candy. No matter how much we love him, he disrespected us with that elevator ho."

"You got no argument out of me."

"Besides, we have to finish what we started with Leah. And you know Rich doesn't want that."

Vanessa's love for Rich was the confirmation Candy needed. Candy had to have Rich back in her life and she was going to do what was necessary to fulfill that need, even if it meant defying Vanessa's wishes.

***

It was hours later that night when Candy screamed out as loud as she could. Her legs and arms flailed in every direction. She accidently kicked Vanessa off the bed. Awakening from a nightmare, Candy was breathing heavy, holding her heart as her eyes rolled wildly, scanning the large room for a sign of the character from her scary dream. Her hand slipped down to her stomach and she began bawling.

"What's wrong?" Vanessa asked as she rose from the floor and climbed on the bed. "It was only a dream." She hugged Candy. "It's okay."

Vanessa's embrace was soothing, but Candy was still distraught. In between sniffles and cries she said, "It's not all right." She slowly pushed Vanessa away.

"What is it?"

Candy took one of Vanessa's hands and pulled it toward her, placed it on her stomach. "I had a dream me and Leah were in a room tied to chairs. And they—" She closed her eyes.

Vanessa attempted to hug her, but she shook her head and kept Vanessa at bay. "You don't have to talk about it now," Vanessa said.

"I watched as Chanel beat Leah's child from her

womb." Candy's head dropped. She was still holding Vanessa's palm to her stomach. She looked into Vanessa's eyes. "Then you . . . you shot me in the . . . the stomach," she uttered the horrific twist of truth that reversed the roles in which she and Leah had lost their unborn children.

Vanessa hugged Candy, rocking back and forth with her, cupping her head in her palm. "It's just a dream. A nightmare."

"It was so real," Candy mumbled, her heart pounding against Vanessa's chest. "It was so real."

"You know I would never hurt you."

Candy slowly pulled back and wiped the tears from her face before gazing at Vanessa. She shook her head. "It's wrong."

"What?"

"It's wrong, Vanessa. What we did to Leah."

Vanessa's eyes closed momentarily. "It was wrong what they did to you."

"You don't understand."

"I don't understand?" Vanessa frowned. "Because it didn't happen to me I don't understand?"

"They beat my child out of me, Vanessa!" she screamed. "And they took something more from me than that. There's a part of me that's gone. It's missing forever. I'll never be the same and I hope you never have to experience this." Candy slid off the bed.

Vanessa followed her across the carpeted floor. "So

what do we do?"

Candy turned to her, more tears building in her eyes. She shook her head.

"I wish I could answer that." Candy walked over to the dresser, grabbed some clothes and began getting dressed.

"Where are you going?"

"Out."

"Out?" Vanessa said in a tone, indicating she was upset.

"I need some air. Gotta clear my mind."

"And you can't do that with me here?"

Candy remained silent.

Vanessa walked over to Candy as she adjusted her belt around her True Religion jeans. "This is not the time for us to be falling apart."

Candy managed to squeeze out a smile. She planted a tender kiss on Vanessa's lips, then their tongues danced in each other's mouth briefly. "I love you, Vanessa." She pointed to the front of the room. "I'm just walking out that door, not out your life."

She wiped her eyes, grabbed her Hermes clutch and headed toward the door. A million thoughts raced through her head. One dominant idea was whether to abort the plan she and Vanessa had for revenge. Candy knew she could not talk to Vanessa about it. The only other person who could give her a rational view on the matter was Rich.

CHAPTER TEN
VANESSA

Vanessa took a deep breath as she watched Candy walk out of the door. She didn't doubt that Candy would be back. What she was uncertain of was if Candy would be willing to follow through with their plan. Candy had been apprehensive about the killings from the outset. She was a person with a history on the streets and experience dealing with hustlers and thugs, so Vanessa expected her to be taking the lead in the drama. But as Vanessa thought about Candy expressing losing a part of her when she lost her child and not being the same, her position made sense. Perhaps Candy's experience had given her intimate knowledge that Vanessa was not privy to, the type of personal knowledge that may have changed Vanessa's outlook on the situation. *I haven't experienced the short end of the stick*, Vanessa thought as she recalled Candy being kidnapped and tortured. Candy was the

96

person who was practically bedridden as she recuperated from that horrific experience. It was Candy who had told Vanessa how she endured physical abuse years earlier by hustlers. How she suffered beat downs from the women they dealt with who felt they were entitled to be the number one woman. Candy had even been pistol-whipped for her jewelry during a robbery at a Brooklyn nightclub. The few incidents that Vanessa had been through left her on top, with the exception of a couple of blows from Chanel during a fistfight.

Vanessa began pacing the room. She was trying to wrap her mind around the ever-changing actuality of their life. Each time she thought of how bad things had turned, she pointed at Leah and the others as the source of her problems. In Vanessa's mind, Leah deserved everything she received and her cohorts were going to get the same.

Vanessa picked up her Droid from the dresser, contemplating whether to call Domingo. She wanted to press him to speed up the process of getting the information she needed to eliminate Leah's cohorts. She didn't want to wait until the Father's Day Tournament. Immediate revenge was the only answer to Vanessa questioning her life. She called Domingo and he answered on the second ring.

"You already know who it is, holler at ya boy."

"When are you going to produce?" Vanessa demanded.

"Why you callin' me, anyway? Where's Candy?"

"I'm filling in for her. Back to my question. When are you going to produce?"

"Let's rewind this." Domingo paused. "You already know who it is, holler at ya boy."

Vanessa's anxiousness was boiling over into rage. "You like two buildings from Vera. Vera's place is Grand Central Station for these skanks. I don't understand why you can't arrange for us to handle all of them at once. Maybe you can enlighten me as to why."

"You need to watch your tone, first. But bottom line is, you want things done right, you need patience. Don't they say that shit is a virtue or something?"

"How about saving the philosophy and giving me facts?"

"Red Hook is not a good place to fuck with them. I live here, trust me. Plus, it's not like everybody and they mother is up in Vera crib like you think. Just be patient."

"I've been patient for two years since these skanks ruined my life. Now I'm asking you to work faster. Bye." Vanessa turned off her phone and clenched it so tight she hurt her hand. She grabbed her iPad. "Fuck!" she blurted. The Wi-Fi in the hotel was down again. Vanessa decided to go to a nearby Internet café she had spotted days earlier.

* * *

After a short walk as the sun was rising, Vanessa stepped into the upscale Internet café named iTrus. She ordered a bottle of Dasani and leaned back in the couch, inhaling the scent of Cappuccino and bagels that permeated the eatery filled predominantly with business people typing away on laptops and tablets. There were nearly as many briefcases as there were computers.

"Is this seat taken?"

Vanessa turned to the squeaky voice coming from the pale, toothpick-thin brunette with oversized glasses perched on her thin nose. "It's all yours," Vanessa responded.

The young woman sat at the far end of the couch and opened her Macbook. "My professor's going to have a heart attack if I don't turn this paper in on time. I mean, some people don't understand that nineteen-year-olds have a life outside of academia." She turned to Vanessa. "Excuse me, I didn't mean to be rude. My name is Peggy Klein, but you can call me Peg. Most people prefer Peg. My grandmother has been calling me Peg since I was just a little Jewish child with freckles and acne. I mean-"

Vanessa interjected to stop the overly expressive fast talker. "Hi, Peg. I'm Vanessa."

Peg smiled and shook Vanessa's hand. "Vanessa, that's a cool name. I once had a friend from Arkansas named Vanessa. We met while I was spending the summer in Illinois. But I haven't heard a peep out of her in a year. I wonder what she's up to now."

Why the hell doesn't this chick shut up!

"So, Vanessa, what brings you to this cafe? I mean,

I'm like one of the most faithful customers here. It's the only green Internet café in town. I actually began spending a good deal of time here shortly after they opened three years ago. I believe it was on a Monday. Summertime. I know every employee here and practically any person who's ever spent money here on a consistent basis. But I've never seen you."

"I was just about to leave," Vanessa lied, anxious to get away from Peg.

"It's my fault," Peg said with sorrow in her voice. "I'm sorry, Vanessa. Sometimes I don't know when to put a lid on it, so people get bored, frustrated or a combination of the two. Let's just say I've driven my share of people away from me."

Vanessa watched the sad look on Peg's face as her upbeat demeanor changed and she lowered her head. Assessing Peg's hippie wardrobe, Vanessa could see herself in Peg. Her old, innocent self, the one who had coped with years of lingering on the outskirts of the in-crowd. The one who had more books in school than friends. There's no need for an apology."

Peg looked up at Vanessa with a smile. "Thanks."

Vanessa glanced at the screen of her laptop, thinking of the days she had spent penning essays like Peg was doing. "So what's the paper about?"

"Stonewall," Peg said, and then explained that the New York City gay bar was raided by police in 1969, causing a riot that resulted in the first public protest by homosexuals. "It sparked the gay rights movement. I'm tying Stonewall in with Governor Cuomo recently legalizing gay marriage. I mean, I'm a single lesbian, so marriage is not in my sight at this moment. But who knows what the future holds."

Vanessa was silent, staring into Peg's dark-brown eyes. Vanessa was rarely attracted to white women, but there was something about Peg's eyes that enticed her. Her openness as a lesbian also appealed to Vanessa. Finding a woman sexy was normal for Vanessa, but knowing a woman was gay always heightened her attraction.

After Vanessa's extended silence, Peg asked, "So, what do you have a problem with? Me being gay, gay marriage or both?"

"I have problems with a lot of people, but women who like women don't fit the bill. Trust me."

Peg smiled. "If more people thought like you, the world would be a better place. I mean, at least my world. I have a mother who doesn't understand me, a father who shuns me and five siblings who debate amongst themselves whether I disgraced our prestigious Jewish family or if I'm to be applauded for my individuality."

Vanessa thought about Candy mentioning how her conservative Christian family had disowned her when she announced her first same-sex relationship. Candy and Peg shared a sense of isolation that Vanessa had felt by virtue of her Bohemian lifestyle long before she discovered her bisexual tendencies. Trading her life in New York City for a drifter wandering from state to state with only Candy and Rich as social support compounded her isolation. But looking into Peg's eyes, Vanessa saw an outlet—a connection to counter the chaos that tore apart Vanessa's three-way relationship.

"I'm confident with my individuality and sexuality, but it's hard being shunned for being attracted to women and having a woman to support me." There was seriousness in Peg's voice as her eyes wandered over Vanessa's body.

Is she coming on to me? Vanessa wondered. She had never been pursued while face-to-face with a woman. There was always something flattering and empowering about a man or woman coming on to Vanessa. Because it rarely happened, when it did she felt validated.

"Is there a lucky someone in your life?" Peg asked.

"Yes and no."

"Open relationship?"

"Broken relationship."

Peg slid her hand over to Vanessa's leg. "Maybe you need to venture out."

Vanessa thought of Candy and Vera, the only two women she had ever been intimate with—Candy by choice, Vera by coercion. But sex with Peg would be out of necessity. There was a fire that burned constantly between Vanessa's legs. And she felt compelled to explore since her relationship with Candy was teetering on destruction and Rich was missing. Vanessa looked into Peg's eyes and placed her hand on Peg's hand.

Peg put her other hand on top of Vanessa's hand, sandwiching it before she stood and helped Vanessa to her feet. Peg closed her laptop.

Vanessa was nervous, but anxious. She was uncertain whether she wanted a one-time affair with Peg or a long-term relationship. But as she gazed at the curly hair lying against Peg's smooth white skin, Vanessa knew she wanted Peg now.

* * *

After leaving iTrus Café, Vanessa found herself lying on Peg's bed, looking at her through the huge mirror on the ceiling. Both women were naked as Peg was gently circling one of Vanessa's nipples with her tongue. Vanessa ran her hands through Peg's hair and caressed her neck.

Peg made her way up, kissing Vanessa's neck before her tongue entered Vanessa's mouth. "You taste so good," Peg whispered, then worked her way down. Her hands cupped Vanessa's breasts, gently squeezing them. She worked Vanessa's nipples with her mouth.

"Ahh, yes," Vanessa cooed. She gritted her teeth and closed her eyes. All she could feel was the sensation in her breasts. It was as if no other part of her body existed. Vanessa winced as Peg engulfed almost her whole right breast and then slowly released it from her mouth after her wet lips sucked intensely on Vanessa's nipple.

She hovered over Vanessa with a seductive look. Turning Vanessa over onto her stomach, she said, "Welcome to heaven."

Vanessa slid a pillow underneath her neck and closed her eyes as she felt the warmth of Peg's body closing in on her. The touch of her lips on Vanessa's neck increased the wetness between her legs. She could feel Peg's soft hands trailing downward from her shoulders, following the kisses that lowered to her spine. In seconds, Vanessa felt Peg lightly slap her rear, before kissing it.

"You like that?" Peg asked

"Love it."

Peg slipped her hands underneath Vanessa and lifted her, while guiding her tongue between Vanessa's swollen pussy lips. The lips on Peg's mouth met the lips between Vanessa's legs.

"Eat me," Vanessa purred as her body wiggled and her world became a small vicinity where only she and Peg existed. She could feel Peg probing her moist insides, her tongue pleasuring every part that mattered. Vanessa reached back, pulling Peg's head until her tongue went as deep as possible.

Peg slipped one of her hands down until Vanessa's clit was snug between Peg's fingers that slid back and forth.

"Please, yes," Vanessa whispered. She bit down into the pillow. Her body became tense, then began to spasm as she released a load of her liquids into Peg's mouth and onto the bed. A surge of energy bolted through Vanessa's body, then she grew tired, her body loose.

Peg pulled back from Vanessa. "How was heaven?"

Vanessa rolled over on her back with a smile. "Simply divine." She stared into Peg's eyes and said, "Let me show you." She leaned forward on her knees.

Peg stood on the bed and stepped forward until Vanessa's lips were kissing her thighs. Vanessa's palms sunk into Peg's cottony ass. "Rub it," Peg commanded.

Vanessa slowly caressed both of Peg's tiny butt checks, covering nearly all of them. Vanessa ran her hand in and out of the crack of Peg's ass and eased her tongue against her clit. "That feels so good."

Vanessa slid two fingers inside of Peg's tight pussy and began working her G-spot while sucking her clit.

"Just like that. Come on." One of Peg's hands fell to Vanessa's shoulders. The other slipped back until Peg was working her own fingers into her ass. "Yes, it feels so right."

Vanessa moved from Peg's clit to the outside of her pussy lips, while still fingering her G-spot.

"Just like that. Ahh, that's great," Peg whispered. Her body began to quiver and her moans turned to roars.

Vanessa sucked hard on Peg's pink mound while stimulating her G-spot.

"Perfect! That's just how I like it. Yessss!" Peg yelled as she came.

Vanessa stepped back as her face, neck and breasts

were hit with the white fluid squirting from Peg's pussy. *What the hell?* Vanessa had heard of women who were squirters, but she had never seen one. She wiped the cum from her face.

Peg bent down and helped Vanessa, by licking her own cum from Vanessa's neck and breasts.

She's a freak for real. Vanessa's nipples grew hard in Peg's mouth. She grabbed Peg and shifted her head between her legs. She clamped them around Peg's head and pulled her toward her. Vanessa balled her fists as Peg sucked her into a second orgasm.

Afterwards, Vanessa and Peg washed each other underneath the warm water of Peg's shower. Shortly after, Peg left the bathroom and Vanessa found herself drying off. She noticed that all of Peg's toiletries were organic, many made from products like oatmeal and hemp. Vanessa called out, "Hey Peg, where's your antiperspirant?"

"You can't be serious," Peg yelled back. "That stuff will kill you. It stops you from sweating, so your body doesn't release the toxins found within the sweat. That means the poisons your body is trying to get rid of remain trapped inside. It's a recipe for cancer. There's a number of studies proving it."

"How about deodorant?" Vanessa asked.

"When you shower three times a day, you don't need it."

No deodorant? She's taking this Bohemian business

106

to another level. Vanessa grabbed some cocoa butter and rubbed it under her armpits. She applied some Shea butter on her 'fro and mineral oil to her body before stepping out of the bathroom and getting dressed. She found her way to the dining room connected to the kitchen.

"You hungry?" Peg asked.

"You suck all of the energy out of me then have the nerve to ask if I'm hungry." Vanessa smiled, looking at the white woman draped in a long multi-colored T-shirt.

"You're welcome to join me for a meal, but I don't eat anything with a face."

Vanessa stood and began walking toward Peg. "You're a vegan too?"

"Since I protested my biology teacher in junior high for failing me after I refused to dissect a frog."

Vanessa smiled and began explaining how she had stopped eating meat and meat byproducts for health reasons about five years earlier.

Peg looked down at Vanessa's leather clogs. "Now all we have to do is get you to stop wearing animals. It's pretty archaic and cavemanish to see us humans wearing animal skin in 2012. Not to mention, it's just plain gross."

As Peg prepared some stir fired vegetables, she told Vanessa how she had been involved in animal rights groups for years. There was something that frustrated Peg about knowing that millions of innocent animals were brought into the world and raised to adults only to be murdered and eaten or worn as clothing by humans. She didn't believe there was a legitimate reason to hurt or kill another being that experiences pain—be they research monkeys in a lab or drug dealers in the hood. She went out of her way to make sure the vast majority of products she bought were not made in sweat shops and were green, from toothpicks to her Toyota Prius.

"So I just had sex with an environmentalist?" Vanessa asked with a smile.

"Consider me a woman who wants to treat the earth right and if given the opportunity, treat you right." Peg leaned over and kissed Vanessa passionately.

As they parted, Vanessa's eyes opened. She stared at Peg. Her thin, pink lips, pale skin, and thin nose. Vanessa was coming to terms with the fact she had just had sex with a white woman and she loved it. She liked what she had seen about Peg as a person, because she seemed to have the morals Vanessa had once clung to so hard. But Vanessa felt guilty for cheating on Candy.

Even though Candy had walked out of the door on a bad note and their relationship appeared to be evaporating like fog exposed to the rising sun, Vanessa still loved Candy, just like she loved Rich.

CHAPTER ELEVEN

RICH

R ich sat poolside on a beach chair behind King's extravagant mansion in the upscale Buckhead section of Atlanta. The sound of Olivia's "December" blared as D.J. Clue rocked the crowd of 200-plus employees from Queens Incorporated and their guests who mingled under the sun. Through his aviator shades, Rich watched the countless models clad in bikinis. Many of them had been flirting with him since he began spending time at Queens Incorporated. But Rich had turned down their advances out of respect and his hope not to cause any problems for Zora. He and Zora had been spending a lot of time together. He found out they shared not only a strong sex drive, but intelligence and ambition too. Yet Rich was trying not to jump into a relationship at the moment. And in the back of his mind were memories of Vanessa and Candy. On many occasions he had fought his urge to attempt to rekindle their once solid relationship. But he was done being a repairman. If they loved him, they would have to undo the damage they caused to their relationship. In his mind, their obsession with revenge had pushed him away.

"You see her?" King asked, rolling his eyes in the direction of a thin, Indian woman in a colorful sundress.

"Honey near the lifeguard?" Rich responded.

"Actual fact."

"What about her?"

"You been to Tasty before?"

"Just two. I slid through the one in Manhattan and the one in LA?" Rich thought of the nights he spent at two of the upscale chain of strip clubs. "I don't remember seeing Pocahontas on the stage at neither one of them."

"You don't strip on stages when you own the club."

Rich nodded, clearly impressed. "I would've never thought—"

"That's why I see things for what they are and not what they appear to be and never take things on face value."

"Okay, drop the science, God," Rich said with a grin. He recognized King's jargon from The Nation of Gods and Earths. For years, King had been a member of the God-centered cultural group, also known as the Five Percenters. But Rich had never taken King's righteous talk seriously, because King was engaged in the street culture that undermined righteousness.

Rich's eyes shifted from the woman to King. "So, besides Pocahontas doing some numbers, tell me

110

something else about her."

King smiled as he removed a bottle of Grey Goose from a bucket of ice on the small table that separated him from Rich. King pulled the collar on his Polo shirt, revealing the hickey on his dark skin. "She's a beast in the boardroom and the bedroom."

"So it's business and personal between y'all?"

"Business and fringe benefits. Katiya Patel."

"Katiya," Rich repeated her name.

"When I say beast in the bedroom, I'm serious. Couldn't keep her still if she was in cuffs and shackles. You'll probably find out, because her eyes were glued to you like rhinestones on a jean jacket in the eighties."

Rich watched the slender woman with the sexy strut. Pearls rounded her neck and filled the piercings in her ears.

"Her money is longer than the Casey Anthony trial and she's about her business. But if you're not into arrogance and spontaneous quickies, stick with Zora."

"You always spoke so highly of Zora, but I don't see her coming home to this mansion or you putting a ring on her finger."

"'Cause I never hit that."

"Fuck outta here," Rich said. "Your personal assistant that travels around with you to Vegas, but you never fucked her?"

"If I was to lay this pipe game on her, it would mess up our business relationship. She's not like Katiya, who's a businesswoman from another company. Zora works too close to me. A love quarrel between us could affect my bottom line."

"So you never had intentions to bag her?"

"If I had the discipline and desire for just one woman, it would be Zora. She's a good woman and deserves a good man to wake up to every morning, but she keeps running into brothers like me that's gone before the sun comes up." King took a swig of the Vodka. "Zora's a queen, but this King needs a harem."

"What makes you think Rich ready to go solo?"

King chuckled. "Candy and Vanessa. After them you need a break."

Rich knew there was some validity to King's statement. But while Rich had turned down passes from women on Zora's job, he had sexed his share of ladies in Atlanta. He had even experience two threesomes. Rich found himself constantly struggling to suppress what had become a natural yearning for sex with two women simultaneously.

"Moving along. What's the science with that business proposition?" King asked.

He had offered Rich the opportunity to invest in the establishment of a second branch of Queens Incorporated slated to open in Los Angeles.

"It's been on my mind," Rich said. He had been living off his stock portfolio of several Fortune 500 companies and a larger stake he had in his uncle's luxury car rental service. Because Rich had no stable residence outside of the cabin he owned in Upstate, New York, he had not settled down long enough to think about new investments.

"It's a one-point-two million dollar project. A thirty percent stake in an established brand is a good look for you. We made a lot of blood money together on the streets. Now we can make a lot of legal money. My marketing team is predicting a return on investment in a year, which you know is unheard of in a lot of companies."

"I'm leaning in your direction, but I need to shoot out to LA and meet with your people and feel the scene before I sign a check."

"So you don't always take things on face value?" King grinned. "Always do the knowledge."

Rich watched Zora saunter over in a striped bathing suit and Fendi shades. On her head was a large white hat reminiscent of those worn by older women attending church on Sundays.

"What's up, baby?" Zora sat on Rich's lap, then leaned down and kissed him before turning to King. "I'm not interrupting anything, am I?"

"It's a little too late for that question, but no," Rich said.

"I'm sorry, Daddy." Zora rubbed her hand on Rich's bare chest, down to his six pack. She grinded slowly in his lap and winked at him. "I can make it up to you."

"It's plenty of rooms inside." King pointed to his two-story, 15,000-square-foot mansion. "Out here we party." He stood and started a slow two-step as Kelly Rowland's "Motivation" came on.

"Damn, I love this song." Zora grabbed Rich's arm and pulled him to his feet. "Come on, baby."

Rich threw his hands in the sky, rocking back and forth behind Zora as she rotated her hips and swerved her small, round butt against his groin. He grabbed the bottle of Nuvo off the table and took a sip before waving it in the air.

Zora snatched the bottle from him and took a swig. She turned around, still rocking to the mellow beat as she placed her arms around Rich's broad shoulders.

Rich's hands wrapped around her gyrating hips. He noticed Katiya gazing at him. She was sipping a Margarita as she moved her body in what looked like a belly dance. Rich saw her inching toward him with the type of grin that often preceded foreplay. She got just a foot behind Zora, then licked her lips at Rich before shifting her ass against King.

"Go, go go," King sang.

Although Katiya's sexy figure and her dance moves were perfectly in sync with the beat, her eyes never left Rich's. He realized how better she looked up close. Thin strands of baby hair trailed her peanut butter complexion. She had a pearly pair of eyes that were naturally seductive and capable of conveying messages that the

114

best orator would have trouble speaking. A curly ponytail hung to the small of her back, where her backside protruded from her dress. Zora was gorgeous and the softness of her body against Rich was intoxicating, but just the sight of Katiya was making Rich more aroused than Zora's closeness to him.

After the song was over, Rich sat. Zora flopped down on his lap again. King and Katiya sat beside each other in front of Rich and Zora. Rich eyed Katiya's toned calves as she folded one leg over the other, revealing a tanned thigh that was far thicker than Vanessa's thighs, but nowhere near as thick as Candy's. As much as Rich tried to free his mind of Candy and Vanessa, they had become the litmus test by which he gauged women.

"Katiya, this is an old friend of mine named Rich," King said.

Katiya smiled and shook Rich's hand.

"It's a pleasure to meet you," said Rich.

"I know." Katiya grinned.

Rich was thrown off. *This broad really on some cocky shit.*

"And this is Zora, my personal assistant," King said.

"Oh, the help," said Katiya with a smirk.

Rich awaited a defensive response from Zora, but she simply smiled. It reminded Rich of the passiveness he witnessed after their elevator adventure when Candy and Vanessa scared Zora senseless.

"Old friend," Katiya said. "I suppose camaraderie

brings you here and not free drinks," she paused and glanced at Zora, "and leftovers."

Zora sighed and looked at Rich as if she expected him to defend her. When Rich remained silent, she stood and stomped off.

"You just had to come at her in a cold current," King said, shaking his head.

"Beauty and class can be intimidating to average women." She turned to Rich. "But my interests lie elsewhere." She leaned forward and removed Rich's smartphone from his waist and began typing. "This is the address to a gated community, Rich. Security will need your driver's license to confirm that you are Jamel Thomas." She slipped Rich's smartphone back in the case attached to his waist, then walked off.

"I just found out your government is Jamel Thomas." said King.

Rich's eyes were on Katiya as she gracefully strutted past a crowd of models in front of the D.J. booth. He was so amazed by her blunt approach and confidence that he didn't know how to respond in her presence or to King's statement. That was a new phenomenon, because Rich had never been left speechless by a woman. As he watched the switch underneath her dress, he knew he had to have her. But more importantly, he needed to know what else she knew about him in addition to the name his mother had given him.

CHAPTER TWELVE
DOMINGO

Domingo parked Chanel's Escalade on the corner of Sutter and Schenck Avenues in front of her East New York home in Sutter Gardens. He scanned the small, three-story apartment complex, then switched his gun off safety as he spotted a clique of youth inside Chanel's hallway.

"Don't start no shit," she protested with a drunken grin.

"I used to start beef. Now, I just finish it."

Chanel pulled out her Sidekick and pressed a few buttons. "I need a cab on Sutter and—"

Domingo grabbed her phone and turned it off.

"I told you I was gonna have a cab take you back to Red Hook. What the hell are you—"

Domingo interrupted her by leaning over and sliding

his tongue into her mouth. He could taste the liquor as she jerked back instinctively and then submitted to him. Within seconds, his hands were everywhere, from her breasts and butt to between her legs.

Chanel pulled back from him. Her eyes were still glassy from the liquor.

"What's good, Ma?"

Chanel looked through her tinted windows to the youngsters inside of her hallway and then glanced back at Domingo. "I wanna see if you can really eat pussy like Vera said. But now is not a good time to come in my crib."

Domingo was anxious. He wanted raw sex where the foreplay began—inside Chanel's Escalade. He started the truck.

"Where we goin'?"

"Don't worry, be easy." Domingo turned down Schenck and rode to Jamaica Avenue and circled around the back of Highland Park. He pulled up in the dark, desolate area. He removed his specs and began unbuckling his belt, then unzipped his pants.

"Damn!" Chanel said when Domingo's dick popped out."Your young ass is holdin'," she said with a childish giggle induced by her intoxication.

Domingo slipped his hand up her skirt. She was not wearing underwear so he had easy access. He began fingering her.

"Umph," she purred, then hiked up her skirt and

straddled Domingo as he steered his stiff pipe into her softness.

"Damn. Oh shit." Domingo's eyes rolled into the back of his head and his mouth opened wide. *The Chanel Legacy is real.* Her pussy was wetter and softer than any he had experienced. It was as if she had extra muscles and flesh that spiraled around his dick like a boa constrictor squeezing the life out of its prey.

Chanel began to pant as she worked up a rhythm, slowly rising the full length of Domingo's long dick, then slamming her pussy down forcefully each time.

Domingo unbuttoned her shirt and pulled her breasts from her bra. As she wrapped her arms around the headrest, one of her nipples fell directly in between Domingo's lips. He ran his tongue over her areola and then swallowed her nipple like it was his last opportunity with a woman.

Chanel sped up her pace, leaning back against the steering wheel as she pushed her lower body at Domingo while he cupped her ass.

"Yeah, Ma." Domingo's eyes opened and he pulled Chanel into him as he came. Sweat dripped from her onto him.

After a few seconds, Chanel climbed off of Domingo. She was upbeat. Domingo had sexed her sober. She looked through the tinted windows of her truck and then opened the door. "Come on."

"Where?"

"Just come on."

Domingo set his gun beside him, zipped up his shorts and tightened his belt, before stepping outside into the warm summer night air. He walked around the front of the Escalade, and found Chanel leaning against the hood. He looked at her thick legs in front of the huge chrome rim.

Chanel hiked up her skirt and hoisted herself up on the hood.

Domingo's eyes stared at the wet layers of hair covering her pussy. He looked around the block. There was no one in sight.

"Come on," Chanel said. "I'm hot, so hurry up." She began squeezing her breasts. Domingo's mind was still thinking of how fleshy and wet Chanel's pussy was, so he was anxious to taste it. He wedged her legs apart and gripped her thick hips before he dove in. He swiped his tongue around until it slipped in between her bulging pussy lips. Her body jolted. He could taste her pussy becoming wetter as his tongue wandered inside of her love tunnel.

"Yeah, eat me. Eat me, baby."

Chanel's erotic cries motivated Domingo. He began massaging her clit as he slurped on each of her pussy lips in between moving his tongue in and out of her pussy. The layers of slippery flesh that wrapped his dick were like a bowl of jelly that his tongue roamed through.

"Just like that." Chanel wrapped one of her legs around

the back of his neck, pulling him close as he worked deeper inside of her.

Domingo applied slightly more pressure to Chanel's clit with his finger and then ran his tongue back and forth across it.

Chanel screamed as her other leg wrapped around Domingo's neck. "Come on. I'm about to cum. I'm cummiinng."

Domingo sucked on her clit until her body went limp. He helped her off the hood of the truck. Palming her ass with both hands, he pulled her skirt down. His dick was getting hard again just looking at her 34-23-40 figure. He was conjuring memories of the supreme pleasure she had given him.

"So Vera was right about your tongue game," Chanel said as she buttoned her shirt. She slipped her hand inside Domingo's pants and ran her hand over the length of his dick. "But she don't know nothin' about this." She pulled her hand out and licked her fingers. "Maybe next time I'll taste it."

"Next time can be right now."

Chanel grinned.

"This ain't no laughin' matter."

"We got plenty of time." She opened the door and climbed into the Escalade.

As Domingo walked around to the driver's seat, he wondered just how much time he would have with Chanel. He had an obligation and was receiving payment to see to it that Candy and Vanessa were given the information they needed to kill Chanel. But that was the old Chanel—the Chanel whom he had no idea would give him a sexual experience he would never forget and the promise of more. Domingo liked Candy and wanted nothing more than to sex her. But Candy was keeping her distance and Chanel was spreading her legs.

* * *

Over a week had passed since Domingo had sex with Chanel. During that time they had explored each other's bodies three times, and each episode had become more intense for Domingo. They had clearly defined their relationship as a sexual one with no commitment to an emotion beyond raw passion. Chanel was vocal that she had a man and Domingo was out of her man's league financially. What Domingo had that Chanel wanted was a tongue capable of awakening feelings within her that she was not experiencing at home.

Domingo stretched out on his bed with a Tec-9 in his hand and a blunt in his mouth. He had just got off the phone with Chanel. He was upset that he would not be able to see her today, because she was in Florida with her man. He was more upset that she had taken a flight to Miami without telling him. But he didn't express his displeasure to Chanel because he knew she had no obligations to tell him of her whereabouts. They were in a discrete and open relationship. But despite his maturity, Domingo was a youth ten years younger than

Chanel. He was outmatched by her know-how in relationships and unable to control the sexual lure of her. Domingo had been a solo player on the streets. He was not used to sharing. And the thought of playing second string to Chanel's man was hard for him to grasp.

Domingo exhaled a cloud of weed smoke and placed his blunt in the ashtray on the nightstand. He removed the long clip from the submachine pistol in his hand and stood up. He was about to take a shower when his phone rang.

"What's up, Domingo?"

"Mamita."

"I'm on speaker. Vanessa is on the other end." Candy steered the conversation. "It's two days away, so we need to make sure everything is everything."

"Yeah," Domingo responded to her cryptic comment seeking confirmation that Chanel, Meisha, Vera and Mimi would be at the Father's Day Tournament.

"Good," Candy responded.

Domingo knew she and Vanessa would be on the scene and he planned not to be there when the bullets began flying.

"Anything on the two missing in action?" Vanessa asked, referring to the Twins.

Domingo had told her and Candy that Jahiem and Tahiem had not been seen in Red Hook lately. "Nothing," Domingo responded. "What's up with Rich?"

"Long story," Candy said.

"Hope it involves him stepping aside and making way for ya boy, 'cause I still got a sweet tooth for some Candy, ya heard, Mamita?"

Candy and Vanessa both laughed.

"What, I gotta be from Harlem to get a shot at that box?"

"What you gotta do is find a girl your age," said Candy.

"All a young girl can do for me is introduce me to a grown woman so I can body that."

"Okay, pussy killer." Candy laughed.

"We gotta go," Vanessa said.

"All right, I'll be waitin'."

"For what?" Candy asked.

"Y'all said y'all gotta go, so y'all must be coming to my crib. Rich ain't the only one who like three-ways."

Vanessa laughed. "Bye, Domingo."

"Later," Candy said, before hanging up.

Domingo tossed his phone on the bed. He thought about the day he met Candy as she headed to Vera's building. Her beauty had snatched him from a conversation he was having with some guys from his projects. Everything visible was perfect, from her face and figure to her walk. She took his flirtatious demeanor as a joke, but every comment lobbed at Candy was designed to break down the age and lesbian barriers she had erected between them. Now, Domingo was older and Candy was bisexual. Those changes coupled with

124

the fact Domingo ate out Vera and was sexing Chanel convinced him that his persistence would also wear down Candy. But his task was to first see her face-to-face. He had no idea if that would be possible after the Father's Day Tournament. He needed Chanel to avoid that tournament and for Candy to survive without getting locked up. Having both Chanel and Candy between his bed sheets would make his life complete.

CHAPTER THIRTEEN
CANDY

I t was just past midnight—one day before the Father's Day Tournament. Candy had been sleeping with Vanessa and woke up after having a wet dream about Rich. She sat on the toilet, washing sticky sap from between her legs. Her dream had evoked every good emotion she ever had because of Rich. She needed him. But the more she thought about the drama set to unfold, the more she pondered the possibility of something going wrong and her never seeing Rich again. She dried herself and stood up. "I gotta talk to him."

Candy left the bathroom and went to watch Vanessa sleeping before she picked up her smartphone and headed back to the bathroom. She phoned Rich.

"Candy?" Rich answered.

She closed her eyes. Every emotion within her leaked from her, before she uttered, "I love you, Rich."

"I love you too."

126

"Not seeing you has been killing me." Candy sniffled, wiping her eyes. "I just wanted you to know that in case something happens to me."

"Something happens to you? Talk to me, baby."

Candy could feel the concern in his voice. She knew he still loved her in spite of their being apart. She wanted to be in the comfort of his safety. But she also wanted to execute her plan. But she was worried. "I need to see you."

"Where are you?"

"Where are you?"

"Down in the A."

Candy glanced at her watch and took a deep breath. "I'm on the next flight there."

"Where's Vanessa? She okay?"

"She's asleep."

"Bring her with you."

"I can't."

"Why?"

"Long story. I'll meet you at the airport. I love you, Rich."

"I know."

Candy hung up and held the phone to her chest while her eyes closed. Being in contact with Rich was overwhelming. She opened her eyes and stepped out of the bathroom. She quickly grabbed her Fendi bag, then scribbled a note to Vanessa. She set the note on the nightstand. She watched Vanessa sleep for another minute, then crept out of the hotel with a sense of guilt for leaving Vanessa.

* * *

Candy arranged a flight by calling a friend who owned a travel agency. A few hours later, she stared at the Atlanta skyline as her plane descended on Hartsfield-Jackson International Airport. She had been questioning herself during the entire flight. Was she wrong for leaving Vanessa? Was she wrong for reaching out to Rich? Was her plan for revenge a wise move?

After the plane landed, Candy walked across the tarmac into the airport. Her heart rate sped up and her knees became wobbly as she saw Rich walking toward her. She picked up her pace and dropped her bag then hugged him. "I miss you."

"Miss you too," Rich responded.

Candy pulled back, getting a look at him. She smiled through her teary eyes.

Rich pulled a handkerchief from his blazer and wiped her tears and smeared mascara from her face. He gave her a passionate tongue kiss. "I love you, girl," he said afterwards.

"I'm sorry about everything."

Rich put his index finger over her lips. "Let's go."

Candy picked up her Fendi bag and stepped off in her matching boots with her arm around Rich's waist and his over her shoulders. They walked out of the airport and into Rich's new Audi R8.

Minutes later, Candy asked, "Where we headed?"

"Don't worry." Rich kept his eyes on 1-85, before hitting Piedmont Avenue and parking on Dallas Street in front of Historic Fourth Ward Park. Rich escorted Candy inside the park to a scenic pond. They walked the surrounding concrete trail and talked.

The cool breeze graced Candy's face, her long weave flowing as she stared at the fountain in the pond. "It's so peaceful."

"Like us, before we went downhill." Rich stopped, tugging on Candy's arms. As she faced him, he said, "You didn't shoot out here on a red-eye to give a commentary on the tranquility of a fountain you didn't know existed."

Candy was silent for a moment. "I had a dream about us."

"Good, I hope."

"So good I woke up wet."

"Sounds more like an adventure than a dream." Rich grinned.

"It was a reminder of us—me, you, Vanessa. It forced me to think hard and question my future."

"Why didn't you bring Vanessa?"

"I love her, but her anger won't allow her to see certain things at this juncture." Candy explained their perpetual debates about how to handle their desire for revenge. She spoke of them killing Leah as well as their plot for the Father's Day Tournament. "I got a bad feeling something is gonna go wrong, Rich." Candy burst into tears again and hugged Rich.

"It's okay. It's all right." Rich rubbed Candy's back. "I'm a bypass the I told-you-sos."

"I appreciate that."

Rich looked into Candy's eyes. "But this vendetta ain't gonna do none of us no good. You know I come from a world where guns do the talking and revenge is mandatory. Point is I fought hard to get out of there, and you and Vanessa helped motivate me." Rich paused, visibly deep in thought. "What happened to you?" He paused again, the dark skin of his forehead wrinkling. He gritted his teeth and shook his head. "That shit had me vexed . . . and scared. Scared that something else might happen to you. So while you was in the hospital, I showed Vanessa how to use a gun so she could protect herself. And I put Chase's gun in your hand so you could get some getback."

Candy remembered what it felt like to exact revenge. Despite society's view of killing being wrong, for Candy it felt right—right like her attraction to women in spite of what society thought of same-sex relations. "Chase deserved to die."

"Stevie Wonder could see that, but I ain't intend for you and Vanessa to be running around slinging hammers like Billy the Kid."

Candy thought of how she had gotten caught up in the spirit of what seemed to be a never-ending cycle of revenge.

130

"You don't think I want everybody involved in this shit put in a casket?"

Candy nodded.

"But I traded in the streets." He put his hand around Candy's waist. "For you, for Vanessa, for a normal life. When I met Vanessa I was on my way out the backdoor and neither one of y'all was in the building. Now y'all paying rent and giving me an open invitation."

Candy stepped back away from Rich and raised her voice. "So this is about you? Never mind all the shit me and Vanessa went through off the strength of you? Shift the blame on us, because it's all about Rich."

"I know you ain't deaf and your comprehension is good, so I'm gonna assume you just wasn't trying to hear me just now."

Candy rolled her eyes. "Ain't no wax stopping me from hearing you. Plus, I can read between the lines."

"Forget the subtext, 'cause I'm giving you this straight up and down like six o'clock. I put that gun in your hand, just like I did Vanessa. I can't point no finger at y'all without kicking myself in the ass. This ain't about no blame game, baby. It's about not seeing no inmate I.D. number behind your last name or having your whole name engraved on a tombstone."

Candy was silent, her thoughts scattered. Rich was saying everything that had been on her mind since she awoke from her dream of him. She knew how deep the hole was that she and Vanessa had dug for themselves. It was why she was reaching out to Rich. But there was still the thought that revenge had to be meted out. She needed an excuse for why she and Vanessa should not kill the people on their hit list, not a scare tactic like brandishing the words prison and death. Candy wanted a logical reason why the people responsible for her life being flipped should not be penalized. But there was no rationale for the wrongdoers. All Candy could conjure was the logic that made visible the strong potential for her and Vanessa to face harsh consequences if their plan was not executed properly.

"Come here," Rich said.

Candy stepped over to him. "I'm sorry, Rich. This shit is just crazy."

Rich smiled. "You learned quicker than me. Took me damn near my whole life running the streets to see the insanity in this shit." Rich looked around the empty park. "Let's slide."

* * *

Candy opened her eyes and lifted her head from Rich's bare chest. After they had left the park hours earlier, she fell asleep in the luxurious round bed inside one of the guest rooms in King's mansion. Candy rose from the large bed, watching Rich. She reached down and carefully pulled his morning erection through the slit of his Polo boxers. She marveled at the dick that had reintroduced her to men. Rich shifted, still asleep. Candy lowered her head, licking the length of his dick and submerging the head in her mouth.

"Umph," Rich moaned.

She looked up as Rich's head rose and his eyes opened. Candy sucked the head of his dick, twirling her tongue around it.

"Damn," Rich grunted, placing his hand in Candy's hair, steering her down.

Candy slowly rode his dick up and down with her mouth, slurping as she savored the familiar flavor of him. She could feel him growing in her mouth. Candy let the head of his dick reach the back of her mouth, the point just before her gag reflexes kicked in. Her pussy got wetter by the second until she could feel her nectar soaking her Victoria Secret thong.

Rich began moaning, mumbling his thoughts about how good Candy felt.

She rose and removed her thong, then crawled on top of Rich and guided his dick into her. "Ahh," she cried as she came down on all ten inches of his thick shaft. She leaned forward and grabbed his ankles, then slowly began riding Rich with him facing her back. She could feel his firm hands gripping her waist as she worked up a calculated motion.

"Damn, Candy. Shit."

Rich's erotic whispers were turning her on. She sped up her pace, sliding down and then grinding momentarily before rising. She tightened the muscles in her pussy each time she rose.

"Yeah, like that. Ride this dick," Rich's voice grew louder.

Candy rode faster, slamming her pussy down harder each time. "Ah. Ahh." Her eyes opened and closed and she gripped Rich's ankles tighter. She squeezed the muscles tighter around his dick. "Yes, make me cum! Rich . . . Rich."

Just as Candy began to climax, the room door opened. "What the—" Zora blurted. She dropped a tray of food she had apparently been bringing to serve Rich breakfast in bed. Coffee and eggs stained the floor. Steam rose from the carpet.

As Candy came and her body was depleted of energy, she realized the familiar face. *The elevator ho.*

"You bitch!" Zora sprung forward, throwing a haymaker that crashed Candy's cheek.

Candy fell onto Rich, whose mouth was open as cum squirted from his dick.

Zora jumped on Candy's naked body. She landed a second punch to her cheek. "Bitch!"

Candy punched Zora in the stomach.

"Ooo," Zora groaned in pain.

Candy grabbed her thin neck with one hand, and then slugged her with the other hand, knocking her off the bed to the floor. "Yeah, ho. Come on." Candy hopped off the bed and began stomping Zora's face.

"Calm down," Rich yelled as he pulled Candy from Zora.

Zora's eyes were swollen and blood leaked from her lips and nose.

"Let me go, Rich."

Rich flung Candy on the bed and pointed at her. "You know I don't put my hands on women, but ain't no woman gonna be disrespecting me either. Calm. The. Fuck. Down."

"You siding with this ho?" Candy questioned. "I can't believe you ran down to ATL with this elevator ho." Candy grabbed her thong and began putting it on.

Zora stood up, stumbling into a tall lamp next to the window. Tears fell from her eyes as she pinched her nose to stop the bleeding. "What is she doing down here?"

Candy laughed, watching blood drip from Zora's lips down the side of her face. "After you get your lips stitched up you can put 'em on his dick." She grabbed her clothes off the coat rack and began dressing.

Rich walked over to her and grabbed her crocodile pumps.

Candy huffed and then looked over at Zora's leopard-print ankle boots. "Rich, don't make me take those Jimmy Choos off her feet."

"Baby, stop making this bigger than it is." Rich tossed her shoes on the bed and grabbed her arms.

Candy was furious. But she knew she had no right to expect that Rich would not involve himself with another woman after they separated. Even with the drama that just unfolded with Zora, Candy was happy to be back in

Rich's presence.

"Baby, ain't nobody gonna come between us," Rich whispered in Candy's ear.

She gritted her teeth, her eyes beaming at Zora. "Get the fuck outta here. Before I fuckin' kill you!"

Zora looked at Rich in silence and then stomped out of the room.

Candy nudged Rich, whose eyes were stuck on Zora. "You act like you want me to walk and her to stay," Candy said, pulling Rich from his daze.

He turned to her. "I ain't never had a problem getting what I want." He rubbed her arms. "And I got it."

Candy closed her eyes as Rich leaned over and their tongues probed each other's mouths. It felt so right. Zora was out of Candy's mind as quick as she entered. She opened her eyes when Rich's lips parted from hers.

"I love you," Rich said.

"I know."

Rich shook his head. "Shit just been different since we separated."

"I see."

Rich sat Candy down on the bed and began explaining the fast chain of events that had happened in his life in a matter of weeks. His relationship with Zora, that he admitted was something more than a mere fling, the time he had been spending with King and their probability of doing business together. "I thought you and Vanessa was gone, so I was trying to build a new relationship. But now that you're here, we gotta get Vanessa and start rebuilding what we had, just on a higher level, minus the bullets and beef."

Rich's voice and the glimmer in his eyes signaled his sincerity. Everything he was saying made sense. It was what Candy had been yearning for, but was uncertain if she could achieve. With her desire for revenge burning her soul and Vanessa giving millions of reasons why they could not move on until everyone on their list was dead.

"Call Vanessa," Rich said.

Candy put on her shoes, then pulled out her smartphone and pressed Vanessa's number.

"So you disappear in the middle of the night and leave a note that you're going to meet Rich?" Vanessa screamed into the phone. "You don't even let me know where he is?"

"Please, Vanessa. Calm down," Candy responded.

"Calm down? You leave me stranded the day before everything is about to go down, and I'm supposed to calm down?"

"Just let me explain."

"Let me explain. I'm going to take care of this by myself."

"Vanessa, please. Hello? Hello?" Candy dropped her phone on the bed and looked to Rich. "She hung up." Tears began streaming down Candy's face.

"What did she say?"

Candy ran her hand over her face. "She's going after

Chanel and the rest of them by herself. We gotta get back to New York and stop her now—"

The door flung open, interrupting Candy's proclamation. "There she is right there!" Zora said emphatically, pointing Candy out to two police officers. "She tried to kill me."

Candy looked at Zora's bandaged face and the police behind her. *Oh shit!*

The police stepped forward. One slapped handcuffs on her, the other began reading Candy her rights.

"Officers, this is a big misunderstanding," said Rich as King stepped into the room.

"This is what I've been trying to tell you," King added.

The officers disregarded Rich and King.

Candy tried to stay strong, but the eerie feeling of handcuffs clenching her wrists was overbearing. She was going to a jail in a city where she knew no one and Vanessa was headed into a situation that could land her behind bars too.

As the officers led Candy out of the room, she turned to Rich, her eyes red and swollen. "Don't worry about me. Take care of Vanessa."

CHAPTER FOURTEEN

VANESSA

Vanessa paced back and forth in the hotel room with Candy's letter in her hand. She felt betrayed in every possible way. Candy left her to commit a multiple homicide by herself. As far as she was concerned, Candy had abandoned her for Rich. "She had a dream about Rich," Vanessa mumbled, thinking of the note. She stopped in front of the window and read the note for the third time.

Vanessa,

I woke up in the middle of the night after having a dream about Rich. It was a good dream. We were all back together. The dream reminded me how much I missed Rich and the fact all three of us are supposed to be together. Anyway, I called Rich. Yeah, I know we agreed not to contact him until this drama was over. But I had to. I love him. I know you love him too, but you're not ready to speak to him. Anyway, I'm going to meet with

139

*him and work things out for us. I didn't want to tell you
because I know you would've just convinced me not to.
But I know you'll be happy when I come back through
the door with Rich and things are back to normal for us.*

A lonesome tear fell from Vanessa's eye onto
Candy's letter as her "She Ain't You" ringtone sounded.
She pulled her phone from her waist. Recognizing it was
Rich calling, she clicked over then hung up as she heard
his voice, ending Chris Brown's crooning. There was
nothing she wanted to hear from Rich or Candy at that
point. In her mind were images of them having sex. She
could hear their conversation about her being gung ho
because of her lack of street credibility. Vanessa knew
she came from a different world. But themes like revenge
and anger transcended class and social standing. That's
why people watched legalized murder from the seats
outside of execution chambers. That's why people
wanted Bernie Madoff to rot in a casket beside Hitler.
Vanessa didn't care about the seemingly sincere nature of
Candy's letter. The fact was Candy had walked out on
her to an unknown place to see the person who was
adamant about them not executing their risky plan. Now
Vanessa was left to complete it by herself.

Feeling neglected, Vanessa pulled out her iPad and
began typing away as she thought of Peg.

She was the one person who knew what it felt like to
be deserted. *And I was actually feeling guilty for
cheating on Candy with Peg,* Vanessa thought as she

called her.

"Hey, Vanessa."

"I need to see you."

"See me? Or see me, see me?"

"Both."

"You can come over now. I'm getting my hair done."

"Okay."

"I'll be waiting," Peg said.

Vanessa turned off her phone with a smile. She needed to unwind and take her mind off Candy and Rich. She had been talking to Peg and they had been sexting each other nearly every day since they met. Vanessa had sexed Peg three times, each experience better than the preceding tryst. Vanessa wasn't sure what attracted her to Peg most, the novelty of a fresh tongue in her pussy, or the connection she and Peg shared as Bohemian vegans. But the growing bond between her and Peg was what she knew would help ease her mind at the moment.

* * *

On her way to Peg's apartment, Vanessa stopped by the health food store and picked up some cucumbers and a strawberry smoothie. After she rang Peg's doorbell, it swung open. Peg hugged her, and then pecked her on the lips. Vanessa's hands ran down Peg's thin waist to her small butt buried beneath her loose-fitting paisley skirt. A black halter covered her flat chest like a headband on a professional runner. What stood out to Vanessa was Peg's pale white skin surrounded by the black halter.

"Come in," Peg said with a smile.

Vanessa took in the scent of fresh pasta as she stepped inside. "Is that ziti?"

"Close. Vegetable lasagna," said Peg as she closed the door and walked past Vanessa.

The image of Peg's hair in curlers made Candy think of her old shop and the good times she had shared with her family-like employees who were now her enemies. Vanessa placed her hand on one of the curlers. It was a symbol of how far she had gone from any sense of normalcy.

"You okay?" Peg asked.

Vanessa shook off her blank stare with a smile. "Yeah. Just daydreaming."

"About me, I hope." Peg slapped Vanessa's butt and giggled. "I mean, daydreams are a sign that your subconscious is in action. Daydreams are so much different from regular dreams. But most people don't know. In antiquity, the Greeks taught that daydreams wer—"

Vanessa pulled Peg close and silenced her with a mouth full of tongue.

"Guess it was me on your mind."

Vanessa set the bag with the cucumbers and smoothie on the dinner table as they walked through the dining room. When they stepped into the living room, Vanessa's eyes widened.

"Heather, this is who I was telling you about," Peg said to the woman in Vanessa's view.

142

"I've heard nothing but good things about you, Vanessa."

Vanessa smiled as Heather shook her hand. Vanessa found it hard not to stare at Heather's healthy legs bulging from her white Spandex skirt and the nipples of her D-cups visible through her button-up shirt she had tied in a knot above her navel. It was the first time Vanessa had met a white woman that had a better shape than Candy. She looked into Heather's gray eyes. "It's a pleasure to meet you." Vanessa held Heather's hand for an extended period. She wanted to do nothing more at that moment than put Heather's hand down her skirt and see if Heather could make her cum. She had already made Vanessa's juices start flowing. Vanessa took another look at Heather's body, thinking of Ice T's wife. *Coco ain't got nothing on this white girl. I hope she's got her lickin' license.*

Vanessa sat down on the couch, and Heather sat on the sofa across from her. Heather crossed her thick leg over the other. Vanessa's eyes immediately shifted to Heather's thighs. The smile on Heather's face told Vanessa the maneuver was designed to entice her.

"You hungry, Vanessa?" Peg asked, heading for the kitchen. "This lasagna is about ready."

"Having home cooked, vegan meals that I don't prepare is a rare treat," said Vanessa.

"Peg sure knows how to treat a gal," Heather said with a sneaky grin. "I've known her for ages, since she was straight and thought me dating a woman was just a phase."

I knew she had her lickin' license. Vanessa felt her nipples getting hard.

"Some of us don't have the guts to act off of our feelings, so we run from them until they catch up with us," Peg called back.

Heather looked at Vanessa. "I've always been bold, and I've always known I loved men and women equally. How about you? Have you spent years inside of the closet or did you come out when your body started to fill out?"

Heather's candidness threw Vanessa off. "You can call me a late bloomer."

"Better late than never," said Heather.

Peg stepped over with two trays containing plates with lasagna, salad and organic applecider.

Heather pointed at Peg and looked at Vanessa. "Her dinner table is just a prop to give her some semblance of the ordinary."

"I wouldn't advise anyone to aspire to be normal," Vanessa responded.

"It's the quirky things I like about Peg," said Heather.

"Have any quirks of your own?" Vanessa asked Heather.

"Besides my penchant for going topless, having multiple sex partners, disavowing the existence of a supernatural being and eating with my fingers, I'm your typical All-American gal who would trade her mother for

144

a chance to have a threesome with Jay-Z and Beyonce and a follow-up with Brad Pitt and Angelina Jolie."

"She never had an editor for the words that come out of her mouth," Peg said, sitting down with her tray of food. "You'll get used to it and eventually love it."

"And hopefully, you'll grow to love me," Heather said, winking at Vanessa.

Vanessa was getting hot with each of Heather's flirts. She listened to Heather rattle on about her part-time job managing her father's clothing boutique. Heather came from a privileged family like Peg and Vanessa.

The women talked as they ate. Vanessa liked not only Heather's bluntness, but her sense of humor. She had an authentic way of making light of anything and any person, including herself. There was a freedom Vanessa saw in Heather that she saw in herself.

The more Vanessa was in Heather's presence, she realized she was attracted not only to her curvaceous figure, but the dominating aura that came with it and her bluntness. Vanessa began to fantasize about what it would feel like to have Heather ravish her, taking control with the sexual force she had experienced from Rich. She wanted to be subdued by Heather's 143 pounds of curves and sexual power.

After they were done, Peg placed the dishes in the dishwasher and returned to the sofa beside Heather.

Heather peered into Vanessa's eyes. "I would be betraying my essence if I didn't tell you the truth Peg's been holding back. We know you're the Vanessa Denay who wrote *Ghetto Love*, the same woman who was on the sex tape with Candy."

"Oh shit," Vanessa mumbled. She had never denied that part of her past. But she had tried to keep it under wraps. She had only crossed a few people in passing that recognized her and sparked conversations with her. Vanessa was simply trying to keep a low profile. The less she remained out of the public eye, the less she would remain in the eyes of Chanel and her cohorts as a suspect in the killing of Leah and the others who would meet their fate.

"You, Candy and Rich dropped off the map for whatever reason," said Heather. "But the bottom line is I've been waiting to fuck you since I saw Candy eating you out on that tape."

"So you're taking this being blunt thing to the next level," Vanessa said.

"I wanna take you to the next level."

"What makes you think you're my type?"

"The way your eyes keep drifting off to my ass and tits."

"Curiosity and attraction are two different things."

"Just because you play hard to get, doesn't mean I won't get you."

"Sometimes you have to take what you want," Vanessa said, licking her lips and opening her legs to give Heather a peek at the bald, pantieless flesh underneath her skirt. "*No* doesn't always mean *no*."

"Humph, it's getting kind of hot in here," Peg said with a smile, fanning herself. "I definitely need to cool off."

Heather stood and began undressing.

Vanessa gazed at Heather's perfectly round breasts fighting to free themselves from her bra. *Damn. She is hot!* Vanessa wanted to plant her face in the center of her cleavage, but she simply crossed her legs to quell the burning sensation in her hot box. She bit her bottom lip as Heather's breasts fell from her bra. Heather squirmed out of her skirt, revealing a set of hips reminiscent of Beyonce. Vanessa's mouth watered at the sight of the meaty white flesh making a gap between Heather's thighs. Vanessa was so focused on Heather that she had not noticed Peg undressing until Heather was naked. Heather's long blond hair hung straight down her back.

Heather asked, "What's wrong with this picture, Vanessa?"

Vanessa looked at Peg and then back to Heather. "For some reason beyond my knowledge, you're undressed," Vanessa said, coyly.

"You're not undressed," Heather said. "That's what's stopping this from being a Kodak moment."

Vanessa leaned back on the couch and stretched her arms out. "I'm done talking."

Heather smirked. She bent down and pushed the coffee table that was separating them across the room.

"Sexy and powerful," Vanessa mumbled.

Heather pointed at her. "Did you just mumble something under your breath?"

Vanessa rolled her eyes and sucked her teeth.

"So now you're mute," Heather raised her voice. She took two large steps forward and her naked body was looming over Vanessa.

Vanessa stood up, only to be flung back on the couch. *Yeah, take this pussy.*

Heather pulled off Vanessa's flip flops and began clawing at her clothes.

"No," Vanessa barked, grabbing Heather's hand.

Heather wrapped her hands around Vanessa's neck and began kissing her. Vanessa shut her eyes. *And she's the perfect kisser.*

Heather leaned back and yanked off Vanessa's skirt with both hands. She grabbed Vanessa by the collar of her shirt and pulled her from the couch. In seconds, Vanessa was on the carpeted floor. "You want it rough? Okay." Heather placed her hands in between a gap of Vanessa's button-up shirt and pulled it apart, sending buttons flying and exposing her perky breasts.

Vanessa almost melted when she felt Heather's mouth engulf her areola. "God."

Heather kissed her stomach and made her way in between Vanessa's legs. She slithered her tongue over Vanessa's clit and pussy lips, sparking moans from Vanessa. She removed her head. "You taste awesome,"

148

she said, then turned to Peg, who was fingering herself as she eyed the action. "Toss me my bag."

Vanessa watched Peg grab Heather's Gucci bag. She handed it to Heather and stood a few feet away.

"I got something for you," Heather said, smiling. She removed a double-penetration vibrator. She set it on her bag and flipped Vanessa onto her back, then began kissing her neck.

Vanessa purred like a cat in heat. The weight of Heather's massive, warm body on her small frame was the overpowering feeling she wanted. The scent of Heather's Flower Bomb perfume made the encounter more enticing. But Vanessa wanted to spice things up, so she tried to struggle free.

Heather grabbed her vibrator and tossed it to Peg. Heather planted kisses down Vanessa's back. She ran her tongue over her butt, kissing and sucking her cheeks until she left hickies on Vanessa's light skin.

"Ahh," Vanessa squirmed. "Stop it," she protested to incite Heather to become more aggressive.

Heather slid her hand underneath Vanessa, sliding her fingers through her wet flesh until she found Vanessa's erect clitoris.

"No. Yes. No, stop it," Vanessa begged.

Heather applied the proper amount of pressure to send spurts of erotic sensations through Vanessa's body. Then she began spanking her ass with her other hand. "That's what you want, naughty girl?"

"Yes, no." Vanessa's tongue ran over her lips in between gritting her teeth as blood rushed to her throbbing clit. She squirmed free.

"Frisky thing, aren't we?" Heather said.

Vanessa looked up at Heather's voluptuous body, while inching back.

Heather pulled at her legs as Vanessa made a feeble effort to kick away while giggling. Heather sat on Vanessa's chest and cupped her head. She pulled it between her legs. "Eat up, Vanessa."

The scent of Heather's wet folds made Vanessa more hungry for her passion as she worked her tongue against Heather's cut.

"Eat me, Vanessa. Yesss."

Vanessa clenched one of Heather's pussy lips between her lips, sucking it. She loved the feeling of Heather's hands roaming her hair, pulling her head closer. She heard Heather scream her name, further fueling her to please Heather.

"Vanessaaa," Heather yelled as she came. Her grip on Vanessa loosened.

Vanessa's body jolted from the tickling sensation of Peg stimulating her by working the lubricated vibrator in her ass and pussy. "Noooo. God!" Vanessa's legs began shaking while she balled her fists.

Peg stood up with a seductive smile on her pale face.

Tears of ecstasy fell from Vanessa's eyes as Peg turned her sideways to dig the vibrator deeper. Peg began working Vanessa's clit with her other hand. "Ohhh. It feels so gggggoooood," Vanessa stuttered.

Heather lay down beside her and wrapped her arms around her, passionately sucking and kissing her neck. She kissed Vanessa, silencing her moans with a twist of their tongues. Then she lowered her head, until her mouth swallowed a large part of Vanessa's small breasts."

"Yes." Vanessa pulled Heather closer, shifting her head to the other nipple. Her body was totally satisfied. Peg continued pleasing her ass and pussy. Before Vanessa knew it, she was clutching Heather's body against hers to brace her quaking frame as it rumbled to a climax. "Yes, yes, ahh."

After Vanessa loosened her arms, Heather pulled Peg away and they began engaging in sixty-nine. Vanessa watched Peg's boney body on top of Heather's hourglass figure. Their mismatched size seemed to mean nothing because their moans and quivering bodies proved they were pleasing each other equally. Vanessa knew their skills personally, as she was trying to recuperate from the mind-blowing sexual adventure. But watching made her insides hotter. Vanessa made her way to the bag she had placed on the table. She removed a smoothie and a cucumber from the bag and came back over to Heather and Peg. She slipped the hard, thick vegetable inside of her own soaking pussy. "Ahh." She twisted it and rubbed her clit with her other hand. Her moans began to match the cries of Heather and Peg in volume. But she didn't beat them to her nut, because they climaxed together.

Looking up, Peg stepped over to Vanessa.

Vanessa now opened the smoothie and began pouring it over her breasts and in between her legs. Before she could finish, Peg was sucking her breasts clean and Heather was between her legs. It took less than fifteen minutes to make Vanessa cum. All three women lie on each other, exhausted, entangled like a bag of rubber bands.

Vanessa looked around her, seeing white skin merged with hers—two sets of pale arms and two sets of pale legs. It dawned on her that her first all-woman threesome was with two white women. Vanessa had never had a problem with white people. She had been raised with them on Park Avenue and had many classmates who were white in every level of her schooling. But the thought of having a threesome with any two women had never crossed her mind. Her mind had only produced images of her and Candy with Rich. But while this was an unanticipated occurrence, Vanessa was pleased with the outcome and looked forward to more in the future.

"God, it's almost ten," Peg said.

"We still have time," Heather added.

Vanessa asked, "For what?"

"We've got a meeting. My group I was telling you about. CSA."

152

Vanessa remembered Peg saying she had founded an animal rights group called College Students for Animals. She said they were newly formed and only consisted of two dozen students that attended Hofstra University with her.

"There's room for you," Heather said, standing up.

"Sure," Vanessa said. She was more interested in being social than being a part of their CSA group. As far as she was concerned, it was time to start a new life for herself since Candy and Rich were starting life over together.

CHAPTER FIFTEEN

RICH

H ours had passed, but Rich still could not believe that Zora had Candy arrested. He was packing his Louis Vuitton duffel bag in preparation for a trip to New York to stop Vanessa from going through with her plan. Candy had given him the location of the hotel they were staying in when she was rehashing everything that happened between her and Vanessa since the day they parted from him. Rich slipped on his Gucci loafers and matching belt.

"Rich." He looked up as King stepped into the room. "This whole cipher with Zora and Candy is crazy."

"Yeah, it put a lot of things in perspective."

King shook his head. "I just finished checking Zora again."

"She gave me a taste of the life I wanted as an average citizen."

"What life?"

154

"The life where people resolve issues through po-po."

King chuckled. "This ain't Lennox Ave. and Zora ain't no ride or die chick."

"That's one of the things I liked about her."

"She's still downstairs crying, tears distilling everywhere."

Rich felt a streak of guilt. Zora had done nothing different than what she was taught to do. Her only crime was falling for a hustler who had retired from the game, but had not fully integrated into the social structure of life outside of the street culture. Rich felt guilty for screaming at her after the police left. He knew she was a fragile woman and his harsh verbal language and confrontational body language would leave psychological scars on her to match the physical wounds Candy inflicted on her.

"You ready to motivate?" King asked as Rich picked up his duffle bag.

"Your cell will be ringing as soon as I touch down. Just make sure you take care of Candy if I don't make it back before they give her a bail," said Rich.

King had agreed to post Candy's bail and he had already sent his attorney to the police station. He admitted to sharing some responsibility for her incarceration, because he had allowed Zora in his house to see Rich, not knowing Candy was there.

Rich and King left the room and headed downstairs, where Zora was seated on a loveseat clinging to a box of

Kleenex like it would save her life. She looked at Rich and shook her head. "I'm sorry, Rich."

As Rich watched her, he saw the innocence he once adored about Vanessa before she flipped. He also saw Candy being hauled off in handcuffs. Rich could not remove the good memories of him and Zora from his mind. He wanted to hug her and accept her apology. Zora was a reminder to Rich that even though he was no longer in the streets, he needed a woman who could relate to the streets from experience. He needed Candy and Vanessa.

"Please, accept my apology," Zora said as she stood up.

Rich paused, then walked out of King's home.

King followed him outside. "Damn, you came at her in a cold current for real," he said.

Rich just sighed and gave King a pound as he stopped beside his rental. He hugged King. "Stay focused."

"Peace."

Rich pulled off wondering what awaited him in New York. He had to first convince Vanessa to abort her plan. But that could only be done if she was still in the hotel room she and Candy had rented.

* * *

After zipping to the airport, Rich was one of the first people to board his first class flight. He was seated beside a window with an empty seat next to him. Looking out of the window, he watched crowds of people on their way to board. Then he pulled out his BlackBerry and called

Vanessa. "Fuck." He hung up when he got her voice mail.

Rich leaned back, took a deep breath, then logged onto amazon.com through his BlackBerry. He typed *Ghetto Love* in the search box and the page for Vanessa's novel popped up. There were a few dozen customer reviews, mostly praising the book for its eroticism and realistic characters. The comments touched Rich, because he had given Vanessa insight on the story and she had modeled the main male character after him. The bestselling novel was a testament to the powerful impact Rich once had on Vanessa's life.

Thinking about Vanessa brought Rich's mind to Domingo. He phoned him, prepared to give Domingo his final warning to end his contact with Vanessa and Candy.

"Who the fuck is this?" Domingo answered.

"Slow your roll and turn the volume down."

"My pops is in Sing Sing and you ain't my moms. Plus, I stopped taking orders when 1 started paying rent, ya heard?"

"All that's irrelevant. Just act like you never met Candy or Vanessa."

"We got business to handle, and as I just told you, I got rent to pay. Matter of fact, act like you never met me."

"What the—" Rich sighed after Domingo hung up on him.

Rich was an O.G. and Domingo was a youngin'.

Respect was due. Rich had earned it on back blocks and projects throughout New York City. Enraged, he wanted to track Domingo down and enforce his will, make him submit and pay homage to a real G. But Rich felt he had transcended the street mentality that mandated such behavior. That was one of the reasons he felt it was his responsibility to pull Candy and Vanessa from that lane where Domingo was driving. Candy and Vanessa were Rich's problems that needed solving.

"Hey, brah."

Rich looked up at the aging black man hovering over him.

"I'm with you for the duration," he said, his wrinkled face covered with a smile. His Kangol and Sean John sweat suit reflected the swagger of a man who was clinging to modern youth in an effort to stop the progressive effects of time on his body.

Rich shook the man's hand. "Rich."

"Cedric, but you can call me C," the old timer responded proudly.

Pops think he the shit. Rich turned off his phone. He listened as a flight attendant who stood at the front of the plane asked everyone to turn off their electronic devices. She began explaining security procedures and referencing the video that flashed on the screen above her head and on the headrest in front of Rich. After she was done and the plane took off, Rich gazed out of the window. Then he called the flight attendant and had her bring him a bottle of Dasani water.

"Brother like you look like he would rather be poppin' bottles," C said.

"Poppin' bottles?" Rich chuckled. "That sound funny coming out the mouth of a man old enough to be my pops. No disrespect."

"You young boys ain't got no monopoly on swag, you dig? Just hope you look this good at sixty-one."

Damn. Rich had placed the man in his early-fifties. Rich did hope he looked as good at sixty-one. Just thinking about that showed Rich how far he had come from the street culture. As a teen, Rich had never contemplated making it past age twenty-one. The life expectancy for a young black man coming of age in Harlem was short, and Rich had made it shorter by making the criminal world his world.

C sized up Rich, looking at the diamond in his ear and at his hand that held a matching bracelet. "I see you ain't got that handcuff on, so that shows you got some sense."

"Doing dirt ain't the only way to pay for diamonds."

"No, no, no, young blood. I'm talking 'bout that wedding ring. That thing right there locked down way more brothers than them boys with badges."

"Sound like you had a bad experience tying the knot."

C removed his Kangol, showcasing his balding gray hair. "This ain't just about time and genetics. Stress is real," he huffed. "I swept honey off her feet, jumped the broom and she cleaned me out for damn near everything."

"They made prenups for a reason."

"Prenups protect your wallet, not your sanity. Once you say I do, women start to transform. You know what the leading cause of divorce is?"

Rich shrugged his shoulders.

"Marriage."

Rich laughed.

"Remember this, if you don't remember nothing I said."

"What?"

"A woman ain't shit whether she riding or walking."

"Riding or walking?" Rich squinted his eyes, confused.

"Whether she got money or she broke, Oprah or that hoodrat in the house party, a woman ain't shit. Riding down Rodeo Drive or walking through the projects in Bankhead. It's some type of genetic disorder that predisposes women to drama. A bullshit gene."

"You ever heard the saying, 'You can't bullshit a bullshit artist?'"

"Of course."

"Well, you can't bullshit the person who teaches bullshit to the bullshit artist," said Rich.

"Ain't nobody got more game than a woman. They make you think you got control. How that Beyonce song go? Who run the world? Girls."

Rich listened to C's philosophy, wondering if there

was some truth to it. He knew that women generally had more game than men, contrary to popular belief. But he had always looked at himself as the exception to the rule. Always, until now. C caused Rich to ponder how he had invested his time in Zora based on their mutual agreement to have an open relationship. Yet, she flipped when she saw Candy. Then Rich had allowed Candy to come back into his life he had restarted. Now, she had convinced him to leave that behind and fly to New York to save Vanessa. Rich's life was being dictated by women. They had the control C spoke of.

"How can I assist you, baby?"

Rich was pulled from his thoughts by C's words to the woman standing in the aisle.

It was Katiya. She directed her attention to C. "You can trade seats with me so I can sit next to Rich." She pointed to her seat a few rows back.

C looked at Rich. "I didn't know you had company."

"Me either."

Katiya scanned C's Sean John suit, then removed a $100 bill from her Hermes Birkin bag. "Perhaps you can find your way to a concert from the man who makes your clothes. It's a fair exchange for another first class seat."

C snatched the C-note. "You paid for what you had coming to you for free." He stood up.

Rich smiled as C left.

"His ability to be in my presence at thirty-thousand feet in the air is the fault of none other than my pilot's tending to an emergency at this last minute and my inability to fly a G6," Katiya said as she sat. "What's your excuse for this crowded seven-forty-seven in lieu of a Gulfstream?"

"Clairvoyance. I had a vision you were going to be the Virgin type today." Rich grinned.

"You seem to be enjoying Virgin Airlines, yourself. But good luck finding some saint with her hymen intact."

"I like my flights Virgin and my women experienced."

Katiya remained silent for a moment. "Women gossip and men do also, but they consider it, what's the phrase?" She paused. "'Putting each other on.' So I'm assuming King revealed to you the nature of our relations and how I comport myself sexually."

"That's a very educated guess."

"Let me be clear, Rich."

"Transparency does us both a service."

"There is very little most men can do for me financially or intellectually. And emotionally, for that matter. Sexually is where I find my only challenge with the opposite sex."

"Interesting." Rich nodded.

"What does this mean in the context of you and I?"

"Your love of specificity should make this response interesting."

"It was obvious from the pool party that I wanted to fuck you," Katiya said. "Hence the address I gave you and you never used."

"Wasn't sure if I wanted to jump into anything right now. Fucking is not a problem for me. Then I was trying to figure out how you knew my name is Jamel Thomas."

"We live in the information age and as a businesswoman due diligence is mandatory. So why not see if you are in a respectable tax bracket and if you're not an ex-con before I decide to fuck you?"

Rich grinned. "Very blunt."

"Well, I also have a fixation with oral sex. And right now, I would like nothing more than to suck your dick and for you to eat my pussy." She looked down at Rich's growing erection. "And I see you feel the same way. My proposition is that we suck each other inside the bathroom and when we land, we can fuck each other properly in the hotel of your choice, my Black Card."

King had told Rich that Katiya was a straight talker, and Rich had often brashly controlled women with sexual propositions in such a clam tone. But he had never been spoken to by a woman so directly and explicitly in similar fashion. Katiya's voice had remained steady during their conversation and her dark seductive eyes had never left his pupils. The irony of the predicament was that she had an aristocratic air that demonstrated her condescending nature when speaking to Zora at the pool party and C minutes earlier. Rich wanted to humble Katiya with a stiff dick and skilled tongue. He wanted to break down her confidence, making her doubt her discipline to have casual sex. Katiya saw sex as a challenge. But Rich was the ultimate competitor between the sheets.

"Hope I didn't scare you," Katiya said, breaking Rich's thoughts.

He smiled. "I just went through a serious situation because a lady friend of mine consented to an open relationship, but she couldn't handle seeing me with another woman."

"I don't have relationships—open, closed or otherwise. I have relations."

Rich grabbed her hand and placed it on his dick. "Can you relate to this?"

"In thirty seconds." Katiya stood and began walking to the bathroom.

Rich watched her ass jiggle underneath her skirt. He was still amazed that he was about to have sex with a multimillionaire on a plane. A woman who had a directness that verged on whorish. After she closed the bathroom door, Rich traced her footsteps.

"Hey, brah." C grabbed Rich's arm and smiled, obviously having peeped the sexcapade in the making. "I told you, 'riding or walking.'" He paused. "Add flying."

Rich chuckled and continued his stride to the bathroom. He opened the door and stepped inside. Katiya was already on her knees. Rich looked down at her long, straight hair and creamy brown skin. She was the third Indian woman he would add to his list of sexual exploits.

Katiya pulled Rich's linen pants to his ankles, then pulled down his boxers. She grabbed his dick with both hands and took the head in her mouth. When her wet mouth soaked the head, she forced the tip of her tongue into the pee hole.

"What the fuck?" Rich jumped back, slamming against the door. He was breathing like he had just run a marathon and his eyes were open wide.

Katiya ran her tongue down the shaft of his dick to her hands, then up before circling the head of his dick and easing the tip of her tongue back into the pee hole.

Rich grabbed both of her shoulders to brace himself as his chest thrust forward and he scrunched his face.

Katiya deep-throated Rich, bobbing her head down once, then freeing his dick from her mouth to tease him. She began juggling his nuts in her mouth while jerking his dick.

Rich's head tilted back and he started breathing faster, panting like a rabid pit bull. He wanted to grit his teeth, but he had no control over himself. Katiya had him in submission. "A, ah, ooh, damn, shit." He twisted his head side-to-side robotically like he was suffering from some sort of twitching disorder.

Katiya began sucking the side of his dick, working her way to the head. She increased the suction each time she inhaled and massaged Rich's balls.

Rich grabbed her head as he felt cum rising from his nuts.

Katiya sucked Rich dry then spit his cum into the toilet.

"Damn." Rich's breathing was slowing as he watched Katiya gargle some water, rinsing her mouth. He grabbed a handful of tissue and wiped his dick, then pulled up his pants.

Katiya removed her panties. She propped her butt up on the sink and pulled her dress all the way up and parted her legs as far as she could.

"Damn, that pussy fat," Rich mumbled as he lowered his face between her legs. There was a small trail of wavy hair above her bald flesh. Rich grabbed her knees and pushed her slim legs further, causing her to let out a yelp. Her clit became visible from the fleshy hood covering it. Rich attacked it with his tongue like a wild animal.

"Huh, huh, huh," Katiya grunted, moaned and cringed as her legs shook in Rich's hands. She clutched the side of the sink for stability.

Rich planted his entire mouth over her pussy and ran his tongue back and forth over the lips to her clit until she was speaking incoherent words in between moans.

"Good, what, who, feels, why, so good, you, so, you good, ahhhh."

Rich pulled back and smiled at the sight of her eyes opening and closing as beads of sweat formed on her forehead. "Turn over." He shifted her body until her arms were outstretched and her palms were flat against the wall. Her ass was poked out just enough for Rich to palm it. He had eased his tongue inside of her slippery pussy lips. His hand shook as her body trembled.

"No, please," Katiya begged. Her hand dropped from the wall.

Rich stopped. He turned her to the side, cupped her butt and pushed her against the side wall. He leaned down, lifted her up the wall and her legs locked around his neck and her hands clawed into his head and neck.

"Huh, huh, please. I'm cumming."

Rich felt Katiya's thighs loosen from around him and he could hear her breathing slow. He gently eased her down the wall as she came in his mouth.

In minutes, she quietly caught her breath and wiped between her legs with a wet tissue. She looked Rich in the eyes for a few seconds, her sweaty face emotionless.

Rich was trying to figure out what was on her mind, then he gave in. "Talk to me."

"I'm speechless."

"I presume that's a good thing."

"If it was a bad thing you wouldn't be able to shut me up."

"I never had head like that before," Rich said.

Katiya flashed a sneaky grin. "It's my tongue tip technique, right?"

Rich nodded. "You might have to get that patented so you can sell it to other chicks."

"You and I can do an x-rated infomercial." Katiya laughed. She pulled Rich to her and gave him a deep kiss.

The type of kiss that most women watched in romantic movies but never experienced. The type that seemed better suited for a newlywed couple.

Rich watched her as she slowly pulled away from him and exited the bathroom. He waited a moment before stepping out of the door. He walked past two people waiting for the bathroom, recognizing one bystander as the woman who had been seated directly across from him and Katiya. He smiled and began walking down the aisle.

C grabbed his arm. "Stay away from that handcuff."

"All right, Dr. Love." Rich smiled and continued walking. He made his way to the seat Katiya had been sitting in, because she was now in his window seat.

During the flight back, Rich and Katiya got to know each other. He learned that she was the only child of a father who was a professor at UCLA and a mother who owned a company that made hair weaves and wigs. She had just celebrated her 37th birthday at the Tasty in Los Angeles—the first of the twenty-strip club chain that she opened throughout North America, including locations in Hawaii and Canada. Katiya had also made millions in commercial and residential real estate she owned throughout the states. Having little time outside of her business endeavors was another reason she said she had no time for relationships.

When their flight landed, they went to the W Hotel. As they stepped through the door of the suite and closed it, they peeled out of their clothes. In minutes, Rich had

Katiya's ankles pressed against his shoulders as he rammed in and out of her. Her back was on the king-sized bed, her eyes opening and closing as quickly as her rapid breaths. Rich watched Katiya grit her teeth each time he pummeled into her.

"Just like that, Rich. Good. Good."

I'm controlling this, not you. Rich flipped Katiya over onto her stomach. Staring at her unblemished skin under the glare from a lamp, he grabbed her small waist and guided himself inside of her soft insides.

Katiya winced and then let out an extended moan.

Rich leaned on top of her. He grabbed the headboard and began pulling himself up into her. He slid up and down her sweat-soaked body. His bare chest against her back. His cadence well thought out. Long strokes. Slow, then fast. Single entries, then short double strokes three times as quick as the long-stroking.

"Good God. Shit," Katiya screamed into the pillow beneath her as she grabbed two handfuls of the sheets. "Take me."

Rich kissed her neck, and then began sucking it as he dropped his hands from the headboard. He bear hugged her and began entering her deeper, his groin slapping against her soft rump.

"Damn, Rich. Riiiich," Katiya moaned.

"Yeah, take this dick." Rich reached under her armpits and cuffed the top of her shoulders with his hands. He pulled himself inside her quicker.

"Yes. Shit. Good, Rich. Good God! Stop!" Katiya begged.

"I'm just starting." He bit down on her neck with enough pressure to turn her on.

"Ahh. Yes. It hurt so good. I love!"

Rich unloosened his grip on her. Just as he knew she was truly enjoying his sex game, he leaned up. Katiya looked startled when she turned around. Rich stared into her eyes, knowing he had subdued her with raw sex. He got off the bed and pulled her toward him. As her arms wrapped his body, he leaned down and wedged his dick into her tight pussy.

"Ahh." Katiya closed her eyes.

Rich grabbed her butt and lifted her. Her legs wrapped around him. He strained his dick as he pushed his lower body up, using all his strength. Each stroke stopped as he was on the tips of his toes, the heels of his foot in the air.

Katiya pressed her lower body down into his strokes. "Yes. Just like that, Rich. Fuck me good."

Rich backpedaled until his back was touching the wall. He pulled Katiya's ass close as he shifted up into her. He could feel her pussy swallowing all of him. She leaned back, her hair dripping from her head, her breasts pushed forward. "Yeah, girl. Come on."

"I'm about to cum," Katiya screamed. "Yes."

Rich pulled her back toward him until one of her breasts was in his mouth. His tongue danced with her nipple. He could feel it hardened in his mouth. "Oh, shit.

Shit." Rich felt a surge of energy take over him.

"Yes, I'm cumming," Katiya gripped him tighter.

"Yeah, girl." Rich stroked one last time as he and Katiya climaxed at the same time. Sweat dripped from his body to hers as he let her down. He leaned back against the wall, exhausted. Katiya was still huffing like she had just been chased by an enemy. Rich knew he had her when she turned to him with a smile.

"You were better than I thought." She licked her lips.

The way she licked her lips reminded Rich of Vanessa. He was impressed by Katiya, but he knew Vanessa needed him.

After they cleaned up, they ordered room service. They ate, exchanged phone numbers, then left the hotel headed in two different directions. They would meet again. But Katiya was in New York City on business. Rich was in his hometown to prevent Vanessa from making a move that could lead her to a death sentence from a bullet or a life sentence from a judge.

CHAPTER SIXTEEN
DOMINGO

Domingo parked his money green Ford Expedition on the corner of Nostrand and Putnam Avenues in Bed-Stuy, Brooklyn. He tapped on the horn four times. Seconds later a sexy Latina in denim shorts and a tank top stepped out of the brownstone he was parked in front of. Domingo nodded to the sound of Wiz Khalifa's "Black and Yellow" as the twenty-two-year-old opened the passenger side door of his truck.

"What's up, baby?" She closed the door, kissed Domingo on the cheek and smiled.

"This money, that's what's up, ya heard?"

"I'm ready to get it."

"It's back there."

The woman grabbed a paper bag from inside the knapsack on the seat behind her. She opened it and pulled out a handful of gift cards. "No Bloomingdales?"

"Macy's. That's three hundred. The rest of the plastic

supposed to come through before the week is out. Bloomingdales and Sak's."

"Give me a week with these. When you gonna come on a road trip with me?" she asked, referring to her cross country shopping sprees in which she and her girlfriends maxed out credit cards and gift cards Domingo gave her from his connect who purchased the account numbers online and churned out cards in his basement. She was the main person who converted Domingo's credit cards into cash.

"Don't get yourself fired, ya heard?" Domingo said.

The Latina squinted her hazel eyes.

"If I go on a trip with you, I could do my own dirt instead of giving you a cut."

"Say no more." She pecked Domingo on the cheek and exited the SUV. "Later."

Domingo pulled off thinking about the woman he just left. He and Jessica were once an item. But he was now trying to keep their relationship strictly business. Women had always been Domingo's weakness. He was controlled by his lower desires and it was easy for women to grab hold of them. Domingo was having problems keeping his relationship with Jessica platonic. But the money she generated for him was a good incentive to keep him from crossing the boundaries they had set.

The only people Domingo now had in his sight were Candy and Chanel. He had Chanel, but not overstepping the boundaries she set between them to exceed booty calls was hard. He realized that the age disparity and distance between he and Candy were roadblocks. Vanessa and Rich, however, were also hindering him from making Candy his. If they were out of the picture, Domingo figured Candy would be open to him. The death of Rich was something that Domingo would enjoy. It was something he had contemplated bringing to fruition after their last war of words. Killing Vanessa was not something Domingo wanted. But he would chalk it up to a necessary evil to advance his goal. He had been a loner for years and his social network revolved around people who killed each other on sight. Domingo had already been facilitating the drama for the team of Candy and Vanessa. Now if he could only manipulate the pieces on his chess board of life and have Vanessa and Rich eliminated without using his trigger finger.

Domingo texted Chanel, letting her know he needed to see her immediately. She texted him back, telling him to meet her at Highland Park in an hour. Since their sexual introduction outside of the park, it had become a regular meeting place for them. The large park was filled with many blind spots where they could meet outside of most people's wandering eyes. The fact that it was in the northern region of East New York, far from Chanel's apartment, made matters better. That reduced the probability of people she or her man knew spotting her and revealing to him that his girlfriend was creeping with a young stallion a decade younger than her. Her boyfriend lived in the Park Slope section of Brooklyn, but kept his ears to the streets of East New York.

As Domingo steered down Fulton Street he thought of Vera's brothers. They were likely candidates to murder Rich and Vanessa. They both had short fuses that Domingo knew how to ignite.

* * *

Domingo parked his Expedition on Jamaica Avenue and rolled down the window. The chatter of children and the voices of adults echoed so loud that he had trouble managing his thoughts. He looked out over the large park, from the basketball court at his level, across the grassy grounds up the hill that housed benches filled with people. The summer sun bore down on the countless people present. Some people had gathered under the shade of trees to have picnics and barbeques. Domingo didn't expect the park to be so crowded.

He pulled out his iPhone and called Chanel. "I'm down at the bottom of the park on Jamaica Ave.

"I'm on the backside, near the reservoir." Chanel was in a serene area of the park where few people went—the area next to where she and Domingo had sexed each other in and on her Escalade.

"Be up there in a minute." Domingo started the engine and drove around the park. He pulled up on Highland Boulevard behind Chanel's truck. After exiting his Expedition, he hopped into her Escalade. "What's good?"

Domingo pursed his lips at her breasts popping out of her BCBG button-up shirt. The contrast of her dark skin and yellow shirt made her D-cups a work of art.

"Them tig old bitties, that's what's up."

"Don't start. I gotta see my man in a minute."

"You already got my dick on swole." He grabbed her hand and put it in his lap.

"Your young ass stay horny." Chanel massaged his dick through his shorts for a minute. "Enough." She pulled her hand back.

"When you become a dick teaser?"

"When you leave, you can get you one of these hood boogers to finish what I started."

"If I don't end up in the hospital from blue balls."

"Come on, now. What you need to speak to me about?"

Domingo's face turned serious. His smile evaporated. His eyes focused on hers. "Good news and bad news. What you want first?"

"The bad."

"Bad news is Rich and Vanessa are planning to kill you. And Mimi, plus Vera and her brothers."

Chanel's mouth was open, her eyes wide and glued to Domingo. "Keep going."

"Good news is they reached out to me for help, ya heard?"

"And Candy?"

"They three-way been a wrap for a minute. They

broke up because Candy wanted to let y'all live. They don't know where she is," Domingo said, then continued building on his lie.

"So I was right?"

"What?"

"Rich. I knew he had something to do with killing Leah."

"Him and Vanessa. Remember Mimi said it was two people. But Vanessa was the one who shot first."

"That Bohemian broad really bustin' her gun?"

"Y'all made a monster, now y'all gotta end her career. Her and Rich, ya heard?"

"This shit is crazy."

"What's more crazy is they planning to move on y'all at the Father's Day Tournament tomorrow."

"How they know we gonna be there?"

"Evidently you must've mentioned it in the shop around Vanessa back in the day."

"You right. I tried to get Candy and Vanessa to come before, but something came up. They know I go every year and Meisha and Leah be there with me."

"Vanessa got a good memory."

Chanel shook her head. "I can't believe this shit. They tried to rock us to sleep for over two years, then get at us."

"My suggestion is that everybody fall back from the Father's Day Tournament, then we meet to discuss this. Everybody involved."

"I'll talk to everybody and set up a place to meet."

Domingo nodded. He rubbed his hand over Chanel's cheek. "Ma, you know I wasn't gonna let nothin' happen to you."

"I know."

"That's why I put you on first before everybody else. On some real shit, I'll hurt something for you, ya heard?"

Chanel smiled.

Domingo leaned forward and kissed her, pecking her lips, then working his tongue inside of her mouth. To his surprise, she submitted. She was usually adamant that kisses were off the menu, because that level of passion was reserved for the type of loving relationship that exceeded their mere sexual episodes.

Chanel's eyes stayed on Domingo's as they parted from their kiss. "Thanks for telling me." She was on the verge of crying. "I could've really got killed tomorrow. I owe you."

Domingo kissed away her tears and hugged her. "As long as I can help it, ain't nothin' gonna ever happen to you." He rubbed her back and then looked her in the eyes. "Don't worry, Vanessa and Rich gonna get it."

* * *

There was a tenseness that permeated Vera's living room. Domingo was sitting on a sofa beside Chanel. Meisha was beside her. Mimi sat in a recliner and Vera was pacing in front of the window. Since people began arriving twenty minutes earlier, there was a lot of small talk to pass the time. Everyone had been briefed on the drama and warned not to attend the Father's Day Tournament that was in full swing. Instead, they began piling into Vera's apartment.

Domingo was tweeting on his iPhone, but his mind was on the meeting set to soon start. He had been preparing all night on how to manage the people in attendance. The objective was to have Vera's brothers kill Rich and Vanessa. Not only were they qualified to murder, they were qualified to track down Rich and Vanessa if Domingo was unable to.

"It's about time," Vera said.

"They here?" Chanel asked as Vera gazed out of her window.

Vera nodded.

"Showtime," Domingo mumbled to himself. He logged off of Twitter and put away his smartphone. While he was the youngest in the room, he knew it would be his responsibility to steer Jahiem and Tahiem in the direction he wanted. The two brutish thugs were renegades-the type of guys who lived within the street culture of crime but had little respect for rules. What they liked they took, with few exceptions. They had no problem shitting where they lived and getting high on their own supply was reality for the gunslingers who often dabbed in selling Ecstasy.

The intercom rang. Vera buzzed her brothers in. Within minutes, they walked into the living room followed by her.

Jahiem and Tahiem were the shortest, but most dangerous people in the room. They each sported baggy jeans in an era of skinny jeans. It was part of their renegade attitude. Jahiem donned a long Inspired By Brooklyn t-shirt with a slew of Brooklyn neighborhoods printed on the back. He walked over and kissed Mimi as Tahiem made his way into the living room. Domingo could see the print of each of their guns on their waistlines.

"What it is?" Jahiem said, before sitting on the empty couch with his twin brother.

Tahiem simply nodded his head. He was the more discrete of the two, but just as dangerous.

Being in their presence reminded Domingo of the caliber of individuals he was dealing with. The Twins were identical in their chocolate skin tone, chiseled faces and short bushy 'fros. But the brothers had different demeanors. Yet they shared a love for drama that was infamous in Red Hook. Domingo had seen them in action. They had been the only two people to walk away from a six-man shootout.

Jahiem turned to Domingo with a sinister look. "This shit true what my sister say about Rich and Vanessa?"

"I don't see why Vanessa and Rich would lie to me."

"Then the question is, 'Why they even come to you?'" Jahiem said, leaning forward, his eyes trained on Domingo with a focus that would intimidate most people. But not Domingo.

"When you 'bout your business, you don't have to chase customers, ya heard?"

Tahiem interjected. "Highest bidder."

His brother looked at him and nodded, then turned to Domingo. "We all know your loyalty is to the highest bidder. But you want us to believe you turned down whatever they threw at you and ain't nobody in this room lining your pockets?"

Domingo grinned. He had prepared for this question all night. "Of course, I like to get gwap. And I'm sure if y'all get your hands on Rich, he'll point us in the direction of that paper he sittin' on."

Jahiem looked at his brother, Vera, then back to Domingo. "So this ain't about saving us from some drama, it's about you cakin' off?"

"It's about killing two birds with one stone. If I didn't care about everybody in this room, everybody who was planning on going to the Father's Day Tournament would be duckin' bullets right now."

Jahiem nodded slightly and then looked at Tahiem before refocusing on Domingo.

"Ain't no reason Rich and Vanessa shouldn't pay with they life and they money, ya heard?"

Jahiem said, "Get at me tomorrow." He looked at the women in the room. "Y'all keep a low profile. This shit will be dead in a minute."

Domingo watched Jahiem pull Mimi to the side and

talk to her for several minutes, before kissing her. He then left the apartment with his brother.

Vera locked the door behind them. It felt unusual for Domingo to be in a room full of women who had watched him conspire to commit murder. He had thought long and hard about having them present. Ultimately, he knew they had all conspired to kidnap Candy, so he felt they were capable of keeping their mouths closed. Domingo also felt it was important for them to witness the Twins commit to handling the problem, because everyone in the room knew the Twins were capable of murder and lived by their word. So having the women present was a way for Domingo to assure that they remained calm about a serious situation, which he may not have been able to assure them of a resolution.

"So you gonna let the Twins take all the money?" Chanel whispered to Domingo.

"That's a small thing to a giant. And this ain't really about money." Domingo paused, then lowered his voice another notch. "This is about making sure nothing happens to you. I don't really care about the rest of these broads. My obligation is to you."

Mimi stood up. "This shit is crazy.

"What?" asked Meisha.

"Everything. I knew Vanessa since she was on some straight lame shit in college." Mimi laughed. "Now this chick out here planning to murder me. I knew she was poison when she flipped on me and started hangin' with y'all." Mimi shook her head and slapped her hands together. "She thinks she's so damn smart, but she never knew I was messing with Jahiem."

Domingo kept his eyes on Mimi. He knew she was the one person in the room who knew Vanessa on a different level. Even though Vanessa's three-way relationship had driven Mimi to cross her in a jealous rage, Domingo still wondered about where Mimi placed her loyalty.

"The crazy shit is they killed Leah," Chanel chimed in.

"Pregnant Leah," Mimi added.

Meisha shook her head and said, "Makes you realize it can happen to any of us."

CHAPTER SEVENTEEN
CANDY

C andy sat in a desolate jail cell thinking about how her life had slipped out of her control. Outside of all the drama she had experienced following her kidnapping, nothing had affected her like what she experienced since handcuffs had been clamped on her wrists. The cramped back seat of the patrol car, the hours she spent being processed in the system, the humiliation of being strip searched, the corrections officers who barked at her, the detainees who saw her as prey because of her New York accent and shapely figure; the list of reasons that caused Candy to yearn change were endless.

She laid back on the thin mattress in the roach-infested cell, gazing at the water stains on the ceiling. "Why and how?" she questioned herself. Why had life been so cruel to her? How had she not seen the women she considered family plotting her downfall?

It was Father's Day, so Candy had been having negative thoughts all day. She was frustrated about what could happen to Vanessa. Candy had called Rich and learned that he was having trouble finding Vanessa. She had checked out of the hotel. Rich had driven past the Father's Day Tournament a few times, finding no sign of Vanessa or her intended targets. But it was only 3:00, so Candy knew there was time left for the beef to unfold.

"Hey." The New York accent startled Candy. She took her eyes off the ceiling to find a pretty twenty-something woman with cornrows and smooth skin that was as black as her hair. "Take this." The woman squeezed a large bag through the cell bars.

"I don't need nothing," Candy said, rising from the bed. She had never been incarcerated before, but her life in the streets taught her that everything came with a price.

"Guess you like having ashy skin and an empty stomach." The woman laughed. "It's some cosmetics and food in there. Ain't none of these country-ass chicks around here gonna give you nothin' but an ass whippin' or a STD, so take it."

Candy walked over to the cell bars, reaching through them to shake the woman's hand. "Thanks."

"I'm Danette. I'm from Brooklyn."

"I'm from Harlem. You can call me Candy."

Danette said she had been locked up for the past nine months after the police stopped her for speeding in her boyfriend's Bentley. He was a dope kingpin from Brooklyn who had moved to Atlanta with her two years prior. "They was lookin' for him for a murder and it just so happened he had a gun under the seat."

"Damn," Candy said, shaking her head.

"Last I heard, he was on the run in Texas."

"That's fucked up."

"Fuck-ups are the story of my life."

"I got my share." Candy told Danette about Zora finding her having sex with Rich and everything that unfolded.

"That's a bullshit assault charge. You'll make bail as soon as you get one in court."

"Shit has a way of not working out as planned for me."

"Long as old boy put a muzzle on old girl, you'll be all right."

"If."

"Even if he don't, a good lawyer can get you probation. But you gotta be easy when you get out, 'cause they'll make a chick do that probation time in here if you slip up again."

Candy listened to Danette speak of her plans to begin her life over. "No more hustlers and thugs for me. If I even think a guy know the difference between China White and Purple Haze, or he got a bulge on his waist instead of one between his legs, I ain't fuckin' with him."

"I hear you."

"You better, 'cause this shit is real in here and I'm not

never comin' back, so ain't no use having no man on his way in."

As Candy listened to Danette, she realized how lucky she and Vanessa had been. They had killed Chase and avoided capture. They had even killed Leah and her husband without a problem. Plus, they had beaten up Zora in the MGM Grand. Candy realized that it was their escape from any repercussions that had convinced them they could continue breaking the law and making enemies. But sitting in a jail cell for her second assault on Zora was a reminder that she was not untouchable.

"I'm a find me a good man that's about his business, that ain't about all this bullshit. Have some kids and raise them right. How my moms tried to raise me before I started chasing behind these guys that bust the gun and sling drugs."

Candy couldn't help but think of Rich. *I already got a good man. A man who was schooling me to all this shit from experience. Only if I would've listened to him.*

* * *

The following day, everything seemed different as Candy walked out of jail, peering at Rich leaning against his Audi. The air seemed fresher, her body seemed lighter. Even her vision was clearer. More importantly, she was thinking sharper. She knew that life was more than what she had settled for and she was destined to get everything good it had to offer.

Rich's face lit up as he stepped toward Candy, kissed

her and hugged her. "Missing you is an understatement."

Candy held him tight, silently savoring the feeling of security and love that she craved. "I'm sorry."

Rich leaned back, his hands around Candy's waist as he gazed into her eyes. "Sorry?"

Candy nodded. "I should've listened to you a long time ago." She began telling Rich about her prison experience and the new outlook Danette helped her discover.

"Forever forward, never backward," Rich said. He opened the door of his car and closed it after Candy got inside.

In seconds, they were rolling. Rich wheeled the Audi with one hand, the other hanging off the door, inside the car. The crooning of "Love Faces" by Trey Songz reverberated at a low level. "I got two tickets to New York," said Rich. "We going straight to the airport."

"Tell me something good about Vanessa."

Rich shook his head. "She ain't returning my calls. And I slid by the Father's Day Tournament a few more times after we spoke. Nothing."

"Chanel and them either?"

"Nothing."

"At least we know Vanessa didn't go through with the plan," said Candy.

"She could've changed it."

"What you mean?"

"What if she decided to get at them at a different

location?" Rich asked. "It would explain why none of them showed up."

Candy pulled out her phone and called Vanessa. "Voicemail," she said. "Vanessa, this is Candy. Please call me as soon as you get this. I'm on my way to New York and I need to see you. Love you." She slammed the phone in her lap and frowned.

Rich rubbed her thigh. "Don't worry, baby. Don't worry."

Candy wiped her eyes and picked up the phone from her lap.

"Who you calling?"

"Domingo."

"Hell no! You know I had words with him about y'all?" Rich asked the rhetorical question before retelling the story of his latest call with Domingo.

"He's all we got as a link to Vanessa."

Rich paused and let out a deep breath. "Call him." He shook his head. "Fuck it."

Candy phoned Domingo.

"Mamita, what's good?"

"You tell me?"

"Did sparks fly on the Fourth?"

"The girls didn't wanna play ball," Candy said, referring to Chanel and the others not showing up at the Father's Day Tournament. "I was hoping you could tell me why they was on the bench?"

"Last minute game in Atlantic City. But they was still

supposed to be back before the last quarter. That's why I asked you about sparks flying."

"All right. Just remember you getting paid good money to ref this game, so we expecting you to make the call on stuff like that."

"Got you, Mamita."

"All right."

"When I'm a get to see you?"

"See me?"

"You won't let me taste that Candy, the least you can do is let me see some eye Candy."

Candy laughed. "Still horny as ever, ain't you?"

"You know I got a sweet tooth, a fetish for Amazons with model faces."

"It's a difference between a fetish and a fantasy."

"Well, I'm clear on my need for a face-to-face."

"When the time is right. Bye." Candy hung up.

"What he talking 'bout besides how sexy you are?"

Candy recounted everything to Rich.

"So, he wanna see you? Probably think we in New York."

"Doubt it. But everything was supposed to go down yesterday, so maybe."

"He ain't say nothing about Vanessa?"

"I wish."

Rich let out a deep breath. "We gotta find her."

"I just hope she's all right."

* * *

190

Hours passed, and Candy and Rich were in New York. They had yet to locate Vanessa. Their phone calls went unanswered and Vanessa had not responded to the messages they left on her voicemail. They had come to New York under the assumption that Vanessa had not left the state after checking out of the hotel on Long Island. But they were now confronted with the possibility of her having relocated to any state in America.

Candy stood at one of the windows in Rich's cabin in Balmville, New York. The hideout was located in Orange County, not far from New York City. Candy stared at the tree Chase had been chained to during Rich's torture of him. Candy had mixed feelings as she thought of her and Vanessa firing bullets into Chase, ending his torture and his life. It was hard for Candy to feel remorse for killing Chase and wanting to kill the others involved with her worst experience. But Candy knew that risking her life or the lives of her loved ones to accomplish this task was not worth a prison sentence.

Rich hugged Candy from behind and kissed her neck. "You okay?"

"When Vanessa gets here with us."

Rich ran his hands up and down her arms to console her. "We put the line out to her. It's just a waiting game until she responds."

"I just thought of something."

"Talk to me," Rich said.

"Let's just have Domingo take care of Chanel and the

rest of them."

"You mean pay the dude who can't keep an eye on them to kill them? The dude I don't trust?"

"We all wanna see them dead. Me, you, Vanessa. But it's no use in us pulling the trigger, especially when we gotta play this waiting game and then get the runaround."

"I don't know about Domingo," Rich said, shaking his head.

"He the only one who can get around them all at once." She turned around and faced Rich. "What you think?"

"I'm thinking about Vanessa right now. Tomorrow. Let me think about it." Candy kissed him and hugged him.

"Let's get some air," Rich said, leading Candy to the porch in the back of the cabin. Rays from the sun beamed down as they stood under the shade of the awning. Rich sat on a chair and Candy sat on his lap.

"It's still beautiful out here." Candy looked out at the acres of grass and trees on Rich's property. Candy and Rich seemed to be isolated in the wealthy neighborhood. The only sounds heard were birds chirping and the ruffling of leaves ushered in with the sporadic breezes. The closest house was a ranch that could be seen in the distance from the front of the cabin.

Rich slid his hands inside of Candy's skirt and into her thong.

Candy took a deep breath and closed her eyes. She began to grind her ass into his lap as his finger crossed

192

her clit and entered her pussy.

Rich massaged her breasts with his free hand.

Her back pressed against his firm chest as she grinded slower and more sensually. Candy could feel his ten inches bulging from beneath his shorts. She turned around and removed her shirt and bra, then lifted her skirt as Rich pulled down his shorts and underwear.

"Hurry up," Rich said. He pulled at her thong until Candy stepped one of her heels out of it.

Candy looked at Rich's dick standing at attention. She was hungry for the sensation it had given her so many times. She had thought about it constantly during their time apart. She felt Rich's strong grip on one of her butt cheeks as she straddled him. "God." She closed her eyes when her insides enveloped Rich's thickness and she plunged downward. She could feel his tongue touch her hardened nipples before his lips pressed against her breast and the suction of his mouth brought a good portion of it inside of his mouth. His arms wrapped her back, pulling her closer to him each time she slid up and down his shaft with a slow motion. His hands ran all over her back, confirming that every part of her body belonged to him. He held her like he never planned to let her go.

"I love you, Rich. I love you," she whispered in a sensual tone.

Rich worked her other breast with his mouth. He went down slightly as Candy leaned back, swerving her hips like she was dancing to a reggae song. Rich kissed the center of her chest, just beneath her breast. Candy moaned as he sucked her soft skin, her long hair touching his hands that embraced her back.

Candy picked up her pace. She reached back, grabbing Rich's knees. "Yeah, Rich."

"Come on, baby," Rich uttered as he swiveled his movements into hers.

"Yeah, ohh. Yes."

"Oh, shit." Rich pulled Candy closer.

"Huh, huh, Ahhh." Candy and Rich came at the same time. As she felt his hands slide down her sweat-soaked back, she looked into his eyes and kissed him. It felt so right to be back in Rich's arms, to feel him inside her. But Candy knew she needed Vanessa in order for their lives to be complete.

CHAPTER EIGHTEEN

VANESSA

T hings had changed drastically for Vanessa in just days. She had been spending nights at Peg's apartment and Heather's house since she checked out of the hotel. When they were not having sex, the majority of their time was spent discussing social issues ranging from animal rights to feminism. Vanessa had even been to a CSA protest at a lab in Ithaca, New York where experiments were performed on cats. Vanessa was not ready to make the pledge to advocate for the issues Peg and Heather did, but she could not deny they had valid points and important causes they supported.

"Killing is wrong and that's the bottom line," Peg said.

"It's a cowardly act," Heather added.

Vanessa was sitting in a health food store watching Peg and Heather debate with a man who was buying several pounds of organic red snapper. But it wasn't the fish that mattered to Vanessa; it was the concept of killing. The arguments Peg and Heather hurled at the man applied to Vanessa's hunger to kill Chanel and her crew. Vanessa had rode past the tournament several times looking for them, to no avail. She was beginning to take it as a sign that her plan was not meant to come to fruition. Listening to Peg and Heather speak of the immorality of killing was confirming that. Vanessa felt like a hypocrite. *Who ever heard of a killer vegan? What the hell has my life come to?* Vanessa was slowly reclaiming her identity that preceded Candy's kidnapping and torture.

Vanessa left the health food store with Peg and Heather. They were in Peg's Toyota Prius heading to a CSA meeting. It would be Vanessa's second time sitting among college students engaging in discourse on animal rights, veganism and other social justice issues. Vanessa had not become a member of the group, but she enjoyed the discussions. The conversations were so far removed from mainstream society that they rendered the group's members as outsiders. It was a feeling Vanessa had coped with for years as a youth. But the group was empowered through their defiance of norms.

"I was checking out your sex tape for the hundredth time," Heather said from the back of the Prius as Vanessa sat up front in the passenger seat beside Peg.

196

"And?" Vanessa said.

"First, I wanna say that Candy is hot. And I know you said Rich is a hell of a cock-slinger, but how did you guys commit to him?"

"Love."

"It just seems a bit debasing as a woman. Of course, I'm all for a threesome. But two women in a relationship with a man reeks of the type of inequality that women have fought against since the era of Susan B. Anthony," said Heather.

"It is a hard pill to swallow," Peg added.

"I actually think having a threesome but not being in a committed relationship is debasing," said Vanessa. In that instance, the women are merely being used, as opposed to a relationship where each party is equally obligated to each other on every level, and not simply for sex."

"But the man is still the one who reaps the benefit that the woman doesn't," said Peg. "He has the benefit of two women. Would Rich have allowed another man to participate in a threesome with you guys?"

Never. She's got a point. Vanessa thought about the time Candy had jokingly asked Rich to allow her to bring another man into their bedroom. Rich laughed it off until Candy continued pushing the issue. For the first time, Vanessa had seen Rich become angry. He raised his voice and slammed his fist on the dinner table, nearly knocking off the plate of food Candy and Vanessa had prepared for him.

The food we cooked. Vanessa reminded herself of all the things she and Candy had done to cater to Rich. The meals they prepared, the hours they spent cleaning his home and washing his clothes. Certainly, Rich had occasionally had some meals ready for them when they arrived home from work. But those were leftover dishes cooked by Vanessa and Candy, simply reheated in a microwave by Rich. *He's no different than any pimp.*

"It's not unusual that you don't see the chauvinistic implications in that relationship," Heather said. "Men have a way of downplaying their role in oppressing us until it seems normal."

"Not to mention they have society on their side," added Peg. "Everything is leaning in their direction. When we think of any position of authority, be it police officer, doctor or lawyer, the image of a man comes up."

Heather said, "What positions come to mind when you think of women? The nurse who takes orders from the doctor and the secretary who caters to the lawyer. So the image of a man being in a relationship with two women may be different, but it's understandable. Yet society can't fathom a three-way relationship between two men and a woman."

Vanessa was growing angry with Rich and he wasn't even in her presence. He and Candy had been leaving messages on her phone for days, but Vanessa simply ignored them when she saw who they were from. She was still frustrated with Candy for leaving her to chase behind Rich. But as she thought of the situation now, in context with the feminist views of Peg and Heather, Vanessa realized Candy was simply under Rich's spell, just as she had once been. *This shit was all his plan from day one.* Vanessa remembered when Rich first broached the topic of a threesome. He had nonchalantly inquired about it in response to a comedian who joked about threesomes on television as he and Vanessa watched.

"You do understand that a woman would benefit both of us, right?" Rich had argued.

Thinking back, Vanessa could not deny that their relationship with Candy had benefited both of them. But Rich was definitely the person to benefit most. Vanessa had thought about this before, but Peg and Heather made the reality vivid. Reflecting on Rich made Vanessa want to call him up and tell him how she felt. But that was simply a thought. She had more important people in her life now: Peg and Heather.

* * *

An hour later, Vanessa sat Indian style on one of the large pillows in the circle of the multicultural group of thirteen CSA members in Heather's carpeted basement. Jasmine incense burned as the students took notes on iPads and writing pads while snacking on fresh fruit and assorted nuts. On Vanessa's right was Peg. Heather sat across from them on the other side of the circle. There was a positive vibe within the room generated in spite of the diverging views that gave rise to intelligent debates. There was a collective openness and willingness to agree to disagree on certain topics. The two black faces, two Latinos and one Asian fit in perfectly with the majority of white students. There was an openness that Vanessa had experienced with Peg and Heather since she met them.

A slender, light-skinned woman with curly hair and a narrow face held up a book titled *Sistah Vegan*. It was an anthology of black women who were explaining their experiences as vegans. "One of the women in here makes a valid point that I've grappled with for years."

"Your mouth still waters at the sight of cooked calf testicles," Peg said, drawing laughter.

"Okay, Tina Fey." The light-skinned woman smiled. "Seriously, as I was about to say, sometimes as an African American I feel white people act as if they have a monopoly on veganism, white affluent people in particular." She looked around the group. "Not you guys, thank God. But some of the larger vegan and vegetarian organizations."

Vanessa added, "I feel like that sometimes also. Even many black people think being a vegan is a 'white thing.' People on both sides need to be more empathetic. There are unique cultural experiences and issues relative to the racial, ethnic and class makeup of people who are vegans. Vegans are not some monolithic group."

"You're right," Heather said. "Vanessa and I debated

yesterday about comparing the living conditions of animals to the living conditions of enslaved blacks."

Vanessa listened to Heather and then the rest of the people speak. She thought about how she had convinced Candy to change her eating habits temporarily. While Candy did not agree with everything Vanessa said about veganism, she had always been interested in hearing Vanessa out.

Unlike Heather, Candy had agreed with Vanessa that the comparison between the treatments of animals and slaves was not the best analogy to convey the seriousness of the mistreatment of animals. Even though Vanessa and Candy came from contrasting classes, they shared a skin tone that helped them connect on many levels where Vanessa could not with Peg and Heather.

"You okay?" Peg asked.

Vanessa snapped out of her thoughts with a smile and a nod. "Excuse me," she announced to the group. She stepped out of the door, went downstairs, exited the house and stood in front of Heather's home. She pulled out her Droid and the battle between her thoughts of calling Candy and her thoughts of not calling her ravished her gray matter. She paced in front of the large flowerbed beside the concrete path leading to Heather's front door.

"The least I can do is check her messages," Vanessa whispered to herself. She began scrolling through her smartphone. She came across one from Rich, then contemplated seeing if he had anything to say about Candy. She played the message. Vanessa stopped pacing immediately, her mouth wide open. She learned that Candy had been arrested in Atlanta for assault. Panicking, she fumbled with the phone, scrolling through message after message. She learned that Rich had come to New York in search of her, before returning to Atlanta to pick up Candy. King had bailed her out and they returned to New York to find her, before leaving back to Atlanta.

Vanessa called Candy.

"Vanessa?" Candy responded.

"It's me."

"You okay?"

"Yes."

"Vanessa, I'm here too, baby," said Rich after taking the smartphone.

"Yeah," Vanessa replied nonchalantly, unlike how she usually responded by telling Rich she loved him. Her perception of Rich and her relationship with him and Candy had changed. "Put Candy back on the phone."

"Okay."

"Vanessa," Candy said, "where are you?"

"Are you still in Atlanta?"

"Yeah, but where are you?" Candy asked.

"On Long Island."

"They said you checked out the hotel."

"I did. I've been staying with some friends."

"Friends?"

"I'll explain when I get to Atlanta."

"When?"

"No later than tomorrow, depending on how soon I can book a flight."

"Okay." Candy paused. "You know I love you, right?"

"I love you too." Vanessa hung up and held the phone tightly. She felt reinvigorated, having reconnected with Candy. Her task was now to save Candy from the clutches of Rich.

"You okay, Vanessa?" Peg asked as she stepped over.

"Yes. I have somebody I want you and Heather to meet."

CHAPTER NINETEEN

RICH

R ich knew there was going to be a problem between him and Vanessa since he spoke to her minutes earlier. He sensed it in her words or lack thereof. Of course, he and Vanessa had parted on bad terms when she walked out of their hotel suite with Candy in Las Vegas. But that was the past. Candy was beyond that and Rich was looking toward the future. So long as Vanessa removed murder from her plans for the future, Rich knew of nothing that could interfere with them rekindling the three-way relationship they once had. But that was wishful thinking based on the bad attitude he got from Vanessa on the phone.

"I can't wait to see her," Candy said as Rich steered down I-85 on their way to Queens Incorporated.

"You'll get your chance soon."

"We can finally get things back the way they were." Candy talked about them relocating to Atlanta. It was something they had once contemplated after Candy's kidnapping. The city was perfect for Candy and her business, because the hair care industry thrived in Atlanta. The leading hair show, sponsored by Bronner Brothers, was hosted each year in the city. There was also a thriving black community in Atlanta from which Candy could find plenty of consumers if she decided to open another salon. And the fact that Rich was on the cusp of sealing a business deal with King, having access to King would be easiest for Rich if he lived in Atlanta.

Minutes later, Rich pulled up in front of Queens Incorporated. "I'll be back in a minute."

"I wanna come in and see what your future business partner has going for himself."

"I'm only gonna be a minute."

"So for a minute, I'll get to see the business my man will be affiliated with."

"You know Zora got an order of protection against you."

Candy was silent.

"Baby, you ain't been out of jail a hot week."

"And I'm not trying to go back, so go 'head upstairs."

Rich kissed Candy. "Don't worry. One minute." He put up his index finger, then exited his Audi R8.

Stepping through the glass double doors, he chatted with the receptionist before making his way to the fourth floor.

"Hey, Rich," one of King's employees called out.

"How are you?" Rich greeted the short white man with a firm handshake.

"Good so far."

"Catch up with you later." Rich smiled and stepped toward King. The two men gave each other dap and hugged.

"My office," King said, leading Rich through a corridor and into a large room backed by floor-to-ceiling windows that overlooked the streets below. African paintings plastered the wall to his left.

Rich sat in the leather chair in front of King's glass desk.

King sat behind the desk and handed Rich a folder. "That's the revised business plan for the L.A. branch."

Rich opened the folder and scanned the Executive Summary at the beginning of the business plan. "I see some good changes from the last one already."

"You negotiate hard like we back on the block," King said with a smile, referring to the debate Rich had with him over some issues in the first business plan King gave him.

"Give me a couple of days with this."

"Time is ticking, brah," King said.

"I know."

"Okay."

"Now tell me something about Zora," Rich said.

King sighed.

"Not good, I guess."

206

"A woman scorned."

"She said she was with the open relationship." Rich shook his head.

"You know women are naturally more emotional than men, right?"

"Tell me something I don't know."

"Well, Zora takes the concept of feeling to another level."

"As my comrade, future business partner and her boss, I'm sure you can make her drop it a notch."

"The only thing that can calm her is time."

Rich huffed. "Even if you can't put a muzzle on her, you can definitely give her a pinkslip."

King frowned. "Fire the person that helped me make millions because she got beat up by your woman?"

"Fire the woman that's trying to make my life so miserable that I can't get the time to put some money up for the LA branch."

"My word is my bond and bond is life. When I was in the VIP at Magic City and Sue's Rendezvous scouting for strippers to manage, Zora was there with me. I gave her my word that when I blow, she'll always be there. She's an assistant making a manager's salary for a reason."

Rich wasn't sure if he could accept King's loyalty to a woman who had helped him make legal money over his disloyalty to a man who knew him before her and helped King rake in blood money. But Rich thought deep as King elaborated on his position. After King's five-minute speech, Rich was seeing things different.

"So, what's the science?" King asked.

"I ain't gonna let no skirt come between us."

King stood and walked around his desk, then leaned on it. "Listen, Rich. I'm gonna talk to Zora. And she's gonna have to understand that you're not the Rich that she was between the sheets with no more. You the Rich that was a boss on the streets and is about to be a boss within this corporation." He gave Rich a pound. "But you gotta understand that Zora is a valued employee at this company."

"I respect that." Rich rose to his feet.

King smiled and walked out of the office with Rich.

As they made their way through the corridor, Rich noticed Katiya talking to a model. He made eye contact with Katiya and she winked. Rich cracked a sly smile, his eyes transfixed on the silk Vera Wang gown that clung to her curves like the label on a classic Coca Cola bottle.

"She's something special," King said as he adjusted his tie.

Rich had been thinking about her since they parted at the hotel after their flight. But he had not had any contact with her. Not a call, not a text message. Definitely no sex. He was confident in his sexual skills and he knew Katiya's reaction to him was genuine, so she would eventually contact him. But under no circumstances did he plan to contact her. She would have to disregard her extreme arrogance and sense of entitlement to have the itch between her legs scratched by Rich. He was planning to eventually become faithful to Candy and Vanessa, but that would be after he was done with Katiya.

As Rich and King approached Katiya, the model walked off. "I guess power is intimidating to some women," said Katiya, watching the woman depart.

"The truth is power and they say the truth hurts," King stated.

"Truth is, account numbers and credit lines are power. And therein lies my strength and your weakness, King." Katiya flashed a shrewd smile and turned to Rich. "You, my friend, may have the name, but your riches are untold thus far, even in the information age."

"Where I come from, you keep your mouth closed and your mind open."

Katiya grinned. "That's cute." She walked away, then turned back. "Excuse me, Rich. It'll only take a second."

There was no way Rich would submit to her order. She had just stepped away from him, so it was clear to him that she was trying to test her power of persuasion. "King was just leaving," Rich said. King looked at him and then walked off. Rich laughed to himself as Katiya returned to him after he refused to move. *You want me, you chase me.*

She reached inside of his Tom Ford blazer, put her hand around his waistline and removed his phone. She typed in her phone number.

Rich liked her confidence. *This chick is different.*
"Anytime after seven, P.M., that is."
Before Rich could respond, Katiya was walking off.
"I got her," Rich mumbled to himself.

* * *

Rich stepped out of Queens Incorporated and into his Audi. He found Candy singing along with "Down on Me" by Jeremih and 50 Cent.

"You sure got in and out quick," she said sarcastically, since Rich had been gone so long.

"It takes time when you're trying to get the person your girl assaulted to drop the charges and not act up in the future."

Candy turned to Rich. "What did she say?"

"Probably a bunch of bullshit if I would've saw her."

"So you never talked to her inside?"

"King. I spoke to him about her."

"And?"

"You should get around the court case, but please don't say nothing to Zora if you see her."

"Don't worry. I'm a quick learner and jail is a good teacher."

Rich turned on the ignition and pulled off. His mind was everywhere. Candy and her friction with Zora, Vanessa and whatever problem she had with him, what awaited him when he got with Katiya the next time. Katiya seemed to be the only woman that came with no drama. But relationships always seemed good at the

210

beginning. It was when he got to know women that Rich had problems with them. When the flaws they concealed at the outset became visible through intimacy and time.

"Vanessa called when you were gone."

"Lay it on me."

"She's in the air and her flight is scheduled to land in an hour."

Rich set his navigational system for Hartsfield Airport and stepped on the gas. They arrived shortly before Vanessa's plane was scheduled to land.

Rich and Candy sat in the terminal beside each other on a row of chairs. "I wonder where Vanessa went when she checked out of the telly?" Rich thought out loud.

"Me too. She said she's been staying with some friends."

"Friends? I didn't get that shit the first time you said it after she called."

"I told you."

Rich was baffled. Vanessa was a loner. The only friends she had became her enemies when they violated Candy.

"Whoever they supposed to be, they live on Long Island somewhere."

"At least she was all right all this time we was looking for her," Rich said.

"She's a trooper. Definitely not that soft chick who came into my shop a few years back."

"A lot of shit done changed since then."

"I think ATL is really the change we need. Judging from how fast Vanessa made a move to come out here, I'm sure she'll like it too."

Rich and Candy continued chatting for a while. They debated whether to take Vanessa out to eat or to the hotel they were staying at. Whatever their destination, they planned to put all of their issues on the table in an effort to heal the wounds suffered in their relationship and to move on. Rich knew that with Candy and Vanessa by his side, he would be able to take on the legal world he had been trying so hard to conquer.

The Miguel ringtone on Candy's iPhone sounded. "What's up, Vanessa?"

Rich watched as Candy paused.

"Okay." Candy turned to Rich. "Her flight just landed."

Rich and Candy sat patiently for a few minutes. Then passengers started piling into the terminal. Rich and Candy stood and watched intently as children, senior citizens and a group of soldiers headed their way.

"I think that's her," said Candy.

Rich spotted Vanessa's afro puffs and smiled. "It is her." She was wearing a patched denim dress and sneakers, walking among a crowd of people.

"Come on," Candy said.

Rich walked beside Candy, both of them smiling when Vanessa noticed them. As they got closer, the crowd around Vanessa disbursed. There were only two people beside her.

Candy hugged Vanessa and kissed her on the cheek. "I'm so glad to see you."

Rich stepped over and kissed and hugged her also, but he didn't feel her reciprocate the hug authentically. "I missed the shit outta you," he said.

Vanessa smiled. "I missed y'all too."

Candy or me? Rich didn't know how to read Vanessa.

She turned to the two white women beside her. "This is Peg and Heather," Vanessa said. The women smiled and exchanged greetings with Rich and Candy.

Rich eyed Heather. *This a thick-ass white girl. She got the crazy fatty.* He noticed her sizing him up also.

"So you two met Vanessa on the flight?" Candy asked.

"No," Vanessa answered for them. "This is who I've been living with on Long Island."

Rich and Candy locked eyes. Then Rich looked at Vanessa. His mind wandered: *What the fuck is Vanessa doing living with two white girls? And why the hell did she bring them all the way down to the A?*

Vanessa looked at Candy and Rich. "I wanted y'all to meet Peg and Heather, because I'm thinking about moving in with them."

"Moving in?" Candy blurted. Her face screwed up like she had just received news of a death in the family.

Rich shook his head. *These white broads must got they lickin' license and they done fucked Vanessa's head up. So much for all the plans me and Candy had for the three of us.*

CHAPTER TWENTY

DOMINGO

Domingo grunted as he slammed into Chanel's pussy. Her legs were pressed against his shoulders, inching forward as the bed squeaked and the headboard slammed against the wall. "You killin' this pussy," Chanel cried.

Domingo let her legs fall to the bed. He turned her onto her side in the fetal position. He stared at the fat lips of her pussy, then grabbed his dick and rubbed it over her lips, teasing her.

Chanel reached back anxiously. "Put it in me."

Domingo wedged the head of his dick into her tight pussy. "Damn," he whispered. He closed his eyes and let out a deep breath. He palmed her ass with his free hand and guided himself inside with the other.

"Ahh. Yes, Domingo," Chanel screamed.

With his knees spread apart on the bed, his hands on her side and the front of her thigh, he began stroking—deliberate, short, powerful strokes.

"Yeah," Chanel whispered as her fleshy tightness engulfed his dick.

Domingo could feel her pussy becoming more wet, allowing him deeper penetration.

"Take this pussy," Chanel begged.

Domingo pressed her cheeks down, sandwiching her pussy tighter around his dick. The feeling of her insides magnified. Her hot juices leaked to his pubic hairs as he sped up his stroking.

"Yeah, faster," Chanel cried. "Hit it faster. Beat the pussy up."

Domingo entered deeper and faster. His neck stretched out as he was about to cum. He pulled out and spurted his white cream all over her large chocolate ass and thighs. Stroking his dick, he exhaled in quick, short gasps. He watched Chanel stand and head to the bathroom. Domingo snatched his sheets from the bed and walked into the bathroom. After placing them in a hamper, he and Chanel showered together.

Afterwards, they dressed and ate before relaxing. Domingo was lying on his couch with Chanel in his arms as they watched Alicia Keys and Bruno Mars perform on the BET Awards. When a commercial came on, Chanel asked, "How much do you think Rich is worth?"

"The question is, how much money he keep laying around?"

"He don't look like the shoebox stash type, so you got two problems."

216

"Oh yeah?"

"Yup. Getting him to withdraw from his accounts, 'cause I assume he got more than one."

"What's the other problem?"

"The Twins. You can't have them regulatin' what you get."

Domingo had long since known Chanel was a paper chaser. But he was just getting used to her straight talk about her interest in the plot. He didn't know whether to interpret Chanel's input as genuine insight into a critical plan or her seeking to exert control over him.

"Don't trust the Twins," she continued.

"Only dude I trust in the streets is Domingo, ya heard?"

"That's right," Chanel replied.

The truth was Domingo had a lot of lust for, but little trust in Chanel. Like him, her loyalty could be compromised if she was confronted by the right number of dead presidents. But Domingo's attraction to her was growing as what had been mere sexual relations between them morphed into personal times spent outside the bedroom. The shift in their interaction changed drastically after Domingo convinced Chanel she was one step away from death and he was essentially her bodyguard. Domingo also knew that her ability to separate her attraction to good sex from the person giving it to her also was working in his favor.

* * *

Most people went to McDonald's to eat. But Domingo had used the fast food restaurant as a place to plot crimes. He remembered the meeting he and Candy had years earlier in the eatery to plot on burglarizing Vera's apartment. It was the sex tape they had stolen from Vera's apartment that was integral to Domingo now waiting in the same McDonalds to plot with Vera's brothers on killing the only two people that Candy loved.

"They still got that bum-ass Taurus," Domingo mumbled to himself as the Twins pulled up just off the corner of Flatbush and DeKalb Avenues in the car they had used to kidnap Candy.

Jahiem walked inside, followed by Tahiem. They sat across from Domingo as he was snacking on French fries.

"What's good?" Domingo greeted them.

Tahiem nodded and Jahiem said, "You tell me."

"I'm waiting on them to get back at me," Domingo said, because he had not yet heard from Candy or Rich.

"You don't wait when it's time to bring it," Jahiem said.

"Everything is a process, ya heard?"

"People speed up processes all the time." Jahiem balled his fists on the table.

"Location," Tahiem said.

"Yeah," Jahiem added. "Still no location?"

"They could be living in a brownstone in Harlem or Forest Projects in the Bronx." Domingo paused. "Listen, man. Ain't no statute of limitations on murder. So people

218

don't murk shit, lay low, then pop up and tell you where they at."

"Your phone?" Tahiem said.

"Yeah, call 'em now," Jahiem demanded.

Domingo shook his head and waved his hands in front of him. "Hold up, hold up. Let me fuck this cow. Y'all just hold the legs."

"What?" Jahiem scowled.

Domingo was gearing up to pull the .45-caliber Sig Sauer from his waistband if things became unmanageable. "And that shit you was hollerin' about what go down when the bread come in wasn't kosher."

"Meaning?" Tahiem asked.

His Twin added, "Yeah, what that 'posed to mean?"

"When it come to Rich's dough, that pie gotta get split three ways." Domingo pointed at Jahiem and Tahiem, then himself. "Three equal ways."

Jahiem grinned and turned to his brother. "I like homey."

"Y'all just give me a minute, ya heard?"

"Just don't let nothin' happen to my sister 'cause you draggin' your feet," Jahiem said.

Domingo watched as the Twins stood and walked out of McDonald's. He questioned if his plan was a wise one. If Rich and Vanessa didn't surface soon, Domingo was going to end up in the crosshairs of the two loose cannons he had pointed at Vanessa and Rich. And if he was able to manipulate the Twins into killing Rich and Vanessa as planned, and unhand Rich of his money, there would almost definitely be a problem over how the money was disbursed.

Domingo pulled out his phone and called Candy. "Ain't nothin' like a pretty face on face time," he said, watching Candy through the small screen on his iPhone.

"I got a lot of shit on my plate, so don't stop me from eating just because you wanna talk some freaky shit."

Oh shit. The OK Café. Domingo noticed the red and white striped awnings on the Atlanta restaurant he had eaten omelets and sour dough French toast at nearly every day of the month he spent in Atlanta several months earlier. Behind Candy was the West Paces Ferry Road eatery Domingo knew was unique to the southern city. "Where you at, Candy? I need to see you. You with Rich and Vanessa?"

"Yeah, we just finished eating."

I knew it.

"Forget where we at. You supposed to be telling me where a few people at."

"All right, all right. I'm onto something, but it's not definite. I'll know in a minute. Just be on point. You'll hear from me."

"Good. Get at me as soon as you hear something."

"I got you, Mamita." Domingo watched a bright smile light up Candy's face. She was sporting red lipstick and a black spaghetti-strap dress. The color contrasted perfectly with her light skin and dark hair.

"Why you staring at me like that?"

Domingo didn't realize that he was transfixed on her beauty. "You know I been flirting with you since I first seen you, right?"

"What else is new?"

"I was seventeen back then and you thought ya boy was just a lil dude with a crush on you, but I was dead ass. And I'm nineteen now, Mamita. On some real shit, keeping it a hundred, I don't know no other way than to say I'm feelin' you."

Candy was frozen.

"I know you still stuck on Rich, for whatever reason, but another man don't stop these feelings I have every time I see you or think about you."

"How do I respond to that?"

"Every statement don't require a verbal response. Just know that as long as you lookin' as sexy as you do and you handlin' yourself on some grown woman shit, ya boy gonna be comin' at you hardbody, ya heard?"

Candy giggled. "You crazy."

"But Rich, you need to put a fork in him, 'cause he done. Old school like Shelltoes and Run DMC. I'm ACGs and Drake, ya heard?"

Candy giggled. "Call him old school, but don't forget to call him dangerous. And you ain't crazy."

"Crazy in love on some Beyonce shit. Real talk, though, I wanna see you."

"You must wanna see Rich go crazy."

"I'll go against a tank with a shank to get to you."

"So you suicidal?"

"People dying all day every day in the hood over dumb shit. Why not die for a cause? For my future wife?"

"Wife? You sure think big."

"Everything about me is big." Domingo winked at Candy.

"I hear you, but I gotta go."

"Just make sure you come back."

"Get at me when you hear something."

"Get at me when you ready to get at me," Domingo said.

Candy smiled. "Bye." She hung up.

Domingo looked around the McDonald's. He felt he was wearing Candy down. He could see himself swooping in and scooping her up once Rich and Vanessa were out of the picture. The fact that he knew they were in Atlanta placed him one step closer to their demise.

Domingo left the restaurant. He hopped in his Expedition and turned on Jadakiss's *I Love You* mixtape. He pulled off nodding his head to the music. He made it to Red Hook Housing Projects, and he headed for his building until he noticed Chanel's Escalade parked in front of Vera's building. He pulled up behind it and walked around to the passenger side.

Chanel let him inside as she dug through her Fendi satchel. "I was coming to check Vera," she said.

"Got good news."

222

Chanel looked up at him.

"Just got off the phone with Rich," Domingo lied. "He down in the A with Vanessa."

"Oh yeah?"

"The ball is in my court. When I say jump, they gonna ask how high."

"So basically, wherever you tell 'em we at, they gonna come and try to get us?"

"You know ya boy call the shots around here." Domingo smirked, adjusting his Cartier specs.

"So basically, my life is in your hands?" Chanel paused, looking down. "This shit is serious. They really wanna kill me."

Domingo gently touched her cheek and shifted her face. Chanel's hazel eyes were on the verge of distilling tears down her dark skin. Domingo could see that beneath all the conceit that defined her personality was a woman fearful of the very streets that molded her, the very streets where she helped scar Candy for life.

Chanel stared at Domingo in silence.

"You all right?" Domingo asked.

"I'll be all right when Rich and Vanessa is dead."

CHAPTER TWENTY-ONE
CANDY

Candy was not surprised about Domingo's attraction to her. What amazed her was that he had momentarily ceased the humorous flirtations for a candid proclamation of his feelings for her. She liked his boldness and could see herself having a one-night-stand with him, but she respected Rich's devotion to her. Still, she had to make a move. As she reflected on Domingo, she was almost certain that her sexual prowess could sway Domingo to kill for her, eliminating the need to finance the multiple homicide.

Despite what the future for Domingo was, Candy had to cope with Vanessa. *She gotta be crazy.* Vanessa had explained to Rich and Candy that she loved them, but she had feelings for Peg and Heather that made it hard for her to leave them behind. Vanessa argued that her relationship with Candy and Rich was virtually nonexistent. Vanessa discussed all of this in the presence of Peg and Heather inside of the OK Café.

Candy stood outside the cafe talking to Rich as they waited for Vanessa to emerge from the eatery with Peg and Heather. "This is some real soap opera shit," Candy said. "Vanessa's leaving us for two white chicks." Candy laughed to shield the pain of the predicament.

"Vanessa wants to do everything, but she doesn't know what she wants. If that makes any sense."

"Since I've known her, she's been like that." Candy thought of how Vanessa was dating Rich when she became ensnared in the love triangle that became their three-way relationship. "A couple of weeks and she think she know these chicks."

Candy watched Vanessa step out of the restaurant with Peg and Heather flanked by her sides. Her eyes honed in on Heather's curves. *I ain't never seen no white girl that thick.* Candy couldn't help but wonder what sex was like with Heather. Then she glanced at Peg and thought of what it would be like to have an all-woman threesome. To Candy, Vanessa's relationship stance said that the all-woman experience was the winner in the battle of the sexes.

"We've decided to stay in Atlanta for a week," Vanessa said. "It's the best way for me to decide where I'm going with my life."

"So we supposed to just sit around like everything cool, while you decide if you wanna give up Coco on steroids and Paris Hilton on crack?" Candy asked.

"Excuse me," Peg said with a look of shock on her pale face.

"Easy," Vanessa warned, putting her hand on Peg's shoulder.

"We didn't come out here looking for problems," Heather said.

"Then why the fuck did you come out here!" Candy barked. "Because that bullshit you said inside the restaurant about supporting Vanessa wasn't convinci—"

"Perhaps it's because you fell short in the support category," Peg interjected.

"What!" Candy pointed her finger in Peg's face. "Don't get fucked up in the middle of this street."

"That's it." Rich stepped in between the women, facing Candy. "Be easy."

Vanessa said, "I'm sorry, Candy." She stomped off.

"Look what you did," Peg told Candy, before following behind Vanessa.

Heather looked at Rich and Candy. "Vanessa really loves you guys. She's just going through a lot right now. Sorry." She stepped off to catch up with Peg and Vanessa.

"Can you believe this shit?" Candy exclaimed. "And you just stood here and let her get that bullshit off."

"If you would've calmed the fuck down, shit would've went different."

A vein popped from Candy's head and her eyebrows slanted downward. "This little white ho talking all reckless and you beefin' about me?"

Rich responded to her rhetorical question, but Candy was so consumed with anger and thoughts of releasing it that she

226

didn't hear Rich. I gotta call Domingo. She walked off.

"So you just breezing too?"

"Everybody else need time to think. I need some time too," she said as she stormed ahead without turning around. All she could think of was how she had traveled down south, made up with Rich and went to jail because of him, only to have him not defend her. She felt betrayed. There was no way she would even stay in the same state as Rich. If he loved her, he would have to catch a flight to New York and find her like she did, coming to Atlanta to reunite with him.

* * *

Hours later, Candy was still vexed. She was so vexed she disregarded the phone calls from her manager. Her declining business would only upset her more. She had decided to stay in Atlanta for a few hours and think her problems out over some drinks. She had expected to receive a call from Rich and Vanessa, seeking to rewind the saga that had played out. Neither of them cared. That was what Candy thought. So she found herself nursing a bottle of Moscato while seated at a table in front of the bar inside of Haven, the upscale Brookhaven restaurant. She decided to call Domingo.

"What's good, Mamita?"

"I need to see you tonight."

"It's like that? Guess our conversation earlier touched you."

"Meet me Uptown. One-hundred and Twenty-fifth and

Morningside."

"That's Morningside Park, right?"

"I'll be on the first bench on Morningside."

"When?"

"Soon. I'll call you back."

"Ya boy gon' be in the building, ya heard?"

"Bye." She turned off her phone and headed for the airport.

During her flight, Candy burst into tears. She felt disrespected by Vanessa and Rich. She could still see Vanessa's face in the back of her mind as she strolled into the airport and introduced Peg and Heather. She imagined Vanessa living with them and having sex with them during the entire time she and Rich were looking for her. And Candy could see the emotionless look on Rich's face as Peg interfered with their personal affairs. Peg had no position, no authority, and no say in anything that went on between Candy, Vanessa and Rich.

These were people who had killed for each other. Candy had once choked out Chanel and slammed her head into a locker in her shop because Chanel appeared to be thinking of laying her hands on Vanessa. Candy had stood by Vanessa's side as they both pumped bullets into Chase's body after Rich had kidnapped and tortured him for his involvement in Candy's torment. But all of that meant nothing, because of two white girls Vanessa had known approximately three weeks in contrast to the three years she had known Candy and Rich.

228

When the plane landed, Candy called Domingo and caught a cab to Morningside Park. The black and silver strap Burberry watch that matched her dress read 10:49. Eleven minutes 'till he gets here. Candy had told Domingo to meet her at 11:00. She exited the cab and sat on the bench outside of the park, just off the corner 125th Street in the heart of Harlem.

Candy felt uncomfortable being back in Harlem. She was like an intruder in her hometown. The old buildings looked different. The new buildings were startling. The people strolling on the summer night seemed to step to a different tune than the Harlemites Candy had grown accustomed to. She had made trips to the neighborhood on occasion with Vanessa since they left the neighborhood. They would steer the streets late at night, peering through tinted windows for any sign of the women that had crossed Candy. But the anger and vindictiveness that fueled Candy clouded her vision more than the tinted windows. Yet things in Harlem did not remain static. Candy had become comfortable everywhere from Long Island and Las Vegas to Balmville and Atlanta. But the streets she was raised in were now foreign.

She watched the street light cause the rims on Domingo's Expedition to glisten as he turned the corner. The sound of Jay-Z's *Brooklyn Go Hard* blasted as his truck came to a halt and the door opened. The fly guy in Prada specs and a matching jean suit stepped toward her in high-top Prada sneakers. Candy had to admit, Domingo had grown since he was last in her presence. His thin frame had filled out and grown tall. His hairline and mustache were perfectly trimmed.

"What's up, Mamita?"

Candy stood and hugged Domingo after he pecked her on the cheek. "Look at you." She smiled, looking up into his eyes. "I used to look down at you."

"I been tryin' to put you on, Mamita. Ya boy ain't no lil kid, ya heard?"

"Even with these heels on, you still taller than me, and I'm damn near six feet."

"I make Rich look like a kid now."

Candy rolled her eyes. "Please, whatever you do, don't mention Rich's name."

Domingo squinted his eyes. "Rich? Rich who? I don't know no Rich." He grinned.

Candy giggled. "You crazy, but you catch on quick." She paused. "We broke up. Rich and Vanessa no longer exist in my world."

"That leaves plenty of room for me."

Candy paused, staring at Domingo, trying to figure him out and figure herself out. She needed to balance her sexual attraction to him with the feeling that she was doing something wrong. As she looked into his green eyes, she could tell he knew something was plaguing her mind.

Domingo gently grabbed her hand and pulled her toward him until his hands were on her huge hips. Their faces were separated only by inches. "Listen, Mamita. I know you got a history with Rich. But Rich is history."

Candy nodded. "A lot of memories."

"Me too. Memories of me seeing you for the first time as you strolled into my PJs in them high heels. Memories of how I wanted to make you mine and give you the world, even though I was only working on locking down a block in Brooklyn. Memories of you in your shop. Memories of me just watching you. Everything from the way your sexy eyes squinted when you were mad to how that smile lit up your face every time Mary J. Blige came on."

Candy blushed. "You actually remember that?"

Domingo's hands slid down to her butt. "I remember everything about you. I remember how I had to sit in that shop and tolerate Rich all over you when I knew I deserved you. When I knew I could please you."

Candy closed her eyes as Domingo's lips locked on hers. She felt a tingling sensation flow through her body. Everything that was wrong seemed right. His touch, the scent of his cologne, even the way he spoke with an air of confidence that said they were meant to be. She knew Domingo had waited years. He deserved her.

As their lips parted, Domingo said, "We got a history too. It wasn't a physical thing, but you was always on my mind, Mamita."

Candy slipped her hand between Domingo's legs. "How 'bout you get a hotel room for us?"

* * *

After Domingo slammed the door to the hotel room and

turned to Candy, he kissed her, then grabbed her ass and picked her up.

Damn. Candy wrapped her legs around his waist, surprised at how easily he hoisted her 140 pounds in the air with ease. She felt so comfortable in his strong embrace and his tongue was refreshing to her mouth.

Domingo guided Candy against a wall and began kissing and sucking her neck.

"Ump," she moaned as the scent of Domingo's Cartier Santos cologne intoxicated her while his tongue brought out a sexual force from deep within her.

Domingo let Candy down to her feet. In what seemed like seconds, he and Candy were naked. Domingo's eyes examined her flawless skin and curvaceous body.

Candy looked up into his eyes as he placed his hands on her waist and turned her around. She planted her palms above her on the wall. One of Domingo's hands left her waist and parted her backside. "Ahh," she moaned as she felt the head of his dick rubbing across the length of her pussy to her clit. Domingo was teasing her, causing her insides to burn with lust. She tried to be patient as he inserted the head of his dick between her lips, and then pulled it out. "Put it in, please."

Domingo rubbed his dick on the inside of her butt cheeks. The juices from her pussy served as a natural lubricant. Candy pressed her hands against the wall harder to brace herself as chills went through her body when Domingo kissed her neck. She felt the hand on her waist again. "Ahh. Please, put it in," she begged.

The head of Domingo's dick pressed against her clit for a few seconds, driving Candy wild. As she felt it slide over her lips, Domingo suddenly plunged all the way inside of her. "Oh shit!" Candy screamed. Domingo pulled back slowly and slammed back into her again, working a slow exit and fast enter mode of strokes.

"Damn, girl. This pussy tight," he whispered, before slamming in hard.

"Yes."

"You like that shit, right? Huh?" he asked.

"I love it."

Domingo put his hands on top of Candy's, pressing them against the wall as he kissed her neck. He sped up his pace. "Yeah. Take this dick like a pro. Take it, Candy."

"It's mine. I'm taking it," Candy exclaimed.

"Yeah, Mamita." Candy felt Domingo's hands trail down her body to her waist. They gripped her tightly. Then she felt his dick begin plunging into the walls of her pussy. "Yes," she panted.

Domingo was striking on an angle, working the left side with several strokes, then hitting the right. "You like that?" he asked. "Tell me you like how I'm fuckin' you, Mamita."

"I like how you're fucking me. Fuck me, Domingo."

"Yeah, I know you like it. Told you I wasn't no kid." He strained his dick, slamming into Candy.

She pushed her ass back and turned around. Sweat trickled down her face, her makeup smeared a mosaic of eyeliner and foundation. She was breathing heavy and getting a good look at Domingo's long dick for the first time. She had planned on dominating their episode, but she was hypnotized by his dick. It stood upwards to the left, like a lamppost after a car accident. She dropped to her knees. "Fuck my ass. Hurry up!" she begged. She wanted to feel the type of pain that came with rough sex. To hell with the KY Jelly and pillow to protect her knees from rug burns.

"This how you want it, huh?"

She felt her cheeks part. "This is your ass," she said as one of Domingo's hands grabbed her by the waist. She closed her eyes as the head of his dick tore through her tiny hole. "Ugh," she grunted like cattle being prodded. Then she mustered all her strength to hold in her desire to scream as he entered her full and began a slow stroking pattern.

"Damn, this shit tight," Domingo said.

"You—" she paused. "Like it, right?"

"Hell yeah." He began stroking harder and faster.

"Ahh. Yes. Fuck . . . my ass." She bounced her ass back into his thrusts.

"Yeah, baby. Yeah."

"Ahh." Candy's head jerked back when Domingo pulled her hair.

"You like it rough, don't you?"

"Yes." Her back arched. She could feel her hair about to be separated from her weave as Domingo's palm began slamming into her ass. "Spank me. I been bad, Daddy."

Domingo slapped her harder and more rapidly, gently

rubbing the stinging sensation away after each hit. He freed her hair from his hand, grabbed her neck and forced the side of her face to the carpeted floor. "Rough, huh? You like it rough, Mamita?"

"Ahh, ahh. Yes, yes." Her face was rubbing against the carpet as were her knees. Her butt was as sore as her asshole. Her scalp was in pain. But Candy loved it. She didn't know why or how, but Domingo had unleashed the beast within her that she didn't know existed. She felt like a slut and she loved it. Sexual fluids streamed from her pussy, down her thigh. "I'm cumming!" Candy screamed with the volume and intensity of her trying to silence someone who was perpetually banging on the front door. "I'm cumming!"

"Yeah." Domingo put both hands on her hips and rammed hard and fast. "Ahh, yeah."

Candy's body exploded in pleasure as she and Domingo came at the same time. Domingo stood and Candy fell on the floor, out of breath. She looked up at his tall, nude body that loomed over her. Her mouth was wide open and her tongue was hanging from the side of her mouth like an exhausted dog. Rich is good, but Domingo is the shit.

Candy knew her plan was to have Domingo do her dirty work. But as she stared at his dick, feeling the after effects of a sexual experience that was unlike any she had imagined possible, she was not ready to have Domingo risk his freedom. Not yet, anyway.

CHAPTER TWENTY-TWO
VANESSA

Vanessa had sat silently in her hotel room for hours. Peg and Heather had tried talking to her, but she needed time…space. Vanessa sat perched on a chair in front of the window. She gazed down on Atlanta from the fifteen-story view of the Comfort Inn. She could not deny her love for Rich and Candy no matter how hard she tried. But Vanessa was fearful that their three-way relationship was no longer viable. And Vanessa was not willing to forego the relationship she was building with Peg and Heather. It was far from formal and none of the women had agreed to anything other than being friends with benefits. But Vanessa was beginning to think undefined relations were what she needed.

Peg walked over, stood behind Vanessa and began massaging her shoulders and neck. "We're here for you," she said as Heather stepped in front of Vanessa.

"Exactly what does that mean?"

236

"It means whatever decision you make, we support it," said Heather. "We have to respect your wishes and live with them."

"Yeah, Vanessa." Peg walked around her and stood beside Heather. "I mean, you know I like you a lot. You're cool to talk with. We're sexually compatible. I mean, if I can just get you out of those leather shoes, everything will be perfect." Peg smiled.

A grin surfaced on Vanessa's face for the first time since they had arrived at the hotel. "The way you were talking to Candy, I thought you were gonna get knocked out of your shoes."

"I don't care how big she is or how quote unquote 'hood' she is, I stand up for what's right," Peg said, her eyes bouncing around behind her glasses. "The surprise was the womanizer interceding. He must've been trying to preserve his miniature harem."

"Maybe he was genuinely interested in not seeing you guys go to blows," said Vanessa.

Peg smirked. "Please. Guys like Rich don't exactly protest the distribution of *Girls Gone Wild* DVDs."

"Womanizer or not, I think he handled himself like a gentleman," said Heather.

"What are you, a cheerleader for the guy?" Peg asked. "I mean, what do you think, Vanessa should subject herself to this oppressive relationship that Rich presides over like some Iranian sultan?"

"Whatever you say, Peg," Heather blurted. "This is

not about what we think about Rich. It's about how Vanessa feels about this entire situation."

Vanessa was a ball of emotions. Anger, love, frustration and fear were just a few of the sentiments that consumed her.

"You okay, Vanessa?" Peg asked.

She nodded. "I love both of them."

"We know," said Heather, squatting before Vanessa and rubbing her arms. "But I can no longer be involved with Rich or another man who feels his gender superiority entitles him to the love and devotion of two women simultaneously."

When tears began falling from her eyes, Peg and Heather gave her a group hug. "That megalomaniac will be out of your system before you know it," Peg declared.

When they unhanded each other, Heather spoke. "He's old news."

Vanessa forced a smile that was more cosmetic than an episode of *Niptuck*. After pausing a moment, she said, "But I need to see Candy." She pulled out her cell phone and called Candy.

"What, Vanessa?" Candy asked with pure attitude.

"I need to see you."

"Did you get approval from Coco and Paris?"

Vanessa looked up at Peg and Heather. They were listening intently to her responses, trying to detect what questions prompted them.

"Kind of quiet," Candy said. "What's the matter, white girl got your tongue?"

"I don't deserve this, Candy."

"How do you think I feel knowing two white girls turned out the woman I love?"

"Turned out?"

"They got you open like a research monkey. They turned you out."

"Turned out or exposed? Like you opened my eyes to feelings I had about women while I was in a relationship with Rich? You exposed me to my true identity, allowed me to free myself. Just like Peg and Heather have exposed me to something about Rich."

"They don't even know Rich."

"They know men, and the last time I checked, Rich was one."

"What the hell are you talking about?"

"I'm talking about the gender inequalities of a male-dominated society that place women on the bottom of the totem pole. I'm talking about Rich living like a pimp off of our backs."

"If he's a pimp, you sure was one happy hooker the whole time he had you on the stroll."

"We both know it wasn't all peaches and cream. Remember Vegas? The elevator ho? In the very same hotel we were in? Just imagine how many other women there were that we don't know of? The day I first met Rich in your shop, you told me he was a womanizer. He's probably got some woman down at that agency. What's the name of that place King owns?"

"Queens Incorporated."

"We mistakenly thought two women could tame him. There's never enough women for a man, Candy."

Silence lingered for a few seconds.

"I still love him," Candy said.

"Me too. But it's about how he feels. How he convinced me to bring another woman into my bedroom because my love wasn't enough. It's about him sexing some slut in the elevator of our hotel because our love wasn't enough. There is no gender equality. Rich took our love and used it as fodder for his belief that he's a god. We created a monster."

"So what now?"

"Join me."

"You mean, you, plus Coco and Paris?"

"Stop wasting your time with Rich."

"You know I've been there, no men in my life for years. But before that I loved men. And even though Rich may be a piece of shit, he reintroduced me to what I was missing. I can't stop myself from having feelings for men and women. And I can't forgive you for turning your back on me for two white girls."

"Candy, that's not tru . . . Candy? Candy!" Vanessa yelled into her phone, realizing Candy had hung up. She dropped her phone and looked at Peg and Heather, then burst into tears.

240

Peg hugged her. "You don't need her."

Vanessa wept in silence. Every memory she had of Candy began flashing through her mind. They shared too much history for Candy to reject her. Vanessa had mistakenly thought Candy had abandoned her before. But the message was clear this time. Candy was gone. Not willing to accept her role in Candy's departure, Vanessa fingered Rich as the person responsible for pushing away the woman who had helped her discover her sexual identity.

* * *

Vanessa lay on her side in bed, her legs trembling. She clenched her teeth around the edge of a pillow while her toes curled. Peg's mouth was invading her pussy while Heather lapped the crack of her ass. The tears in her eyes made her vision blurry as her eyes blinked uncontrollably. "Woooo." Her scream was muffled by the pillow as she came.

Vanessa felt Peg and Heather leave the bed. By the time she wiped the tears from her eyes, Heather was strapping a dildo around her waist.

"Come." She pointed to Peg's hand as she lay on some pillows strewn on the floor.

Peg straddled the long, black dildo and began a sensual, slow grind. She clasped her hands behind her head and rode as Heather rubbed her small ass. "Fuck me, Heather." Heather pushed her ass up slightly off the floor." Just like that." Peg's small hands landed on

241

Heather's huge breasts. She squeezed them gently as she rode.

"Ohh," Heather roared.

Vanessa watched Heather's swelling nipples between Peg's thin fingers. Vanessa slipped one finger into her own wet slit. Within seconds, she had two inside and she was rubbing her clit with her thumb.

Peg leaned back and grabbed Heather's ankles. She thrust her chest forward as she grinded her lower back against the dildo. "Yes, yes. Shit. Heather. I'm gonna cum."

Heather leaned up and pulled Peg into her embrace. She slipped her tongue into Peg's mouth. Their hands roamed each other's backs as they engaged in a wet kiss.

Peg began riding quickly, slamming down on the dildo. "Ahh."

Heather grabbed Peg's butt, pulling her closer as she climaxed.

Vanessa came at the same time, her finger tugged at her G-spot. "Uh, uh," she panted, breathless.

Peg looked at Vanessa and smiled. She helped Heather to her feet. "The Jacuzzi awaits."

Vanessa slowly pulled herself from the bed and followed them to the Jacuzzi. She sat in the soothing water, thinking of how days had passed and her calls to Candy and Rich had gone unanswered. Vanessa was ready to return to Long Island and continue the life she had begun building with Peg and Heather, but she needed to confront Rich before she left.

After the Jacuzzi, the women showered and quickly dressed. Vanessa grabbed her Droid and scrolled to Rich's phone number. "Voice mail."

She clicked off, then logged onto Google. She typed in Queens Incorporated and found the address of the company. She looked at Peg and Heather. Peg was wearing a checkered dress that fell to her ankles, just above her sandals. Heather was sporting a Dior mini-skirt and over-the-knee-boots with shades. She looked like a movie star strolling the red carpet. "Y'all ready?" Vanessa asked as she adjusted her multi-colored sundress.

"What's the itinerary?" Heather asked.

"Rich. Destination Queens Incorporated."

Heather's eyes lit up. "Oh yeah?"

Vanessa nodded.

"You don't need to have the last word in person," Peg said. "I mean, you can send him some hate email or an unsavory tweet."

Heather shook her head. "No, I think she should tell him off in his face."

"Exactly," Vanessa confirmed.

Peg huffed. "If you insist."

* * *

Vanessa, Peg and Heather walked side-by-side onto the crowded floor that housed Queens Incorporated. Heather took precedence over everyone.

Vanessa could see men and women lifting their heads from computer screens to focus on the white woman with features just as shapely as any black or Latina model that had ever stepped through the doors of Queens Incorporated. The conversation at the water cooler turned into conspicuous whispers and discrete finger pointing at Heather.

This place disgusts me," said Peg. "It's a den of feminine exploitation. Just look at them." She rolled her eyes toward two scantily clad models speaking with a photographer.

"Judging from the ogling eyes of damn near everyone, looks like you have a future in the next hot rap video, Heather," Vanessa said.

Peg grimaced. "I can see Heather practically lap dancing on some guy who thinks his perversion of poetry is actually art."

"It's really empowering, if you think about it," Heather said.

Peg sucked her teeth. "You can't be serious."

"These Fifty Cents and Jay-Zs claim to be the greatest gangsters and hustlers and fans love them. But they need the power of a woman's sexuality for their videos to become popular. We mesmerize millions of video viewers who could really care less about what the rapper is saying. It's the only venue where a woman can actually seize the power men hold over society."

"So shaking your ass virtually naked is an image you

implore women to aspire to?" Peg rolled her eyes. "I mean, come on. Get real."

They stopped at the receptionist's desk. "Excuse me, I'm here to see King," Vanessa said, hoping he would be with Rich.

"Your name?" the receptionist asked.

Vanessa watched her scan the computer screen, presumably for Vanessa's name. "My name is Vanessa Denay and I don't have an appointment." As the receptionist looked up from the screen, Vanessa noticed Rich and King through her peripheral vision. Vanessa began walking toward them.

"Miss! Miss, you can't go back there," the receptionist raised her voice, drawing the attention of the few employees who had not already honed in on Heather or those near her. Vanessa looked back, finding Peg and Heather on her tail.

Rich stopped when Vanessa was a few feet in front of him.

"The snow bunny is crazy thick. I can get her on the cover of *Straight Stuntin* easy," King whispered.

"That's the pink toe I was telling you I'll smash," Rich mumbled.

Vanessa's eyes squinted in anger when she heard the comments. "First you fuck me, then Candy, then the elevator ho. Now you wanna fuck Heather?"

Heather stared at Rich with her mouth wide open.

"There's just not enough women on the planet for

you," Vanessa said.

Rich surrendered his palms to Vanessa. Baby, this is the wrong place and wrong time for soap opera drama."

Vanessa smirked. "If I can't talk about women inside of a modeling agency, where can I?"

"Please, Vanessa. This is a place of business," King countered.

"What? A house of ill repute?" Peg asked sarcastically, stepping beside Vanessa. She and Vanessa were faced off with Rich and King as Heather and the room full of employees looked on.

Rich said, "Sweetheart, you invading my space and trying to play a character in a story that ain't even yours."

"Your chauvinistic superiority trip won't allow you to see that the story you starred in is over," Peg said and pointed at Heather, then herself. "We're in the sequel, not you or any other man."

Rich looked at Vanessa. "These freaks spinning you in circles with this textbook feminist shit, huh?"

It hurt Vanessa to know their relationship had been reduced to a boisterous public spat. "The sad part is I still love you, Rich."

"Baby, let's discuss this somewhere else." He put his hand on her shoulder.

Vanessa slapped his hand off. "There's nothing else to talk about." She felt tears building in the corners of her eyes. She pointed at Rich. "You'll never get the chance to touch me again." Vanessa turned and walked away. She noticed Heather froze, gazing at Rich.

King stepped over to Heather and slipped a business card in her hand. "When you're ready to see your face on magazines, call me."

Vanessa grabbed Heather's arm. "Come on." They stormed off with Peg.

When Vanessa reached the door, she turned and watched Rich still eyeing her. It hurt knowing this would be the last time they would see each other in person. But she was ready to cope with that pain in order to rid him from her system and move on.

CHAPTER TWENTY-THREE

RICH

Show's over. We got models to manage and money to make."

Rich watched King direct his employees, but the damage was done. Rich had just watched his first love walk out the door, headed home with two gay women that she had been living with. The irony set in. It was Rich who had introduced Vanessa to threesomes. He had not answered her calls, because he had decided it was best that he move on. But that decision did not suppress the feelings he had developed for Vanessa, and he feared he didn't have the heart to dismiss her in person. Now, as he stood in the center of the business that was helping introduce him to a new life, he realized that Vanessa had publically dismissed him and it hurt.

"Let's talk about it," said Katiya as she stepped over between Rich and King.

248

"I thought I saw you by the conference room," said Rich, forcing out a bogus smile. "You catch the whole performance?"

"Pretty much. Come on. I'm treating you and King to lunch."

Rich could feel the eyes on him and hear the whispers from the staff as he stepped off with King and Katiya. They entered the elevator and were waltzing out of the office building in minutes. Rich was silent most of the ride as Katiya wheeled her new Bentley Continental Supersports Convertible. But Rich began to loosen up when they pulled up in front of Floataway Café.

By the time they were seated inside the dimly lit bar and lounge area, Rich was comfortable. His appetite had gone out the door with Vanessa, so he ordered a bottle of Moet Rosé. King dined on halibut with locally grown vegetables and pesto. Katiya toyed with the plate in front of her that contained Risotto with English peas and morel mushrooms. Rich leaned back in a large multi-colored chairs and placed his champagne flute on the small orange table beneath the glimmer of the sunrays beaming through the windows in the ceiling.

"Your life is a movie," Katiya said after Rich revealed all he had been through with Vanessa and Candy, minus the killings.

"I was thinking about pitching the idea to Scorsese," Rich joked.

"Seriously? I have a couple of associates behind the

scenes in Hollywood that owe me favors," Katiya said.

"I'll think about it."

"Brother, I don't know how you handled two women under the same roof."

"You'll be surprised at what good dick and a sharp mind can do." Rich beamed. "Ask Katiya."

"You both are merely boy toys of mine. I'm a grown woman who possesses everything she needs and uses everything she desires."

King said, "If you can't be used, you're useless."

"You can use me, just don't abuse me," said Rich, looking into Katiya's eyes.

"A word of advice, from one manipulator to another, Rich: the goal of the game is to be a puppeteer without strings attached."

"Have relations, but not relationships?" Rich asked.

"That's the first step and I think you know that already."

"Control your emotions," King said.

"Almost. Don't allow emotions to develop."

"I'm a master at controlling my emotions. But stopping feelings from arising is a big difference," said Rich.

"Impossible." King shook his head and stuffed a piece of fish into his mouth.

Katiya giggled. "You have to lose yourself to control yourself."

"Sounds real philosophical," Rich said.

"I'm gonna assume you've probably shot someone,

possibly killed someone in those many years in the street. We'll call it collateral damage of the street pharmaceutical industry."

Rich laughed.

"Assumptive, but you gotta respect that she's a straight talker," King said.

"Here it is, Rich. The way you were able to sell drugs to people is no different than many slaveholders were able to enslave blacks and prison guards are able to lock people inside of cells day in and day out."

"They dehumanize their subjects," King said.

"Step one," Katiya confirmed, "you objectify the human being. Transform that human who smoked crack into a crackhead. Some disgusting beast. You make that human being who is enslaved into a slave. Remove his humanity like Thomas Jefferson called blacks orangutans. You make a human being into a Negro. The human being in prison becomes a prisoner, a number. It's not hard to sell poison to a crackhead beast, or lynch an orangutan known as a Negro, or lock an identification number in a cell every night. It's much harder to do that to a human being."

"That's an actual fact." King nodded.

"But what happens is, the person dehumanizing the subject loses their own humanity in the process," Katiya said. "It's why I said you have to lose yourself to gain yourself. Every time I see you," she pointed at Rich, "and you," she pointed at King, "I don't see human beings. I see a dick and a tongue."

Rich laughed.

Katiya's grim look remained. "I'm serious. And I don't see a human when I look in the mirror. I see all of the attributes it takes to dehumanize people, because that's what it takes to win."

"I ain't trying to deal with that type of science," King said.

"That's why my net worth is more than your business grosses. I'm not concerned about blood diamonds, climate change or sweatshops. It's why I have the audacity to tell a man, a stranger I don't know, that I want to fuck. I don't care if people call me a capitalist whore, because my eyes don't see human and I got rid of my humanity a long time ago." She looked at Rich. "Once you do, you'll never have to worry about a broken heart again."

Rich never saw Katiya's philosophy coming. As heartless and as brash as it was, he could identify with it. He had been the guy who sold drugs and killed for years without as much as a second thought. He had set up his opponents to be robbed and extorted by King, because he saw them as crooks, not humans. He had broken the hearts of more women than he could count, because his childhood was marred by the experience of his drug-addicted mother renting him to pedophiles. So he didn't see his mother, and by extension any woman, as human. It was only when he was confronted with the fear of prison and death and when he was introduced to

Vanessa's love that he began to develop a morality that designated women as human beings. Before that, he had no memories of being a normal human being.

Katiya set her fork on the table and took a sip of champagne. She looked at King, then Rich. There was not a semblance of emotion on her face. "Class is over and it's time for us to have a ménage a tois."

* * *

The queen-sized bed on the roof of King's mansion was surrounded by four large plants that could pass for infantile palm trees. They shielded some of the sunrays. King was seated on the bed facing Rich on the chair a few feet away. Rich clutched a white bottle of Remy Martin V from the bar behind him. The sound system cranked "Look at Me Now" by Chris Brown.

Katiya strutted over with a seductive smirk and nothing on but a pair of six-inch Christian Louboutin heels with straps wrapped up just beneath her knees. She stopped between Rich and King, then bent over and touched her toes.

Damn. Rich's dick grew hard beneath the pinstriped pants of his Armani suit. He unloosened his tie as Katiya rose, shaking her perfectly round ass. Rich could see ripples of her smooth skin form like it was a pond distributed by droplets of water.

Katiya turned around and began massaging her breasts and feeling her body as her eyes locked with Rich's eyes. She stepped back, flopped her ass on King's lap and began giving him a lap dance. She licked her upper lip, and then bit down on her bottom lip as she continued gazing into Rich's eyes.

This freak is wild, Rich thought as he grabbed his dick through his pants, anxious to sex Katiya. She stood and strutted over to Rich, hoisted her left leg on his right shoulder and danced seductively to the beat of Chris Brown's song.

Rich's mouth watered as he stared straight into her pussy. A thin layer of her wavy Indian hair covered it, along with the glaze of her wetness. Her hot pink hole became visible each time the lips of her pussy parted while she danced.

Katiya slid a finger inside of her, licked it, then put it in Rich's mouth. "Don't touch," she instructed as he reached for her butt.

Rich obeyed, trying to control himself since in the restaurant Katiya had given a long lecture about controlling emotions.

Katiya took her leg down and wrapped her arms around the back of Rich's neck. She straddled him and began dry humping him. Her moist pussy left wet marks on the costly fabric of his pants where his dick rose.

Rich closed his eyes as her breasts collided with his face. His dick felt like it was about to burst.

Katiya began removing his unloosened tie. Then she unbuttoned his shirt, before removing his blazer. Within a few minutes, she had undressed Rich and began undressing King. She dropped to her knees and began sucking King's dick.

Rich could hear the slurping as her round ass invited him toward her. He raised her ass to meet his dick, slid behind her and rammed himself inside of her pussy. "Damn." He felt the muscles in her pussy lock on his dick like handcuffs on a suspect's wrists. He watched her head bob up and down in King's lap. *A freak-ass millionaire.*

A minute later, Katiya lifted her head and looked back at Rich.

Rich stroked harder.

King slapped her in the face with his dick and grabbed her head until she was back to sucking him off.

Katiya managed to please King while maintaining her pace by shifting her butt into Rich's strokes and tightening her pussy.

"Come on, Katiya. Uhn." King's eyes closed and he fell back on the bed as he came.

Katiya stood up and propped one of her legs on the bed. Her back was to Rich as he engulfed her in his arms and cupped her shoulder in his palms. "Ahh, fuck," Katiya screamed as Rich jumped inside of her with carefully orchestrated strokes. "Yes!"

King stood on the bed in front of Katiya. His dick rose to attention and she gripped it with both hands and began sucking it again. He palmed the back of her head with both hands, guiding her.

Rich was in another zone, lost in the sensation of

Katiya's soft wetness. *Damn, this pussy choking my dick.* Chills ran through his body. Then his strokes subsided. "I want you to ride this dick." He laid on the bed.

Katiya let go of King's dick and climbed on Rich. "Oh, God," she uttered. Her body shook as her pussy swallowed his stiffness. She leaned forward, placing her hands flat on the bed above Rich's head. With her body outstretched, Katiya's breasts dangled into his mouth as she slithered her body up and down in a snakelike fashion.

"Yeah, girl," Rich whispered in between her nipples sliding in and out of his mouth.

"Put it in me, King. Get the KY out of my bag and fuck me in the ass," Katiya demanded as her cries of ecstasy reverberated.

Through the corner of his eye, Rich could see King fiddling through Katiya's Birkin bag. In seconds, he felt her body shift down as King slowly wedged his dick inside of her ass.

"Yes! God!" Katiya yelled. "You guys are killing me!"

"Oh shit." A surge of energy bolted through Rich's body as he climaxed. "Damn, Katiya. Whooo."

"Give me what's left in that dick, Rich." She sped up her pace as King slammed slowly into her ass. "Yes, yes, yes . . . ahhhhh," Katiya screamed as she came from the double penetration.

King pulled her from Rich. He coaxed her to the edge

of the bed. "Put your hands on the floor." As soon as Katiya's hands hit the floor, King grabbed her waist, reentered her ass and began stroking.

"You're killing me. God. King! King!" Katiya clawed into the rug that the bed sat on.

King rammed her with more force and sped up until they slid off the bed. He climbed back on top of Katiya on the floor, continuing what he started. He smashed into her ass until he came, pulling out and nutting all over her ass and lower back.

Rich laughed to himself. *King is wild.* He looked at Katiya lying on the rooftop, exhausted, wearing nothing but high heels. *This freak is worth millions.* Rich had heard stories of world-famous actresses fucking their way to stardom and celebrity couples who were swingers. But this was his first experience with a woman so wealthy who he felt most people would consider a slut. *A woman ain't shit, whether riding or walking.*

***

The following day, Rich lounged in King's office with him. All of King's employees had gone home and he was about to close the business when his cell phone rang. He looked at the screen on his BlackBerry and squinted his eyes.

"Who is it?" Rich asked.

King shrugged his shoulders and answered the phone. "It's King." He paused. "Who?"

Rich leaned back in his seat.

"Oh, Heather, Vanessa's friend." King smiled.

Rich leaned forward with a scowl.

"So you wanna be a cover girl?"

"Tell her to come over," Rich instructed in a low tone.

"Why don't you come over so we can discuss it?"

Yeah. Rich nodded. *I got something for her ass.*

"Okay. See you in a little while." King hung up.

"I definitely need to see her," Rich said. He had already told King of his vindictive plot to sex Heather as payback to Vanessa. King was considering doing business with Heather. But he told Rich that he owed him a favor since it was him who had allowed Zora into his home, and from there things had become chaotic for Rich.

Rich smiled. "I know you trying to make this snow bunny the next Coco."

"I keep telling you, she still gonna wanna run with the team after you slut her. Won't be the first time a chick got her back blown out to advance her career through this company." King picked up his office phone and called security downstairs. He told them he was expecting Heather and to let her in.

"I'm going out front to wait on her." Rich left the office and went to the waiting area outside of the elevator. He flopped down on the long leather couch in front of the coffee table littered with books and magazines. He flipped through them, picking up

258

Brooklyn Born. He began reading the coming-of-age tale of a drug dealer and a stickup kid that rose through the ranks on the streets, not much unlike he and King had done. Rich was engrossed in the story, only realizing that over an hour had passed when the elevator sounded.

Heather stepped off the elevator in a black dress with sequins and a matching watch. Her long hair flowed over her chest, just above her melon-sized breasts.

That's a bad-ass white chick. Rich could smell the Prada Milano perfume she sported as she neared him. He knew the scent well, because he had introduced Candy to it. He was attracted to Heather, but knowing she was part of the duo that influenced his first love to dump him made Heather his enemy. Rich knew she liked him from how she had stared at him while Vanessa and Peg attacked him verbally. Her ogling eyes revealed a weakness Rich was determined to exploit.

"Rich," Heather said, with a partial smile of interest and apprehension. "I'm sorry about what happened between you and Vanessa."

"All good things come to an end." He patted his hand beside him on the couch. "Rest your feet."

"Looks deserted in here," Heather said as she sat, crossing her legs. "No sign of King."

"He just left. I told him I wanted to meet with you first." He placed his hand on her thigh. "You seemed interested in me yesterday, so I figured we'd get to know each other." Heather placed her hand on top of Rich's hand, slowly guiding it up her dress, between the gap in her crotchless panties and into her pussy.

Rich pulled his hand out and toward her face. She jerked her neck back slightly. Rich continued, placing his fingers in her mouth.

Heather reluctantly began sucking her own liquids from Rich's fingers. She licked his fingers like a hard dick until Rich continued pushing his hand down her throat. She gagged. Heather began coughing like a bronchitis patient.

Rich unbuttoned his pants and pulled out his dick. As soon as she was done coughing, Rich stood and helped her to her feet. He pulled her over to the nearby receptionist desk. "Get on top."

"Huh?"

He looked at his Rolex. "I ain't got all day, baby."

She looked at the desk for a moment, then slowly climbed on top of it."

"On your knees." Rich climbed on the long, mahogany desk behind her. He was careful not to knock down the computer. He grabbed her ass and dug his dick between the crack of her ass until the head of his dick was in her rectum.

"Ahhh. Fuck. Goddamn!" Heather moved forward as she screamed.

He pulled her back, ramming into her until all ten inches of him was up her ass. "Fuck, yeah. Fuck!"

Heather's screams hyped Rich. He threw the force and

weight of his lower body at her, stretching her rectum with each pump.

"Fuck. Ohhhhh."

Rich smiled as he watched Heather's forehead bang into the wall the desk was posted against. He grabbed a handful of her long, blond hair and pulled it back until it was wedged between his palm and her waist as he stroked.

"Fuck. It hurts, Rich. Yeah!"

Rich used his free hand to slap each of her fat, white butt cheeks.

"Fuck! Goddamn!" she blurted as pain resonated from Rich's hand.

He let go of her hair and rammed into her savagely, banging her head against the wall one last time. He watched the red welts on her ass swell and show the form of his handprint. He pulled his dick from her asshole, sat on the edge of the table and guided Heather's face into his lap. She sucked his dick clean of the shitty, bloody remnants of her asshole. He pulled her head down as he was ready to cum. Her gag reflexes kicked in again. As soon as she leaned back, globs of cum shot from Rich's dick in her mouth and eyes. Her face resembled a pastry topped with stripes of vanilla frosting. Rich nonchalantly strolled past her, picked up her Marc Jacobs dress and cleaned his dick with it. He tossed it on the floor beside her. "Wipe your face and get dressed so I can shut the office down."

Heather exploded with tears as she noticed her reflection for the first time on the computer screen. She looked down at the silk dress worth over $1,000, then stared at Rich and shook her head.

CHAPTER TWENTY-FOUR
DOMINGO

D omingo was cruising through Bed-Stuy when he parked in front of Jessica's house. He sounded his horn four times. Domingo watched her exit her home and lock the door. She sported a colorful sundress and black pumps. She put on her Gucci shades and began strutting toward Domingo's Expedition with her handbag held close to her.

Domingo bopped his head to Maino's "Let it Fly" as the video played on the small screen in front of him.

Jessica opened the door and got in. "Hey, baby." The shapely Latina smiled and kissed him.

"How you?"

"It's all about you, not me."

"It's all about this road trip," Domingo said, adjusting a fresh pair of Cartier specs he had recently bought. "You ready?"

"I'm always ready for you."

263

Domingo pulled off, thinking of how fortunate he was to have Jessica on his side. Even though they were no longer an item, she was loyal to him. She had his back even after she dumped him when he was arrested for a gun while he was supposed to be on a date with her.

As Domingo stopped at a red light, he handed Jessica two Visas. "Keep one for you, ya heard?"

"That's what's up."

"You sure you wanna do this in New York?"

"Sak's Fifth Avenue is another world, even though it's technically in Manhattan." Jessica giggled, then placed her hand on Domingo's shoulder. "Don't worry about the law."

"If you say so." Domingo pulled off when the light turned green.

"You just point out the clothes and let me handle the rest."

Domingo steered over the Brooklyn Bridge into Manhattan. Heading through Little Italy and a couple of other neighborhoods placed him in Midtown, Manhattan. He struggled to find a parking space, ending up in a garage not far from his destination of 50th Street and 5th Avenue.

"The land of milk and honey," Jessica said as they stepped in front of Sak's Fifth Avenue. "Every woman's dream. Follow me."

Domingo trekked behind her. They strolled through the wood-trimmed ground level for a second, then headed upstairs for the exclusive designers. Jessica helped Domingo pick out a Chanel dress and handbag for Chanel along with a leather body suit by Bottega Veneta and a Moschino bag for Candy.

"That's it?" Jessica asked.

Domingo nodded. "I'll be outside."

As he went downstairs and outside of the store, he contemplated how unusual it was for him to have his ex-girlfriend help him shop for two women he was now involved with. Then there was the reality of him having become more than sexual partners with Chanel and Candy. He had been spending a lot of time with both women. Neither had officially become his woman. But the nights they spent together and mornings they cooked for Domingo spoke volumes. Having the Twins kill Rich and Vanessa was no longer a priority for Domingo. He had the women he had hoped to get without having to cause anyone harm.

Jessica pranced out of Sak's Fifth Avenue with two handfuls of bags. Domingo grabbed them. "See you loaded up too."

"That's what stolen account numbers and bogus credit cards are for," Jessica said, flashing her perfect teeth. "Now let's fill our stomachs with the balance."

Domingo and Jessica made their way back to the garage. After loading the back of Domingo's Expedition, they were on their way.

A short trip placed them inside of the prominent

Upper East Side restaurant Bolivar. They ended up in a huge hacienda-style room sparsely filled with patrons. The walls were sprinkled with leaves, giving the Latin restaurant a rural feel. After finishing the main course for lunch, Domingo snacked on freshly made chocolate as Jessica sipped wine from a Mexican glass.

"What's up with your sister?" Domingo asked.

"She'd lose her mind and question how well mine is working if she knew I was out shopping for your girlfriends."

"Girlfriends is too strong a term."

"You don't drop almost ten stacks at Sak's on some fuck buddies."

Domingo grinned. "Friends with benefits is a better term." But the reality was, Domingo had feelings for Candy and Chanel—feelings that he knew were leading him somewhere. But he did not know the destination.

* * *

Later that evening, Domingo walked through the door of the house he had recently began renting in South Ozone Park, Queens. He locked the door and eased through his spacious living room, hall and into his bedroom. He put the bag with Candy's outfit away. Then he pulled the 9-millimeter Smith and Wesson from his waistline and set it on the nightstand as he sat on the bed in the air-conditioned room. From his iPhone, he ordered some Chinese food from a local restaurant. After it arrived, he showered and waited in the living room for Candy to show up.

Domingo was lying on the couch lusting over Lisa Raye and Stacy Dash on *Single Ladies* when the doorbell rang. He sprang to his feet and looked through the peephole. *Damn.* Domingo's eyes honed in on Candy's cleavage bulging through her lace bra beneath her blouse. He opened the door, kissed and hugged her before letting her in.

"Chinese?" Candy said, taking a deep breath and spotting the bag of food on the dining room table. "Smells good."

Domingo reheated the food, then he and Candy began eating at the table.

"So what you been up to today?" Candy asked.

"Shopping."

Candy giggled lightly.

"So Domingo going shopping is a joke?"

"No, no, no." Candy shook her head. "Just thinking about when I first met you in Red Hook. You was a fly-ass little cat. Had like fifteen-hundred worth of gear on."

"You remember that clearly, huh?"

"Down to the Gucci shorts and diamonds. It threw me for a loop because you was so short."

"Come on, Mamita. You know you wanted to give me the pussy right there."

"If you was older and I wasn't strictly dealing with women, maybe."

"Now you can't get enough of me." Domingo took a

bite of his beef rib.

"Now you're a grown-ass man." Candy walked around the table and sat on Domingo's lap. She gave him a long kiss, gazing at him with her seductive eyes.

Domingo's heart raced. He loved everything about her. Her sexy eyes, her smooth skin, her juicy lips, the baby hair that trailed the long curls dangling past her shoulders. She was perfect. She opened her mouth to speak and Domingo silenced her with a kiss. "You look so good I just wanna stare at you in silence for a minute. Really appreciate your beauty."

Candy blushed.

"Okay," Domingo said moments later. "You can talk."

Candy giggled. "You crazy."

"I just recognize I got a good thing, ya heard?"

Candy took one of Domingo's ribs, bit a piece and then fed him the remainder of it.

After eating, Domingo went into the bedroom and returned with the outfit he and Jessica had picked out for Candy.

"Oh, this is hot." Her face lit up as she held up the body suit, then inspected the handbag. "Thank you so much." She hugged Domingo.

"Thank you."

"For what?"

"For being you." He kissed her. "For being real."

Candy stared at him in silence, clearly surprised. "I'm

gonna put this up."

Domingo sat on the couch and kicked off his slippers. He laid on his stomach, and gazed at the wide screen television.

Minutes later, Domingo was flicking though the channels, when Candy sauntered in the room wearing a nightgown. She climbed on his back and laid there. Her soft, warm body wrapped around Domingo, her head resting on his shoulder, her fingers rubbing his neck. Domingo thought of questioning Candy about their relationship being defined in concrete terms. But as they lie there together on his couch in silence watching television in his home, it was clear to him that he had invited Candy into his world and she had accepted the invitation. No proclamation or designation of a formal relationship would make the intimacy they shared any more real. Candy was a significant part of his life and that was all that mattered.

* * *

The following morning, Domingo opened his eyes, finding the television on from the night before. He could feel Candy's warmth, because her body was still on top of his. He could feel the beat of her heart against his back. When he felt her body shift, he tugged on her arm. "Wake up, Mamita."

"Huh? What?" she mumbled while holding him tighter.

Domingo glanced at the time on the clock above his

television. "It's almost ten o'clock. We gotta get up, ya heard?"

Domingo and Candy slithered off the couch and showered. After dressing, Candy cooked Domingo breakfast, then they prepared to leave.

"Where you going?" Domingo asked.

"Back to the telly." Candy had been living in a hotel in Mount Vernon.

Domingo kissed her neck. He whispered in her ear. "Why don't you stop making the Hilton rich and rest your head here?"

"After I get situated," Candy said. She mentioned an appointment she had with a realtor later that day to discuss her finding some commercial property in Mount Vernon to open a hair salon. Candy felt it was time to work harder at making money, because Rich was no longer around.

"Come on, Mamita."

Candy turned around and kissed Domingo. Her tongue slid around in his mouth. "In due time, baby."

Domingo watched her step off and grab the Sak's Fifth Avenue bag. She held it up. "Thanks again." Candy stepped out of the door.

Domingo went into his bedroom and removed one of the handguns from underneath his mattress. He inspected the clip, then cocked the .380-caliber Walther, before tucking the small handgun in the waistline of his jean shorts and pulling his Polo shirt over the slight bulge. He looked in the mirror, adjusting his Cartier frames. Then he removed a thin, black diamond bracelet from its jewelry box and put it on. He left home and got in his Expedition.

As he rode through Queens on his way to Brooklyn, he got a call from Chanel.

"What you up to?"

"Gotta take care of some biz, ya heard?"

"You need to come take care of your business with me."

"Kind of frisky this morning?"

"All I need is a quickie to hold me over 'till later."

Domingo laughed.

"I'm not joking. Plus, I wanna see you."

"My crib at twelve," he said, referring to his apartment in Red Hook. He had yet to tell her about his Queens home. The level of trust that Domingo had in Candy was not a reality for Chanel. She had no loyalty to her man and Domingo never lost sight of the fact that she had crossed Candy after years of friendship they had.

"Your crib at twelve. I'll be there," Chanel confirmed.

As Domingo drove, he thought of sex with Chanel. He had shared intimate moments with her that did not revolve around bumping and grinding. But unlike his attraction to the mere presence of Candy, Domingo was driven toward Chanel by their interaction in the bedroom. As he thought of how juicy and wet her pussy was, he remembered her boasting about The Chanel Legacy. She had never defined the term with clarity while in his presence. But her sex game was definitely a legacy that was unsurpassed by every woman Domingo had been with.

By the time Domingo made it to Red Hook, he was horny from thinking about Chanel. He exited his truck, then took a Sak's Fifth Avenue bag from the back as he began his trek to his apartment. When he entered the elevator, the Twins were exiting. "What up?"

"You," Jahiem said. "We been waiting to hear from you."

Domingo had been drawing out the process of sending the Twins at Rich and Vanessa, because he was not certain where Vanessa was and their deaths were no longer of personal interest to him, because he had Candy and Chanel in his life. "I got y'all."

As Domingo attempted to step on the elevator, Jahiem jumped in front of him. "If you don't got us in a minute, you gon' get got soon."

"What?"

"Motherfuckers tryin' to murk my sister and you got access to the motherfuckers, but you not playin' ya cards right."

Before Domingo could respond, the elevator was closing and the Twins were leaving the building. *They act like I don't get busy.* Domingo had made a lot of threats during his life. But he hated when they were hurled at him. Domingo was being threatened because of a plan he had concocted. He had created a lie that had the potential to destroy him.

He made it to his apartment, then pulled out his phone and tried calling Vanessa, but got her voicemail. He flopped down on the living room couch, frustrated.

A while later, his bell rang and he let Chanel inside. After closing the door, she kissed him and began loosening his belt.

"Whoa," Domingo brushed her off. He removed the .380 from his waist, then dropped his jeans.

Chanel hiked up her skirt and bent over, placing her forearms on the dining room table. "Hurry up, I'm on fire."

Domingo entered her throbbing pussy. He exhaled as her lips sucked him deeper inside. He started slamming into her quickly with a force that made her wetness feel like oil coming to a boil in a frying pan.

"Faster. Fuck me harder."

Domingo gripped her waist tighter and ravished her insides like a madman. Chanel reached under herself and began rubbing her clit. "Yes, yes, yes."

"Yeah, that's what you want?" Domingo asked.

"Fuck me, Domingo!"

Minutes passed and before Domingo knew it Chanel was screaming like she was being viciously attacked. "Stop . . . stop. Ahh, ahh. Ahh, noooo."

Domingo propped one of her legs on the table and

stroked harder until he came shortly afterwards.

Chanel turned around with a smile wider than Domingo had seen in a while. She kissed him. "I really needed that. I was fantasizing about you and I ended up horny as hell!"

"Fantasizing about ya boy, huh?" Domingo asked the rhetorical question as they both headed to his bathroom to wash up.

"We was on this yacht and got stranded at sea."

"Oh yeah?"

"Just me and you."

Domingo soaped up a rag and began washing himself in the sink. "What was it like? Just us?"

Chanel was silent.

When Domingo turned around, she had a distant look on her face. A look like she was in some zone where nothing else mattered but what she was experiencing. Bad experiences. Domingo waved his hand in front of her face.

Chanel shook her head.

"You zoned out on me," Domingo said.

"Thinking about us."

"What about us?"

She nudged Domingo, then looked into his eyes. "I'm scared. Scared something is gonna happened to me like Chase and Leah. You make me realize I got someone to live for." She gently kissed Domingo, sliding her tongue between his lips.

"Everything gon' be all right." Domingo had never seen Chanel so vulnerable and fearful. All of the high fashion and tough talk that defined Chanel masked a sensitive woman who was looking to be shielded from the harsh realities of life. It didn't matter that she had participated in Candy's kidnapping and torture. Domingo had known countless men in the hood who were Average Joes that committed isolated acts of violence. Chanel was no more of a bonafide killer than Vanessa and Candy.

"I'm losing hope in the Twins." Chanel paused. "You gotta get 'em, baby. Get Rich and Vanessa before they kill me."

First, the Twins had pressured Domingo to work harder at finding Rich and Vanessa. Now, Chanel was pushing for him to kill them. He had bent the truth about Rich and Vanessa to suit his needs. But now he was beginning to question if his tall tale was becoming more of a problem that could destroy what he was trying to build with Chanel and Candy. He needed to keep Chanel calm and decide if he would have to dole out the same violence on the Twins that they had planned for Rich and Vanessa.

CHAPTER TWENTY-FIVE
CANDY

C andy held onto the Sak's bag as she strode past a group of soldiers stepping out of Hartsfield Airport in Atlanta. She had left Domingo's home a few hours earlier. Candy had walked off on Rich days earlier, because she needed some space after the spat with Vanessa, Peg and Heather. She also needed time to think because she planned to coax Domingo into picking up the plan for revenge where she and Vanessa had left off. But Candy found herself unexpectedly falling for Domingo. He had a vibrancy that Rich lacked and a desire to please her that was stronger than Rich's. It was as if he was trying to prove himself sexually, having known Candy viewed him as a kid at one time. That hunger for validation translated into a sexual drive that was unparalleled.

Candy stood outside of the airport and pulled out her

276

smartphone. It was time to fix what she had broken between her and Rich. The two had spoken to each other several times while she was in New York. Rich was under the perception she was in Atlanta in an undisclosed area, because she needed some space to think. He was furious, but willing to cope with Candy's antics, because he feared losing the second of the only women he had ever loved.

After scrolling through her iPhone, Candy called Rich.

"Tell me something good," he said.

"I'm coming to see you," she said. "Where are you?"

"The company. Just got back from lunch."

"We need to talk."

"You know where I'm at, so see you."

"I love you."

"Love you too," Rich said before hanging up.

Candy hailed a cab and went to the hotel room that she and Rich had been sharing. She showered and changed into the outfit that Domingo gave her. After spraying on some perfume, Candy stepped out of the door.

She took a cab to a luxury car rental company and stepped out with the keys to a BMW 760. Candy drove to Queens Incorporated and found Rich on the elevator.

Rich kissed her and they hugged for what seemed to last forever. "I missed the shit outta you," Rich said as they parted.

"Miss you too."

"So now that your mind is clear, what's on it?"

"You."

"That's a good start."

"I spoke to Vanessa."

"And?"

"She wants me to leave you and I can't do that."

"So you're ready to let her go and be with me?"

"I wanna speak to her one last time. Try to talk some sense into her."

"Do you really want to after that stunt I told you she pulled here in front of everybody?"

As they stepped off the elevator, Candy remembered what Rich had said about Vanessa coming to the company with Peg and Heather. "I love her, Rich."

They walked through the corridor. "Love don't always cut it."

"We'll see."

Rich led her through a few clusters of people, then into the large conference room. He helped Candy to her seat and sat beside her.

She took Rich's hand into hers. "Tell me what's on your mind."

"I'm used to winning, but I took a L." Rich let out a deep breath. "The deck was stacked against me from day one, but I thought I could do it."

"You're losing me."

"This three-way relationship we had. I knew we were defying everything society says about male-female

278

relationships. I fought hard to make it work. Trained hard, went in the ring with a fresh set of gloves, but some amateur, hatin'-ass broads from your shop dazed me. Then a couple of suburban snow bunnies knocked me out in the last round."

Candy was silent, but she felt the same way. Rich had given up a life of fast women and fast money and gave himself to her and Vanessa. Each of them had supported and protected each other with trust and love. But Chanel and her cohorts had swung a haymaker that knocked down everything they had built and left them vulnerable to defeat.

Candy felt what was left of her relationship deteriorating. *It's just not right without Vanessa.*

* * *

Candy was focused on giving one last shot at trying to pull Vanessa back into the fold. Vanessa had left several messages on Candy's phone saying she needed to speak to her, so Candy was hopeful that they could rekindle the relationship they once shared with Rich.

Candy agreed to meet with Vanessa at North Point Mall in the Alpharetta section of Atlanta. She found Vanessa waiting outside of American Girl Boutique and Bistro like she had promised. As Candy neared, she noticed Heather was present, dressed in a black dress and matching-colored shades that covered most of her face.

Vanessa greeted Candy and they began walking. Heather remained silent as she walked alongside Vanessa.

"I thought we were meeting alone," Candy said.

Vanessa stopped, grabbed Candy's hand and removed the large designer shades Heather was sporting. There were bruises on Heather's forehead, just above her right eye. "That's courtesy of Rich."

"Vanessa, we both know he doesn't hit women."

"Overly rough sex, Candy. Heather tried to convince Rich to patch things up with me, and he manipulated her into having sex with him. He left her ass bleeding, Candy."

Candy stared at Heather, who pulled her shades back over her eyes to cover the emerging tears. "So Rich manipulated you?"

Before Heather could respond, Vanessa said, "You know he's a master slick-talker who takes advantage of women."

Candy was still focused on Heather. "Or maybe you thought you was gonna get fucked by a black stud and that Mandingo was more than you could handle." Candy laughed and turned back to Vanessa. "Manipulated? So Rich just tricked her into falling on his dick?"

"So what, I wanted to fuck him," Heather blurted. Her mouth was wide open as Vanessa's eyes beamed at her.

Candy laughed. "This is the girl who got you thinkin' all men are dogs, Vanessa? She put her hand on Vanessa's shoulder. "What happened to you? You let these white girls put a battery in your back with all this feminist bullshit."

"To hell with you, Candy," Heather barked and then turned to Vanessa. "I'm sorry, Vanessa."

"That's obvious." Vanessa walked off, leaving Heather and Candy behind.

"Vanessa," Candy called. She walked behind her and Vanessa sped up her pace. *That's it. She's gone.*

Once Vanessa was out of Candy's view, the reality that Rich had sexed Heather set in. The same Rich who had told her about his dedication to their relationship just hours prior. Candy needed to confront him. Not to afford him the opportunity to talk his way out of him having sex with Heather. Candy wanted to watch his reaction to her revelation. She wanted to see him for the last time and rid him from her system before she headed back to New York to be with Domingo.

After zipping through traffic in her rental, Candy stopped by their hotel and gathered her belongings. She stuffed them into the BMW and drove to Queens Incorporated. Candy made her way upstairs, through the corridor and into the open floor.

"Son of a bitch." Candy watched Rich at the water cooler. He was positioned behind Katiya with his dick against her ass as he whispered in her ear, bringing a smile to her face. Candy darted through an aisle between a row of cubicles and tapped him on his shoulder.

He turned around and his mouth opened nearly as wide as his eyes. "Candy."

She snickered. "First the white broad, now some

Indian ho. I see you're into diversity."

Katiya stepped off in silence.

"Baby, this ain't—"

"Save it for one of these broads that you got hypnotized with your dick." Candy stomped off, brushing past King and a number of other spectators. She was hurt by Rich and it was a pain she had not anticipated. Just as she had not anticipated finding him with another woman. Candy felt her knees buckling with each step. But she mustered the strength to march her Amazon figure with pride.

After the elevator door opened and closed behind her, she sunk into a corner and burst into tears. She knew she had to end her relationship with Rich. Adding to her misery was the memory of Vanessa walking off from her and out of her life. The only people she had total trust in and love for were gone out of her life. The unique relationship she once thought was impossible had been defeated. Someone had to pay.

She headed to the airport. After the flight landed the tear-smeared mascara and puffy eyes were things she tried to conceal as she rode in the backseat of a cab to Domingo's home. What little success she had battling her emotional scars was undermined by the tears that flooded her face when Domingo opened his door and she dropped her bag and hugged him. In silence, she basked in the comfort of his embrace for several minutes.

Candy looked at Domingo, thinking long and hard

about what to disclose to him. Possibilities bounced around her head like balls in a pinball machine. In his eyes she saw innocence, although she knew he was no saint. She saw the feelings he had for her. Genuine feelings. Feelings that Vanessa and Rich no longer had for her.

Candy thought of everything she had observed of Domingo, from the young teen with the audacity to press a woman beyond his age and height, to the young man who had grown taller and more confident than her in just a couple of years. The young man who had invited her into his home and pleased her in every way she could think of sexually. The young man who had helped her and Vanessa kill Leah.

"I don't wanna rush you if you ain't ready to talk, Mamita. But seeing you like this got me nervous."

"There's a lot that's been going on that I didn't tell you."

"Whatever it is ain't gonna change how I feel about you."

"How do you feel? Honestly? And where are we going with this? Us?"

Domingo leaned up and kissed Candy passionately. He placed one of her delicate hands between his. "We goin' wherever you wanna take this, Mamita."

Candy flashed a partial smile, then the frown she was trying to hide surfaced. "It's about the future. Us." She looked into Domingo's eyes. "I can't go on like this. Not until everybody that destroyed my life is dead. Chanel,

Vera, her brothers, all of 'em."

Domingo kissed her lips, then gently rubbed her cheek with the back of his hand. Don't worry. I'm a take care of everything."

The following morning, Candy's eyes opened slightly as she lay in bed. She was lying on her back when she was overcome by sexual bliss. She licked her lips and began massaging her nipples, before squeezing her breasts. She shook her head and wiped the cold out of her eyes to make sure she was not asleep. She guided her hand down and felt Domingo's wavy hair. She looked down and saw him between her thighs. Her back stretched out and she hissed like a viper. Candy grabbed a handful of the sheets and closed her eyes as Domingo brought her to a climax.

When she opened her eyes, Domingo was looking down on her, licking his lips. "That's wifey treatment."

She watched Domingo step out of the bedroom. He had outdone himself and any man she had been with. She had never awakened to the feeling of her pussy being eaten. It was the type of thing she had never even fantasized about. The thought of a man that was so concerned with pleasing his woman seemed unreal.

Candy got out of bed, showered and then went into the dining room. Domingo had the table set with Egg McMuffins, apple pies, coffee and sausages. Candy sat down with a grin.

"It's the thought that count, Mamita. If I could cook, I

would've. But you know I'm a fast food fanatic."

"You affirm that every time I'm over here."

"My motto is fast food, slow sex, ya heard?"

Candy laughed. "One out of two ain't bad. I'm gonna start doing the cooking around here. You just handle the slow sex."

"Deal."

Candy and Domingo started eating. She found it hard not to look at him. There was so much she had learned about him over the years, but residing under someone's roof reveals aspects of a person that go unseen by friends and associates.

"Why you keep lookin' at me like that, Mamita?"

"It's not against the law for me to look at my man, right?"

"If you can touch, you definitely can look, ya heard? But that don't stop me from being curious about what you curious about."

Candy chewed on her Egg McMuffin. "I was wondering how many women can say they woke up to you eating them out?"

"It's only one woman can say that she woke up in my bed."

"Yeah, right."

"Two things usually happen the morning after me and a woman go to bed."

"What?"

"I'm gone before she wakes up and she wonderin'

285

why."

"What makes me so special?"

Domingo looked at Candy in silence, sipping his coffee. "I don't know. I been tryin' to figure that out since I first saw you strut into Red Hook. I don't know what it is. I just know how good you make me feel."

Candy could feel the truth resonating from Domingo. She had no reason to think he was lying. She needed his word to be authentic, because she was planning to invest every bit of herself in him.

CHAPTER TWENTY-SIX
VANESSA

V anessa had been trying unsuccessfully to justify the hypocrisy of Heather having sex with Rich. She had known the story was flawed when Heather first explained it to her and Peg. But both women were so adamant about Rich being a player and Heather being unmatched for the street savvy womanizer, that Vanessa began to rationalize in favor of Heather. But after Vanessa watched Candy dismantle Heather's story, all the suppressed feelings of betrayal resurfaced. First Rich had disrespected her by having sex with Zora, then he and Heather had violated her by having an affair. Rich's actions were unexpected, but not unbelievable. His bond to Vanessa was nearly nonexistent and when it was tight, he had proven his dick was liable to turn up in places it wasn't supposed to be.

Even Heather's actions began to make sense. Although she had egged Peg on in her opposition to Rich, there was always some underlying hints of her empathy for Rich. Heather had also made it clear that she loved men and women equally, unlike Peg who despised men. It was Heather who seemed mesmerized by Rich when she saw him at Queens Incorporated.

Vanessa was silent as she sat in her hotel room with Peg and Heather. A day had passed since her faceoff with Candy in the mall. Vanessa had nothing more to say to Heather. But Peg had been trying to mediate a truce between both women. That was after Peg and Vanessa agreed to disagree if Heather was manipulated into having sex with Rich.

Heather was leaning against the window, toying with her collection of credit cards when Peg walked over and sat beside Vanessa. "Come on. We've overstayed our welcome," she said, looking at the open suitcase on the bed that Vanessa had begun packing.

Vanessa stared at Heather and rolled her eyes.

"Oh please, Vanessa. I mean, we don't have time for you to start this again," said Peg. "We've got a flight to catch. Besides, all fingers should point at Rich. You don't blame the victim for being oppressed."

"You're too smart to believe that," Vanessa said. "Heather didn't trip and fall on top of Rich's dick."

"I mean, so what are you going to do, Vanessa? Hang Heather and let the chauvinist go free? He's a manipulative scumbag who put you under his spell and he did the same thing to Heather."

"I'm not stupid, Peg."

"Just gullible," Heather said as she stepped over.

Vanessa pointed her finger at Heather. "Fuck you."

Heather grabbed her hand and Vanessa slapped her. Her second swing was blocked and Heather grabbed her neck. She flung Vanessa's petite body to the bed.

"Get the fuck off me!" Vanessa screamed.

"Heather, stop it!" Peg pulled on one of Heather's arms.

Vanessa squirmed to free herself, but she felt helpless against Heather's thick frame. She watched tears begin to fall from Heather's face.

"I'm sorry, Vanessa. I'm sorry." Heather's face descended toward Vanessa's until their lips met.

"No." Vanessa twisted her face as Heather's long hair fell to her neck. Then Heather's soft lips touched Vanessa's, immobilizing her. Vanessa opened her mouth, allowing Heather's tongue inside. She felt Heather's hands loosen from her neck and roam through her hair as they kissed. Heather's lips made their way to Vanessa's neck. Vanessa's back arched and she cried out whimpers of joy. Her arms enveloped Heather, her hands roaming over the silk covering and the delicate skin of her back.

Heather leaned up and Vanessa's eyes opened. "I'll never hurt you again," Heather said, then kissed her.

Vanessa's body was heating up. She slid her hands up

Heather's skirt and rubbed her huge bubble.

"Ahh," Vanessa moaned. As her nipples hardened in Heather's mouth, Vanessa felt Heather's hand roam in between her thighs and rub her clit through her soaked panties. Vanessa put her hand on top of Heather's hand and worked up a rhythm as she grinded her pussy into Heather's hand.

Heather's head dropped, kissing Vanessa's stomach and twirling her tongue over her navel.

"That feels so good." Vanessa was overwhelmed with pleasure.

Heather pulled down her tights and panties, then ran her tongue over Vanessa's clit and into her pussy. She cuffed the inside of her thighs to prevent Vanessa's legs from clamping around her and to allow her to eat Vanessa's pussy precisely. Her tongue and lips provided the lubrication and suction on Vanessa's clit that caused her body to jolt and shake sporadically.

"Stop," Vanessa cried, clawing at the bed sheets as her lips shivered and her breathing accelerated.

Heather inserted her index finger inside of Vanessa's pussy and began stimulating her G-spot.

"Ahh, uhh." The feeling consumed Vanessa, causing her to try and pull Heather's hand away. But Heather kept hitting her G-spot and sucking her clit. "No, yeah. Ahh. Ohhhhh." Vanessa's body trembled into a climax that she felt throughout her entire being. She was taking quick, short breaths and mumbling incoherent sounds like a churchgoer catching the Holy Ghost.

Heather kissed Vanessa and hugged her, calming her body into stillness. When Vanessa opened her eyes, she noticed Peg fingering herself and rubbing her small breasts. Vanessa wrapped her arms around Heather and closed her eyes, enjoying her warm, soft body pressed against hers. All thoughts of Heather crossing her by having sex with Rich were gone. Vanessa found it hard to be mad at someone who made her feel so good. She knew Heather's feelings for her were real. She just made a bad decision, but she didn't do it to hurt me. Vanessa had made enough bad choices in her life to empathize with Heather. What mattered to her most was that Heather understood where she went wrong, so Vanessa was willing to give her another chance. She knew Heather and Peg were officially an integral part of her life and happiness. And she was not willing to let anything or anyone interfere with what they were building. She was still recovering from the last three-way relationship that was dismantled by outsiders. Although she was done with that relationship, she was not done with the culprits who destroyed it. Vanessa no longer needed the approval or support of Rich and Candy to execute the plan she and Candy had devised. She had the only phone number she needed—Domingo's.

* * *

During the flight back to New York, Vanessa had found it impossible to suppress her thoughts of revenge.

The notion of Chanel and the other guilty parties not being penalized was something she could not grasp. *People have to pay for their actions.* What angered Vanessa most was not that she had been affected by the actions of Chanel and the others, but that their actions were the result of senseless jealousy. Candy had done nothing that warranted her being kidnapped, tortured and molested.

After the flight and ride to Long Island, Vanessa stepped through the door of Peg's apartment along with Heather. She dropped her bags and looked around, realizing that this would be her new home. During the flight, she had accepted Peg's invitation to live with her. To outsiders, they would be merely roommates. But Vanessa and Peg had become lovers along with Heather. While flying back to New York, the women had solidified their relationship. They were a threesome that had feelings for each other, but were not committed solely to each other. They were free to have sexual relations with other people, but not individuals close to the three of them.

Vanessa flopped down on a couch alongside Heather, while Peg entered the kitchen and returned with some orange juice and three glasses. As the women drank, they talked about the saga that unfolded in Atlanta. Vanessa found herself facing the truth that she would never see Rich or Candy again. "Excuse me. I have to use the bathroom," Vanessa announced as she stood.

"Vanessa," Heather called.

Vanessa turned around.

"I'm sorry," Heather said. "In spite of everything, I know Rich and Candy meant a lot to you. I can see it in your face."

Vanessa smiled and stepped off. Once in the bathroom, she pulled out her Droid and phoned Domingo.

"Long time no hear from, my soul sister."

"They say 'better late than never.'"

"What's up with my future wife?"

"Don't worry about Candy." Vanessa paused for a few seconds. "You're talking to me and I have a proposition."

"In relation to what we already have in play?"

"Same situation, more activity on your part."

"The more I play, the more you pay."

"Understandable," Vanessa said.

"We need a face-to-face to iron this out."

"I'm on your clock."

"Tomorrow. You'll hear from me tomorrow on the location and time."

"Domingo, this is between us, not Candy."

"I never had loose lips."

"Good. Tomorrow." Vanessa hung up her phone, preparing to hire Domingo to kill the people she and Candy seemed to be unable to touch.

***

The following night, Vanessa pulled up in front of

Domingo's Expedition on a desolate block in the Bronx. She exited her cab and entered Domingo's truck.

"Damn." Domingo smiled. "Show me some love." He kissed her on the cheek and hugged her. "You lookin' a lot better than the last time I saw you in person, my soul sister."

"A couple of years did you some good too." Vanessa observed how Domingo had added some inches and muscles to his frame along with some hairs to his chin that connected to his sideburns.

Domingo turned down the Jay-Z and Kanye West song "Otis" that was thumping from his surround sound car stereo. "So what's this proposition for me?"

"You, one gun, six bodies, sixty-thousand."

"So you and Candy gave up the hands-on approach to revenge?"

"I told you, you're doing business with me now"

Domingo laughed. "Not at ten stacks a head."

"Oprah and I don't share a bank account and we're talking about the lives of six creeps that are worth far less than ten grand each."

"My freedom's worth a lot more and I'm sure you can dig up at least twenty stacks a head."

Vanessa's eyes widened. "One-hundred and twenty grand?" She took a deep breath and exhaled. "I may be able to scrape up a hundred, maybe."

"Then you got a twenty-stack problem."

Fuck! Vanessa's eyes rolled to the minivan parked in

front of her, then through the tinted windows and around the empty block lit by a few street lamps that hardly pierced the trees hovering around Domingo's truck.

"I wanna help you, but you gotta help me," Domingo said as his eyes locked on Vanessa's eyes.

She stared at him for a while, then reached for Domingo's belt.

"Whoa, tiger. Watch your paws." He blocked her hand, gazing at her like she was an enemy set to kill him. He removed his .380-caliber Browning from his waistline and smiled.

Vanessa unloosened his belt, then pants before his underwear. She pulled his long pipe out. Staring at his dick, she couldn't believe she was reducing herself to this level in the name of revenge. She slowly leaned down and swallowed the head of his dick. She began bobbing her head quickly, trying to finish the job as fast as possible.

Domingo shifted his head deeper into her mouth. "Damn, Ma. You serious," he whispered.

Vanessa felt the head of his dick probing around every part of her mouth, from her cheeks to the roof of her mouth and the bottom of her tongue. Before she knew it, she was enjoying the feeling. There was something about having a mouthful of dick that turned her on. She could feel emotions stirring inside her. She rose to the head of Domingo's dick, maneuvering her lips and tongue around the rim of it rapidly until Domingo gripped her head tighter and came.

"Shit, Ma. Damn." He held her tighter as she tried to move her head away.

After Vanessa's mouth was full of cum and Domingo was done, he let her go. She opened the door and spit. She coughed a few times and closed the door. What the fuck am I doing? Reality set in as her hormones subsided and she stared at Domingo. "You better kill all of them bastards."

Domingo nodded his head as he grabbed some tissue from the glove box and began wiping his dick. "I need half my money before it go down."

"We can find a Citibank right now."

"Tomorrow." He grabbed his dick, then rubbed his hand between her legs. "I need to feel that too and see if it's worth that twenty stacks you short on, ya heard?"

Vanessa stepped out of the truck and slammed the door. "Call me tomorrow. And be prepared to tell me when am I going to get my money's worth." She walked off feeling used, but she knew she was using Domingo also. As much as she hated to give into him, she was willing to, because her hunger for revenge outweighed everything.

* * *

The following night, Vanessa exited a cab at the same place and made her way into the passenger seat of Domingo's Expedition. She opened a brown paper bag and showed Domingo five crispy $10,000 stacks of money. "That's fresh out of Citibank's vault," she said.

Domingo placed the bag on the seat behind him, removed his gun from his waist and began unbuckling his belt.

Vanessa sighed. "Shouldn't we discuss business first?"

"This is part of the payment, so it's definitely business, ya heard?"

Vanessa reluctantly lifted up her skirt. She knew what was in store, so she was not wearing underwear. She climbed on top of Domingo and worked his dick inside of her tight pussy. "Ahh." She closed her eyes to take her mind off of her surroundings and circumstances.

Domingo grabbed her ass and pulled her each time she descended on his dick."

"Ahh." Vanessa could not fight the fact that the thickness of Domingo's dick was stretching her tight pussy and making her more wet and horny each time he entered her. She could feel his face pressed against her breasts through her sheer blouse. The scent of his Cartier Declaration was stimulating. Before she realized it, she was swerving her hips and riding Domingo like he was a faithful lover. "Yes, ahh." Her breathing grew heavy as she cringed.

"Come on, Ma." Domingo pulled her closer to him as her pussy swallowed his dick. After a minute, he loosened his grip, then turned her around.

Vanessa gripped the steering wheel of his truck and

began slamming her pussy into his thrusts as he guided her with a solid grip on her hips. She melodically rocked her body back and forth while staring through the windshield at a car in the distance. "Fuck me."

Domingo lifted her blouse and began kissing her back. He wrapped his hands around her, squeezing her breasts.

"Umph, umph," Vanessa cried. "Yes."

Domingo sucked on her back in between kissing her.

Vanessa moaned as his thrusts sent sparks throughout her body. Her mind was in another world. A utopian sphere saturated by passion and pleasure.

Domingo leaned back as Vanessa grinded harder and they both climaxed at the same time. She fell into his embrace. Both of their bodies were drenched in sweat. Their breathing slowed.

I can't believe I just fucked him and I liked every moment of it.

"Get up," said Domingo.

Vanessa eased over to the passenger seat and pulled down her skirt.

"You sure put your back into that." Domingo laughed. "That pussy could throw me off if it wasn't a payment and I wasn't about my business."

"Yeah, let's get down to business," Jahiem said, climbing from under a blanket in the back row of the Expedition.

"Oh, shit." Vanessa turned around and stared down the long barrel of the .22-caliber Ruger Jahiem held. She

298

turned back to Domingo. "What the fuck is this? You bastard."

Domingo turned on the truck and pulled off.

"You set me up," Vanessa said.

"You set yourself up," said Domingo. "I thought I was gonna have to come get you, but you came right to me. And you paid me fifty stacks, sucked my dick, plus rode me like a Great Adventure ride. You set yourself up."

Vanessa looked back into Jahiem's eyes. Her heart was already in overdrive, but her hands began to tremble from the thought of what awaited her. She was almost sure that she would face the same torture and abuse that Candy had.

Looking at Domingo, she realized he was right. She had brought herself to him. Her trip to him was the culmination of a long series of events that began with her failure to heed Rich's calls for her and Candy to end their plot for revenge. Now, they had moved on, but Vanessa's rebelliousness would possibly result in her demise.

CHAPTER TWENTY-SEVEN
DOMINGO

Domingo would have preferred not to have gone inside of te vacant building in the Bronx. But he walked behind Jahiem and Vanessa, past the "FOR SALE" sign outside of the empty innards of the two-story home on Jerome Avenue. Tahiem had opened the front door and slammed it behind Domingo. Domingo watched Jahiem push Vanessa into the wall, face-first. She fell to the wooden floor.

Tahiem snatched her from the floor by her 'fro and pointed at her before turning toward Domingo. "This the little bitch that's schemin' to murk my sister?"

Domingo nodded, hearing Tahiem speak a full sentence for the first time. He wanted to laugh at the sight of the miniature madmen. They were half his height. But they were twice as bulky because of the

300

bulletproof vests that bulged from their chests. But despite their humorous appearance, Domingo never lost sight of how dangerous they were.

Tahiem slapped Vanessa off her feet, sending her crashing back into the wall before hitting the floor.

She looked up, her bloody lips quivering. She curled up in a corner like a wounded puppy.

"Lil' bitch a freak too," Jahiem said. "Fucked the shit outta Domingo a little while ago."

"Yeah?" Tahiem said.

"Had my dick hard than a motherfucker the whole time." Jahiem handed his gun to his brother and began unbuttoning his pants.

I know he ain't 'bout to take no pussy. "Fuck you doin'?" Domingo asked.

Jahiem smirked. "Same shit you did."

Domingo shook his head. "Nah, nah, nah, nah. I don't jump outta trees, ya heard? Stupid ho gave me the pussy."

"And she gonna give it to me," Jahiem said.

"You said you brought her here to get some info on Rich. Not to get a nut off," Domingo added.

"Domingo, who the fuck you questioning?"

Domingo looked at Tahiem. "Yo, Tah, calm your brother down, ya heard?"

"What?" Tahiem trained his brother's gun on Domingo.

Domingo surrendered his palms, his hands at shoulder-height. "Vanessa the one y'all wanna kill, not me. I helped Jahiem get her here, remember?"

"So," Tahiem blurted.

"I'm just sayin', get the info on Rich, body her, and then handle Rich. I'll murk her right now."

Tahiem turned to Vanessa.

Domingo noticed the lit screen on the phone she held in her hand.

"I know that ain't no phone," Tahiem said.

Fuck! She might be tapin' us, callin' the police, anything, Domingo thought. He pulled his gun, drawing Tahiem's attention.

Tahiem fired a shot and then Domingo began shooting. The dim room became a center of sparks and gun smoke. Domingo squeezed off every bullet in his .380 as he bolted out of the door. He made it to his truck and pulled off, trying to figure out exactly how such a simple plan went wrong and if anyone was killed. He replayed the scene in his head as he drove. There was no doubt that he could soon be faced with problems from the police or the Twins.

He didn't know which was worse. Then there was the frightening possibility that he would be a wanted man by the police and the Twins.

* * *

Domingo circled his block for a third time, then parked around the corner from his home. He was confident he had not been followed after fleeing the shootout. But his confidence was not enough when his life was at stake. He could still hear Tahiem's bullets whizzing past his ears. It was a deafening sound he had experienced before, but had never gotten used to. He had seen Vanessa's body tumble over as it was met by at least one of the slugs that flew through the room. But what mattered most to Domingo was if she was dead, who was on the other end of her phone, and what had they seen or heard. The police? Rich? Or them two white girls Candy said Vanessa was fucking with. Domingo's mind was speeding.

He opened the gate to his front yard and treaded over the concrete pathway onto his porch. His eyes scanned the block, then he keyed his front door and stepped inside.

Candy walked to him slowly, her eyes locked on his. She kissed him. "What's up?"

Domingo silently tried to gauge Candy. There was something in her kiss and stare that seemed abnormal. Her smile wasn't as inviting as usual. She seemed guarded. "Ain't nothin'," Domingo responded, before finding a seat on his couch.

Candy stood across from him. "What's in the bag?"

Domingo held up the brown paper bag containing the $50,000 Vanessa had given him. "The root of all evil." He smiled. "That brown paper bag under your mattress drug money," he quoted Jay-Z's "Imaginary Player" and chuckled.

"Guess that's a joke, because I've dealt with enough

hustlers to know they have a 'don't ask, don't tell' policy about where they get their money."

Domingo leaned back on the couch and placed the money on the coffee table. "It's a safety measure. You can't be held accountable for what you don't know."

"So I've been told. Anyway, I remember when I first met you and you said you don't sell drugs."

"I remember."

"You said you get it any way you can."

"Jack of all trades."

Candy was silent, staring at Domingo. "Any way?"

"There's exceptions to every rule. Now you done with the twenty-one questions?"

Candy giggled. "Yeah, Dave Chappelle."

"Come here." Domingo pulled his gun from his waist and put it on the couch as he guided Candy onto his lap."

She grabbed the gun. "Nice."

"Dangerous."

She removed the clip and cocked the gun back. Her eyebrows arched and she looked at Domingo. "Not if it's empty."

Domingo unhanded her of the gun and set it back on the couch.

"You don't strike me as the type who would have left home with an empty gun."

"Sometimes when I'm in the streets I have to do more than carry it."

Candy looked at Domingo in silence.

Domingo could feel her body tense up. There was apprehension in her eyes. It was the type of look he expected from most women. But Candy was not most women. She had held and used guns to their fullest extent. He placed his hands in hers. "What I do in the streets is to make things better for us. Ain't no 'me' no more, ya heard?"

Candy slowly nodded.

Domingo removed a $10,000 stack from the bag and placed it in her hand. "What's mine is yours, Mamita. And it ain't never been like that with me and no woman. Just like my doors never been open to no woman before you. When I say I'm feeling you and I been feeling you since I met you, I ain't playin'." He kissed Candy, allowing her to taste his tongue for a moment.

She hugged him. When she pulled back, her eyes were verging on watery.

"You all right, Mamita?"

She nodded.

"Talk to me." He began to ponder if Candy was the person on the other end of Vanessa's phone.

She shook her head. "It's nothing. I was just thinking about Rich and Vanessa and what happened when I put my trust in them."

"I ain't Rich and I definitely ain't Vanessa, ya heard? You don't have to worry about them no more."

"What do you mean?"

"It's about us." Domingo ran his hand through her

hair, down to her back.

"Sometimes I still think about them. I don't hate them. I just understand we could never be together."

"Feelings don't go away overnight, but eventually they gotta go away." Domingo kissed her.

Candy stood when they finished. She gazed at Domingo. "You want something to eat?"

"Yeah. After I get out of the shower." He grabbed his gun and inserted the clip before grabbing his bag of money and walking off. He undressed, then entered the shower. As he lathered his body, he thought about Candy and how awkward she was acting. He realized that they had made an agreement to be faithful to each other relatively quick. So he assumed she was simply caught between the emotions attached to her, Rich and Vanessa. Then there was the fact she still had a lot to learn about Domingo. *She must've been thinkin' about all of this shit before I came home.*

In spite of his interest in Candy's thoughts, Domingo had more pressing issues to deal with. He remembered shooting, but not the details. The haze of gunfire had made everything a blur. Domingo was unsure who had gotten shot.

If Tahiem survived, Domingo knew he and his brother would seek revenge. If he died, Jahiem would dedicate his life to tracking down Domingo.

Domingo assumed Vanessa was dead. There was no way the Twins would let her walk out of that building alive. But the problem was who was on the other end of her phone when hot lead took her life? Was her camera on? Was there a video of Domingo participating in a kidnapping and the shootout that caused one or more deaths?

It was ironic because the situation was rooted in a videotape of Candy and Vanessa having sex years ago. If Vanessa was videotaping her kidnapping and the shootout, Domingo was done if that tape landed in the hands of police. He had seen plenty of crimes caught on camera and shown repeatedly on the nightly news followed by reporters asking people with information to call the police. There would be no fair trial by a jury of Domingo's peers. Every potential juror in New York City with a television would have the image of a gun-toting Domingo in their minds long before they saw him in a courtroom. No words he could utter and no strategy his attorney could concoct would outweigh the footage of Domingo firing his gun.

I gotta get at these dudes. After he showered he decided to head out to Red Hook in search of the Twins. He would first call Chanel to see if he could sense anything in the air about the shootout.

He went into his bedroom after drying off. As soon as he closed the door, the sound of Uncle Murder's "Warning" chimed from Domingo's iPhone. He silenced the ringtone and answered the call.

"They lookin' for you? Where you at, Domingo?

What you did? I'm worried."

Domingo peeked out his window. "Calm down, Chanel. Slowly. What you talkin' bout?"

"These crazy ass Twins. I just left Vera's crib and they came through mad as hell, lookin' for you. They vexed."

"Oh yeah?"

"They was trying to act like it wasn't nothin', but I overheard them in the room tellin' Vera they gonna murder you."

Domingo began pacing. "What else?"

"What else?" Chanel asked rhetorically. "Killin' you ain't enough?"

"Me and death got a while before we meet, so that's the least of my worries."

"I don't know what you did and who you think you fuckin' with, but these motherfuckers ain't playin'. You know how Jahiem and Tahiem is."

"Where they go?"

"What the hell I look like, GPS? I don't know?"

"I'm a call you later,"

"That's it?"

"I'm gon' be all right, ya heard? Just be easy and I'm a holler at you later."

"Be careful," Chanel said, then hung up.

Domingo dropped his phone on the bed and peered out of the window, making certain there was nothing out of the ordinary. He knew he was growing paranoid. But

Domingo had miraculously escaped being killed by Tahiem and he was willing to do whatever it took to continue to avoid being struck down by a bullet.

Domingo got dressed and walked into the kitchen, following the scent of Candy's fried pastrami. After she prepared him a sandwich, he said, "Good lookin'. I gotta be out."

Candy was stiff as Domingo kissed her. She grabbed his hand as he turned to walk off.

"What up?" he asked.

"Be safe." She pecked him on the lips.

Domingo watched her face drift away as he walked off. He wondered what was on her mind, but he didn't have time to pry it out of her. *She acting all weird again, but I'll get at her later about that.*

Domingo left his house, sped around the corner to his Expedition and pulled off. He weaved through traffic until he was in Red Hook. He rode past the building where the Twins lived, seeing no sign of them. After rounding the block several times and steering throughout the projects, Domingo gave up on finding the Twins at that moment.

He looked at his watch. It was just past midnight, a few hours since the shootout.

Domingo phoned Chanel.

"You okay?" she asked.

"Of course."

"What's up?"

"That's what I'm tryin' to figure out."

"You sound good, so I assume you didn't cross paths with the Twins."

"So you ain't hear nothin' else?"

"Vera actin' funny, so I left and went home."

"What's funny?"

"Like she hidin' somethin', but she wanted to let it out."

"And this is after you heard the Twins talking about me to her?"

"Yeah?"

"What about Meisha and Mimi? You seen them?"

"Left them at Vera crib."

"Nothin' unusual about them?"

"Nah."

"All right," Domingo said.

"I wanna see you."

"Tomorrow. Gotta take care of some business right now."

"Call me."

"Tomorrow." Domingo hung up. He rode into Queens, destined for his home. It was late, so he planned to get some rest and regroup. He needed to develop a clear course of action to handle the Twins. And he needed to find out exactly what happened to Vanessa and her smartphone. The sooner he found answers to those questions, the sooner he could handle the Twins.

CHAPTER TWENTY-EIGHT

RICH

W hen Domingo walked through the front door of his home, a .50-caliber Desert Eagle crashed his temple. He fell to the floor. As he looked up and tried to reach for his gun, Rich said, "Pull it out slow and drop it on the floor."

Domingo looked at the huge handgun in Rich's hand and did as he was told.

"Get the fuck on the couch," Rich barked. As Domingo sat on the couch, Rich picked up his gun and tucked it inside his waistband.

"What you do to Candy?"

As Domingo's question left his mouth, Candy walked slowly into the living room.

"Oh, hell no." Domingo's head dropped momentarily. Then he looked up at Candy. She could hardly look him in the eyes as she stood next to Rich. "This is how it's goin' down, Mamita?"

Candy managed to look directly into Domingo's

311

eyes. "Why?"

He scowled. "Why? I'm supposed to be asking that."

"You didn't have to kill Vanessa."

Rich watched Candy as he contemplated. He knew she was fighting her feelings for Domingo. He blamed himself for allowing her to slip away from him and into Domingo's hands.

Candy turned to Rich.

Rich glared at Domingo. "I was the one on the phone when you was talking about killing me and Vanessa. Then you started shooting."

"Man, Tahiem started shooting and I was tryin' to clap him and his brother. You ain't see through that phone that Tahiem backed out a gat on me?"

Rich didn't care about anyone's gun being pointed at Domingo. Since the gunshots that echoed through her phone shattered his world, he had gone straight to the airport and caught the first flight to New York. During the flight, he called Candy and explained everything he heard over the phone. After she stopped crying, she confessed that she had been involved with Domingo and she told Rich where Domingo lived. Rich thought he had cleared Vanessa and Candy from his system. But with the thought of their safety being compromised, he realized he would always have feelings for them.

"So when you came here earlier with that empty gun, you telling me that was because you had a shootout with Tahiem?" Candy asked.

"I knew something was wrong with you. I could see it in your eyes. I could feel it, ya heard?"

"Answer my question," Candy demanded.

"I ever lie to you since you been in this house? I had a shootout with Tahiem." Candy looked at Rich. "What if he's telling the truth?"

"It don't matter. He set her up to get killed and he planned to kill me too."

Domingo was silent as Candy stared at him. His facial expression spelled guilt. It was obvious Domingo would rather not debate with the man who heard him voice the plot to kill Vanessa and Rich.

"But what if he didn't do it and Vanessa is alive?" Candy asked Rich.

"Where y'all had her at?"

"Some spot up in the Bronx."

"Where the fuck is some spot?" Rich asked, raising his tone.

"I don't know."

"This the last time I'm moving my lips. Next time my trigger finger gonna move."

"It don't matter how many times you ask me the same shit, the answer don't change, ya heard?"

Rich fired a shot in Domingo's leg.

"Urgh. Motherfucker!" Domingo yelled as he grabbed his leg.

"Where ?" Rich asked.

Domingo remained silent, shaking his head and

gritting his teeth.

Rich fired another .50-caliber hollow point into his other leg.

"Fuck, shit! I been there one time. I don't know where that shit is at." Domingo leaned forward in pain, gasping as blood ran between his fingers that covered his wounds.

"He don't know, Rich."

Rich turned to Candy as her voice faded. "Don't be his voice box." Rich could see she was concerned about Domingo's wellbeing. Rich knew it would be hard for her to overcome the feelings she had for the youngster. His experience with her taught him how attached she could become to a person she felt. Staring at her, Rich said, "He fuckin' murdered Vanessa, Candy."

"That's what you think," she countered. "All we know is you heard some gunshots over Vanessa's phone."

"So I'm a liar now?"

"You're uncertain. Trying to put a damn puzzle together that's missing way too many pieces."

"I know he was there with the motherfuckers that kidnapped Vanessa and was about to rape her."

"Didn't you tell me he stopped them?"

"So they could just kill her. He said they plan was to kill Vanessa and me. He even volunteered to kill her instead of them raping her. I heard that so I know that for a fact."

Candy looked at Domingo, whose pants were bloody. He was curled up in pain.

"That's the same motherfucker who lied to you," said

Rich. "Told you he was gonna protect you, kill the Twins and Chanel. What he do? Get with the Twins and murder Vanessa."

Candy turned to Rich with tears in her eyes.

She bought this bullshit Domingo hit her with. Rich stepped a couple of feet in front of Domingo. "Last chance. Where the fuck is Vanessa?"

As Domingo shook his head, Rich put his Desert Eagle to it and squeezed off a slug. Blood splattered on the couch and wall as Domingo's lifeless body fell to the couch, and then the floor.

Rich turned to Candy. Her eyes were shut as she slowly dropped her head. "This fuckin' dude killed Vanessa," Rich said.

"You don't know shit!" she screamed, pointing her fingers in Rich's face. "You don't know shit about me or about what happened to Vanessa."

"Calm down." Rich attempted to move her hand and she smacked him. He grabbed her in a bear hug and held her tight.

"Get the fuck off me!" Candy screamed as she attempted to break free. She eventually submitted, embracing Rich.

"Everybody's dying. Vanessa . . . Domingo. I'm scared. Tired of losing people."

"Don't worry. I'm a make sure nothing happens to you." Rich had long since known Candy's and Vanessa's vulnerabilities. It was one of the main reasons he tried as hard as he could to stop them from seeking revenge. He knew that they were out of their league when it came to seasoned vets like the Twins and Domingo. There was more to street killings than simply pulling triggers. To survive and thrive in the world of gun slingers required a psychological capacity to subdue the internal demons that haunted those who were not desensitized to death.

Candy and Vanessa were women scorned by the streets, but they were still women defined through a life of sensitivity and emotion that made them affectionate lovers. They had only dabbled in the ring where fighters sparred with bullets. They had endured a lot, but not enough to harden their hearts to the point where they could kill anyone—even a person like Domingo, who Candy had feelings for. It was that criminal mentality that allowed Rich to aide in Chase's murder because of his violation of Candy. As Rich held Candy in his arms, he hoped that she never reached the level of disregard for life that he had.

Rich looked down at Domingo's body lying in a pool of blood. *What the fuck am I doing?* He knew that trying to console Candy was jeopardizing their freedom. His loud .50-caliber gunshots may have alerted neighbors to call police. There would be no justification for him and Candy inside of Domingo's home with him dead.

Candy stepped back, gazing at Domingo's lifeless body.

"Baby, you gotta go get your shit. Come on," said

Rich.

Rich and Candy went to Domingo's bedroom and began packing her clothes and any potential evidence belonging to her.

"Just thought of something," Candy said, before sprinting out of the room. She returned with Domingo's keys and iPhone. She slipped them in the pocket of her jeans.

Another phone. Rich thought of how they had learned of the plot resulting in Candy's kidnapping and torture by scrolling through Chase's phone before killing him. There were messages from Chanel and her cohorts.

"You ready?" Rich asked after Candy zipped her luggage.

She nodded, and then Rich grabbed her bags and followed her out of the bedroom. As they stepped into the living room, Candy stopped, then Rich. They took one last look at Domingo. He had long since outgrown the smooth kid that Rich had met years earlier. He had morphed into a snake like many of the teens Rich had saw coming of age in Harlem where Rich learned that trust was more than a word and something that could be earned only through high stakes.

Candy looked at Rich, then headed for the door.

Suddenly, the front door flung open after a loud thump.

"Oh shit," Rich said as he saw Jahiem raise a Mac-11. Rich dropped the luggage, jumped in front of Candy and pushed her back as he reached for his Desert Eagle.

"Got your ass." Jahiem squeezed the trigger.

Two bullets hit Rich's shoulder, slamming the left side of his body back as he aimed his gun with his right hand and squeezed over three thunderous claps. "Go!" Rich pushed Candy back as Jahiem took cover.

Candy ran into the bedroom as Rich backpedalled behind her.

Rich surfaced as a barrage of 9-millimeter bullets blew past him. While he turned and stepped into the bedroom, two more bullets hit his back, dropping him. He looked up at Candy in shock.

"My God." She pulled him deeper inside of the room and shut the door.

Rich's body was on fire. Candy helped him to his feet, but as he staggered he could feel his energy quickly depleting. "Jahiem must've followed Domingo here," Rich said. He handed Candy the gun he took from Domingo.

Candy was hysterical, tears smearing what little eyeliner she had left on her face.

Rich looked out the window. Finding no sign of Tahiem, he told Candy, "Open it and go. His brother not out there."

As she opened the window, several bullets tore through the bedroom door.

Rich and Candy fired back, silencing Jahiem. Rich fell down and was having trouble getting up.

"Trapped," a voiced resonated from behind the door.

"I know that shit gotta be a bad feeling," a second voice sounded.

"Damn." Rich sighed. "That must be both of the Twins."

Candy grabbed Rich's hand as Jahiem sent some more shots through the door. Rich shot back. "You gotta go."

"Hell no!" Candy said. Beads of sweat and tears covered her light skin. "No, Rich."

Rich noticed the puddle of blood forming beneath him. The burning sensation consuming his body was as scary as how hard it was for him to simply move his fingers. He looked at the woman he loved. "Only one of us gonna make it outta here alive and it ain't gonna be me."

About five more shots tore through the wooden door and Candy fired back.

"Go!" Rich yelled at Candy, cringing as his gunshot wounds dominated his will to live. He looked at Candy and managed to smile. Even with the fear on her face, she was the same beautiful woman who had brought him a level of joy and love that most men would never experience. Rich had lived his life well.

Candy looked at the holes in the door, then back at Rich. She leaned down and kissed him. "I love you," she said through a whisper and tears. She rubbed her hand on his face and shook her head slowly. She pulled his face to hers, cheek to cheek. "I'll always love you."

"I know," Rich mumbled before coughing up blood on his shirt.

Candy let him go and began climbing through the window.

Shots fired again, tearing through the door and breaking the window.

As the glass cascaded down on Candy, Rich fired through the door. When he looked up, Candy was out of the window. The door opened and Rich fired again. A single shot. His heart sunk as he realized his gun was empty. *It's over*. He saw a lifetime of memories in 3D. A montage of pain and pleasure. The people he had killed. The shootouts in which his bullets had ripped through flesh, but he never found out if they ended life. All the drugs he had sold that contributed to death, destruction of families and imprisonment. The women he had wronged. His ability to make it out of the game only to be pulled back. He thought of how he was so close to joining King in a life of normalcy. He thought of Vanessa and Candy—the two people who had introduced him to love. His only love. An unconditional love that most people didn't know was possible. *I lived my life*. Rich closed his eyes and waited for the Twins to finish what they had started.

CHAPTER TWENTY-NINE
CANDY

As Candy started Domingo's Expedition, she heard gunfire. She looked at the window she had just climbed out of and she could see the bedroom lit by the sparks of what she knew was the Twins' guns. She pulled off slowly with a lump in her throat as she tried to swallow a cruel truth. She had experienced the worse day of her life. Worse than the day she was tortured. *The only three people I cared about, all murdered in one day.*

Candy steered out of the neighborhood and pulled over on a desolate street to cry, to gather her faculties. It was the only thing she could do at the moment to release some of the pain. To cope with something that she felt no one should have to endure. Candy thought of what Vanessa was put through. Then she remembered Domingo as Rich slowly took his life away. No matter what Rich said, Candy could not envision Domingo murdering

Vanessa. Candy was caught in between the love she learned she had never lost for Rich and the relief Domingo had given her when she had no one to rely on. She saw images of Rich in her mind. Images of him shielding her from Jahiem's bullets. He had given his life instead of allowing her to risk hers to save him. She questioned would she have given her life for Rich? She knew that she loved him, but she could not answer her own inquiry. The hot bullets whizzing by her inside of Domingo's house gave her a different perspective on the value of life. An intimate experience with beef. Not just what it meant to take life, but what it meant to lose life.

But at the same time, Candy was contemplating whether her life was worth living. There was no one to live life with or live life for. Vanessa had aborted her unborn child as a testament to her loyalty and love for Candy. Rich had given his life for Candy. Finding people of that caliber was almost impossible. No one would ever replace them.

Candy started the truck and turned on the radio. "December" was playing. Olivia's soothing voice added to Candy's stress, so she turned from Power 105 to Hot 97. K-Slay was playing 50 Cent's "Outlaw." She pulled off, destined for the long drive Upstate to Rich's cabin.

When she began her ride through Brooklyn, she grew angry. The borough evoked thoughts of Vera and Chanel, two of the people who were integral in making Candy's life an insignificant existence. Two people alive while Vanessa and Rich are dead. As she rode down Atlantic Avenue in Bed-Stuy, Candy tried to keep herself calm and ward off her growing desire for vengeance. She recognized that it was her vindictive attitude that had contributed to her sad predicament.

As Candy pulled up in front of Rich's cabin, an eerie feeling overcame her, because she knew she would never again spend time there with Rich or Vanessa. She parked the Expedition and went inside the cabin. Candy dragged herself over to the couch in front of the fireplace and laid Domingo's gun on the couch. Staring at the semi-automatic, she was reminded that it was in the back of the cabin she now sat, where she killed Chase. The surge of power that went through her body as she emptied her clip into Chase was the spark that had ignited the hunger within her for the revenge that she now tried to suppress.

Candy walked over to the bar and grabbed a bottle of Crown Royal Black and a bottle of yellow Nuvo. She mixed them into two large glasses. "Black and Yellow for those who didn't make it." She toasted, both glasses chiming on contact before she sipped from one, then the next. She leaned back on the couch and gazed at the flameless fireplace. One sip led to another. And another. And another. Before Candy grasped what she was doing, she had run through the entire bottle of Nuvo and half of the Crown Royal. Her head was spinning. Images of Rich, Vanessa and Domingo made their rounds within her head. She stood, only to stumble back onto the couch.

Candy laughed in an attempt to mask the pain of loss as she began sobbing. It wasn't simply the death that haunted her, it was the isolation. Candy felt trapped in solitude like a terrorist confined in the annals of a Guantanamo Bay cell for 23 hours a day. There was no shoulder to lean on like the one Domingo provided for her after she parted with Vanessa and Rich. There were no firm arms to hold her close like Rich had done on countless occasions. There was no tender voice to say, "Everything's gonna be okay" like Vanessa had done time after time. There was only Candy and the bottle of alcohol she was swimming in.

* * *

The following morning Candy awoke with a massive hangover. She cooked breakfast—a vegan meal of soy sausages and tofu eggs in honor of Vanessa. Then she showered for almost an hour, trying her best to wash away the tears that emerged the more she contemplated moving on without the people that mattered to her.

Candy's head was wrapped in a towel and she was lotioning her flawless skin when she heard Drake's voice. She looked at Domingo's iPhone on the nearby dresser as the "I'm On One" ringtone played. She walked over and discovered a sext message from Chanel stating she needed to see Domingo immediately at Highland Park, because she was horny. There was a close-up of Chanel's pussy and her legs spread wide open.

324

"Fuck," Candy mumbled as she gawked at Domingo's phone. *He was fucking the broad he said he was gonna protect me from.* Candy could still see the straight face Domingo had when he told her he would handle Chanel and the others who had violated her. Candy had been fooled. There was no doubt in her mind now that Domingo had killed Vanessa.

Candy stared at Chanel's message. Acting as Domingo, she texted Chanel back. The message led Chanel to believe that Domingo would be picking her up at Highland Park at midnight.

The internal fight Candy was having about Domingo was over. Her emotional side had successfully been knocked out by her intelligent side. The possibility of incarceration occupied a space in her thoughts. But the probability of Candy successfully murdering Chanel was the only outcome she saw.

Candy put on some Prada jeans, sneakers, and a long button-up shirt. She went into the closet in the bedroom and removed a large trunk. She pulled it beside the bed and began unloading guns. Within seconds, she had a 40-caliber Glock, Tec-22 and a .380-caliber Beretta on the bed. She grabbed the Tec and loaded it with a 50-shot transparent banana clip with a brown tint. She cocked back and put it in her D&G backpack. Next, she loaded the Beretta and tucked it in her waistband before putting a second clip in her pocket. Lastly, Candy loaded the Glock and tossed it inside of the knapsack along with an extra clip.

Candy pushed the trunk back into the closet, then grabbed her knapsack and went outside. The morning sun bore down on her as she made it to Domingo's Expedition. Starting the car, she adjusted the mirrors.

Candy pulled off and turned on Biggie's "Somebody's Gotta Die." She nodded her head to the beat, trying to cultivate the mindset she would need to kill not only intended victims, but anyone who interfered, be it good Samaritans or police. Candy was aware that plans had a tendency of not working out to perfection.

Candy made her way into Queens. She drove past Domingo's house and saw yellow crime scene tape just about everywhere. A few tears trickled down her face as she stared at the window she had jumped out of, leaving Rich behind to die. She had abandoned him in the worse way. Although he had insisted she leave, Candy now felt more than guilty for his death.

She flipped on the news, peeking at the screen in the dashboard in an attempt to see if there was any coverage on Rich or Vanessa. Making her way out of Queens, she drove through Red Hook in search of her prey. With no sign of them, she drove Uptown to Harlem. As she steered through her old stomping ground she reflected on the shifts that her life had taken. Bonds she had built and broken. Friends and family she had loved and lost. She slowed down as she gazed at the barbershop fashioned from the storefront that was once Candy's Shop. Leah's conniving attempt to take over the shop is what had boiled over into the tragedy that had changed Candy's life.

Candy continued driving around New York City until night. She rented a room at a small hotel in Coney Island and watched the news.

"Oh shit." Candy began to fidget as she saw a news reporter in front of Domingo's home. She felt little emotion when the reporter announced Domingo's death. Luis Dominguez. She had already been through the emotional whirlwind of watching him die, only to later conclude that Rich was right when he said Domingo deserved to die. But when the reporter mentioned Rich's government name, Jamel Thomas, Candy's heart sunk into her chest and she began wheezing. The televised confirmation of Rich's inevitable demise was almost as shattering as if it were breaking news for her. She could no longer watch the television. Candy turned it off and closed her eyes. Blood would soon spill and she would cherish the sight of every crimson drop that befell the flesh of her victims.

Domingo's phone sounded and Candy opened her eyes. It was another text message from Chanel saying in two hours she would be at the Ark nightclub in East New York along with Mimi, and Meisha. "She's gotta know he's dead. I'm sure the Twins told Vera and she told Chanel," Candy mumbled to herself. "Plus, his death is in the news." Candy knew the Twins had seen Domingo's dead body in Rich's home when they killed him. But

Candy was the only person who knew Domingo's birth name. At least that's what he had told her. So a reporter announcing the death of Luis Dominguez would mean nothing to Chanel. And she remembered Domingo saying Vera had denied the shootout between Domingo and the Twins when Chanel asked about it. *Maybe the Twins told Vera to keep Rich and Domingo's death on the down low,* Candy thought.

Candy made it to the club with an hour to spare. She was parked on the corner of the block, watching partygoers headed inside the Ark. Candy waited impatiently, her fingers tapping against her thighs. Her mission was beyond mere desire. She needed to kill. It was the only way she would begin to feel whole again, the only way she could live with herself. Candy was not leaving until each of the women were dead.

Fifteen minutes prior to when Chanel and the others were set to arrive, Candy texted Chanel. Acting as Domingo, Candy said he would be parked outside of the club and that he needed to speak to her before they went inside.

About ten minutes later, Candy watched Chanel's Escalade park behind Domingo's Expedition. This is it, Candy told herself. She put on a skully hat and pulled it over her eyebrows, then down both sides of her face as far as she could. Next, she pulled out the Tec-22 from the knapsack and clutched it in her lap. Simultaneously, the women exited the Escalade and began walking toward the

328

passenger side of the Expedition. This is too easy. Candy grinned at how naive the women were, blinded by the dark tinted windows separating them from death.

Candy looked around the street, finding only a few stragglers nearby, making their way to the club. She glanced down at the banana clip in her gun. Her feet tapped away at the floor of the truck. "Come on, come on, come on," she whispered anxiously as the women got closer.

Chanel was leading the pack. Candy eased up from her seat, prepared to shoot and exit as fast as possible. As soon as Chanel tapped on the window, her face was in clear sight. Candy raised the Tec-22 and squeezed the trigger on the fully-automatic machine pistol. Five bullets shattered the window and the smile on Chanel's face as they tore through her pretty dark skin and Gucci shades. She dropped to the ground as Candy opened the passenger side door and stepped over her.

"Oh my God!" Meisha froze, her fingers gripped her handbag and phone. Her eyes grew wide as her lips quivered.

Candy pumped ten shots into Meisha's face, neck and chest before the Tec-22 jammed. She tossed the gun inside the Expedition and pulled out the Beretta from her waist. Mimi was running as Candy fired at her. Mimi darted into the street and was hit by a speeding minivan.

"Oh shit!" the driver yelled as he skidded to a halt.

Candy ran over to Mimi, who was curled up in the

middle of the street in front of the van. Blood was leaking from the side of her mouth and head. Her slanted eyes were closed. Candy didn't care that Mimi was unconscious. She took aim and fired six shots into the neck and face of Vanessa's ex-best friend.

The minivan sped off in reverse, leaving a cloud of smoke from its burning tires.

Candy traced her steps back, firing two more shots into both Meisha and Chanel. She jumped in the truck and backed off the block as people flooded the scene. While Candy drove away, she felt as if a surmounting pressure had been pulled from her shoulders. The need for getback was gone. But the truth was that Rich and Vanessa were also gone. No matter how elated Candy felt because she knew her victims warranted what she had given them, no penalty on any perpetrators would bring back the people Candy loved. There was still the feeling of guilt for Rich's death. And there were still the Twins and Vera alive. Judging from the pain that still ached Candy's heart, she was sure that more murders would not stop the feeling. They would only compound the feeling with the twisted thrill that came with revenge killings. But Candy was mindful that the Twins wanted her dead, and allowing their desires to come to fruition was not an option.

* * *

A month had passed since Candy committed the triple homicide. During that time, she had been cooped up in

Rich's cabin, trying to come to terms with her life. She feared being alone, but needed time alone to become in tune with herself. She knew that she would never be able to be any good to anyone unless she became mentally fit. The absence of Rich and Vanessa had diminished her ability to love and trust others. The loss of someone to a relationship gone bad would do nearly as much damage to Candy as the death of a loved one.

But through all her fears, Candy needed someone to trust, someone to be a part of her life. There would never be another Rich or Vanessa. But Candy was ready for someone new in her life.

Candy had just spoken to the manager of her hair care business. He was the one person who had brought some semblance of socialization to her life, yet they had only been speaking by phone. Candy had been through enough of merging friendships with business to know the results could be deadly, so she maintained her distance.

As Candy sat on the porch of the cabin, she surfed the internet, researching for a new distributor for her products. Her manager had just informed her that one of their top distributors was downsizing and their diminishing staff would slow down Candy's business. Her phone rang, but she didn't recognize the number. She answered anyway.

"Candy?"

"Who is this?"

"Peg."

"Peg?"

"Yeah, Vanessa's friend."

"I remember you."

"I don't think you are aware, but Vanessa has been in a coma for a little over a month."

"Oh shit." Candy jumped to her feet. Candy smiled because she was happy to know that Vanessa was alive, even if she was in an unconscious state.

Peg said she and Heather had been by Vanessa's side since she had crawled from a building in the Bronx where she was shot in the head. Peg's phone number was listed in Vanessa's phone as a person to contact in case of an emergency. Medics at North Central Hospital had called Peg and Vanessa. They remained at the Bronx hospital since the shooting.

"I gotta see her," Candy said.

"I wish I could've told you sooner. I just found your phone number as I was going through some of Vanessa's things in my apartment."

"I'm on my way," Candy said. She hopped in the old Toyota Corolla Rich had kept at the cabin. She hit the gas and zipped down to New York City. She flew through traffic in the Bronx, until she was in the parking lot of North Central Hospital. Peg and Heather were waiting downstairs for her. They hugged Candy like long lost sisters. None of the women showed a sign of discontent from their last meeting in Atlanta that resulted in Peg and Heather virtually pulling Vanessa across the country.

Now there seemed to be an unspoken, collective agreement that Vanessa was more important than any of them and their old friction.

"She's a fighter," Peg said with a smile.

Heather added, "The doctors say she's strong like that Gabrielle Giffords, that congresswoman who survived being shot in the head by that madman in Arizona."

Candy smiled, thinking of the pint-sized woman who walked into her shop a few years earlier. Vanessa had appeared so fragile and innocent. Precious. Not the type of person with the capacity to cause death or fight it off.

The women found their way to Vanessa's room. Candy trailed Peg and Heather as they entered the pristine white area filled with beautiful bouquets. When Peg and Heather parted, Candy stepped forward. Her eyes were transfixed on Vanessa, whose head was wrapped in a bandage as she rested underneath a white sheet. There was a clear mask-like device covering her nose and mouth. It was attached to a nearby respirator. Vanessa was a poor imitation of the beautiful woman Candy had grown to know and love. Her naturally smooth, light skin was pale. Her lips cracked. Her bushy 'fro was reduced to small patches of hair surrounding her stitches that sealed the signs of brain surgery.

Candy gently grabbed one of Vanessa's hands. She leaned over and planted a kiss on her forehead. Candy was elated at being in Vanessa's presence, but Vanessa's condition scared her. It angered her. Candy felt weak, as if her legs were going to give out and she would curl up into a helpless ball of flesh. She could feel tears stream down her cheek.

As Candy sniffled, trying to ward off tears, she turned to Peg and Heather. They gave her a group hug. Candy felt what she yearned, what she missed. The strength of someone else's body transferred to hers. She felt comforted, cared for, supported. Candy didn't have Vanessa or Rich to hold, but she had two people who knew both of them.

After they parted, Candy watched Vanessa again before stepping out of the room. She leaned her back against the wall outside of the door. Candy wondered if Vanessa would make it out of the coma.

Peg and Heather walked over to Candy. "This has been my life for the last month," Peg said, tears dripped beneath her glasses.

"We never got a chance to fully reconcile," Heather said. She began telling Candy about the conflict that had arisen because she had sex with Rich. "We talked about it and made up, but I still think Vanessa never really forgave me."

Candy listened as Heather and Peg rekindled memories of Vanessa—good and bad. Candy laughed and engaged the women with personal tales of her own about Vanessa and Rich.

"Wow," Peg said, glancing at her Casio watch. "We've been talking for hours."

"Yeah, I'm starving," Heather added. "You guys wanna grab a bite to eat?"

"Sure," said Peg.

"I'm with it," Candy said, looking at the two white women she was growing to like. They were nothing like the women she had grown up around in Harlem. But neither was Vanessa. Candy understood how the three of them had jelled so well.

The women went and observed Vanessa for the last time for the day, then left the hospital. A short drive left them in front of Candle 79. They found seats at a square table perched against the floor-to-ceiling windows inside the exquisite, duplex restaurant located on Manhattan's 79th Street. It was a favorite of Heather's, because of its organic vegan cuisine.

After ordering, they began eating. Candy listened to Peg and Heather discuss issues ranging from feminism to environmentalism. Candy joined in, interjecting views that often conflicted with the women's. But there was no debate. Candy found that Peg and Heather were as empathetic and understanding as Vanessa. But Peg was clearly the more vocal of the two, and Heather the easygoing one. It felt good to Candy to be in the presence of women again. Her past month of solitude in Rich's cabin had taken a lively woman with a strong sex drive and subjected her to isolation and sex deprivation.

"Excuse me," Candy stood, gaining her balance after too many drinks. "I have to use the restroom."

"It's that way." Heather pointed at the ladies' room.

"Thanks." Candy walked away. Once inside of the restroom, she entered the last stall. She closed the door behind her, but it flung back open. "What the—"

Heather stepped inside with Candy and closed the door.

Candy's eyes locked on Heather's. She had been attracted to Heather and she could tell that Heather was attracted to her by the way she had stared at her for extended periods. Candy's thought produced guilt, because she couldn't help but think of Vanessa and she was still grieving over Rich. But as Candy looked into Heather's eyes, she succumbed to her desires. Desire to be touched. Embraced. Sexed. They locked lips without as much as a word.

Candy's hands were all over Heather. She had never been intimate with a woman as tall and thick as Heather. Candy let out a slight moan as she titled her head back and Heather's lips and tongue probed her neck.

Heather's hand rubbed Candy's inner thigh, making its way up her miniskirt. And beneath her thong into her wet pussy.

Candy's back sunk in as she felt Heather's fingers invade her insides while her thumb stimulated her clit. Candy grabbed Heather's head and pushed it downward until Heather's tongue was pressed against her clit.

Heather's hands cupped both of Candy's butt cheeks. She pursed her lips around Candy's clit and sucked it softly.

"Whoa." Candy pressed her open hand against the wall of the stall and her lips began to quiver. She felt like she was floating as her legs locked around Heather. Candy's hands were trembling. Her heart rate accelerated. Her toes curled and she gnawed on her lip as she came in Heather's mouth. Candy's heart rate slowed as she unlocked her legs from around Heather and her feet hit the floor.

Heather kissed Candy. Then smiled before leaving the stall.

Candy's body was still hot. She wanted to taste Heather, but she patiently waited. There was plenty of time left before the night would be over. Candy used some tissue to clean up and she fixed her clothes before leaving the bathroom. Heather and Peg were eyeballing her as she made it back to the table.

"You've been a naughty girl." Peg smiled at Candy.

Candy countered, "What does that make Heather?"

"Extremely naughty," said Peg.

Candy sat and engaged in the most sexually explicit conversation she had been in since she was on good terms with Rich and Vanessa. Candy was amazed at how nonchalant Peg and Heather were about sex. Candy could see how Vanessa fit perfectly among them.

Candy ordered some more wine as she became increasingly comfortable with the women. Neither Peg nor Heather were drinkers, so Candy ended up downing almost the entire bottle. The alcohol made her all giggles.

She transformed into a comedian. She had become touchy feely, flirting with both Peg and Heather.

After they finished eating and paid the bill, they each stood. Candy paused to catch her balance.

"Careful now," Heather said, laughing. "Somebody's sipped a little too much white wine."

"White wine?" Candy pointed at Heather and laughed as if Heather had just told the funniest joke in the history of comedy. Candy grabbed her stomach as she laughed.

The women stepped outside into the night air and Candy snatched Heather's keys to her preowned Range Rover she had driven the women to the restaurant in. "I wanna drive," Candy said.

"Not like that liquor lady," Heather said, grabbing her keys back. "I'm driving you home."

"Who said I was going home?" Candy responded, laughing. "I might wanna hang out at your place or Peg's."

"Okay," Peg said.

"I'll do the driving," Heather said. The women piled into the truck. Candy stretched out in the second row, while Peg sat beside Heather who pulled off. Outstretched and giggling, Candy continued telling jokes as the women cruised through Manhattan.

"It's time to quiet you up," Peg said as they began riding over the Brooklyn Bridge. She climbed over to the back seat and on top of Candy.

Candy cuffed Peg's small butt. "I like what I feel."

She giggled.

Peg gazed into her glassy eyes, slowly leaned down and locked her lips on Candy's neck.

Candy closed her eyes and moaned. The feeling of Peg's tongue on her neck heated her up. Then, as her eyes opened, their lips met. Their tongues danced. Candy titled her head back, while Peg went back to her neck, placing light kisses on it. Her lips were sobering Candy. "Your lips are so soft," Candy whispered.

"And you taste just like Candy." Peg smiled as she said it. She lifted her head and kissed Candy again. She reached down and lifted Candy's miniskirt, then pulled her underwear to her ankles and over her heels. Peg lifted her own skirt and removed her panties.

"Hurry up," Candy purred.

Peg turned Candy onto her side. She slid her leg between Candy's legs until their pussies made contact. As she positioned herself, the truck hit a bump, pressing Peg's pussy against Candy's clit.

Peg reached forward and grabbed a handful of Candy's delicate ass. She eased her hand between Candy's crack, and then slipped a finger inside of her asshole.

"Oh, damn. Umph." Candy's body jolted as Peg's touch sent a chill through her being. Candy grinded into Peg's humps and fingering.

Peg leaned back and swerved her hip faster. "Yes, yes."

"Ahh," Candy panted.

"You guys are making me hot in here," Heather said as the Range Rover stopped at a light.

"Ahh. I'm almost there," Candy whimpered.

"Yes. Me too. Yes."

"Ahh, shiiiit!" Candy climaxed seconds before Peg did. They both grinned while the overwhelming sensations of their sweaty bodies subsided.

* * *

They following morning, the women awoke and showered. Candy was still stunned. She had never been in an all-female threesome.

After showering, the women got dressed and rode to the hospital.

"Breaking news and good news," Vanessa's doctor said to Peg as she led the women into the hospital. "She regained consciousness an hour ago."

Candy was so happy that she cried. She listened as the doctor said there would have to be several tests done on Vanessa and she may be ready for visitors in a couple of hours.

"Thank you," Peg said to the doctor. She turned to Candy and Heather with a wide smile. "I knew it. I mean, she's a fighter. Told you so."

"I'm like ecstatic," Heather added.

"I need some air." Candy stepped back outside and inhaled the fresh summer air. She looked up to the sky, then around her. The trees, the people, the sun, everything was beautiful. Having Vanessa back was like having a new part of her. Candy was rejuvenated.

Heather walked outside, followed by Peg.

"She's back," Candy said. She hugged Heather, then Peg. "I can't wait to see her."

"We'll be one big happy foursome," Peg said. She placed her hand on Candy's shoulder. "Once we get you to stop consuming carcasses, everything will be copasetic." She laughed.

Candy smiled, because the comment reminded her of something Vanessa had once said. But Peg's first statement resonated with Candy. They could actually be part of a foursome. But Candy hardly knew Peg and Heather. Sex with them was good and their conversations interesting, but living under the same roof was a huge step. Having Vanessa back in her life and both Vanessa and her staying away from the streets is what Candy was focused on. Candy looked up. *I know Rich is proud, looking down on us knowing that we're done with the streets. Vanessa can get back to writing. You gave your life for me while you were trying to go legit and you kept trying to steer me and Vanessa down the right path, Rich. Well, it wasn't in vain.* Candy smiled.

***

When the two hours were up, they went upstairs in the hospital. They waited outside of Vanessa's room for a minute, then the doctor came. "She's ready for visiting, but—"

Candy bolted off into the room as the doctor spoke to Peg and Heather.

Candy closed the door and rushed over to Vanessa. Candy had almost forgotten what it felt like to see Vanessa's eyes open. She smiled at Vanessa and kissed her forehead. "How you doin', baby?"

Vanessa burst into tears.

"What?" Candy blurted, holding onto Vanessa's hands.

"Clant wllallk," Vanessa slurred and then pointed at her legs.

"You can't walk?" Candy repeated, causing Vanessa to cry more. "I'm sorry."

Vanessa's head began shaking slightly. "Iiii clant evlllen ttlalk fffuckin' right."

Tears flooded Candy's eyes. She had never seen another person in such a debilitating state. Vanessa was a helpless fragment of the vibrant woman Candy had grown to love. All of the plans made for Vanessa were suspect. This wasn't the happy ending Candy had in mind. She knew there must have been brain damage from the bullet that pierced Vanessa's skull.

Peg and Heather came into the room and Candy turned to them, sobbing as they stared at Vanessa shaking.

Peg pulled Candy close. "The doctor said there is a chance that she could overcome being paralyzed and that speech therapy can help. He says she could be normal in time.

Candy dropped her head, then turned back to Vanessa. She leaned over and hugged Vanessa. "I'm so sorry."

Vanessa's shaky head rubbed against Candy's face as she whispered into Candy's ear. "Don't bbbe sillory. Gllet ttthe pleoppple thlat dlid thllis too mmme."

Candy's head slowly rose from Vanessa. She thought of Vanessa's request for the murder of those responsible for her affliction. She stared through her own watery eyes into Vanessa's bloodshot eyes as her head shook.

Vanessa's eyelids shut and she turned her head. Candy knew it was out of the shame of being seen in such condition. Candy thought about it and realized the same people who had taken Rich's life had done this to Vanessa. The same people who had tried to murder Candy—Jahiem and Tahiem and Vera were the people Vanessa wanted dead. The people who deserved to be dead. How could Candy not fulfill Vanessa's wish?

Candy kissed Vanessa on the cheek, then turned to walk away. She stepped past Peg and Heather. She wanted to stop. The two innocent women reminded her of all the good life had to offer. All the things that normalcy provided which Rich gave his life for her to enjoy.

"Candy, where are you going?" Peg's voice called out.

Candy was too angry, too hurt and too scared to turn around.

"Candy!" Heather yelled.

Candy stepped out of the door with murder on her

343

mind. She finally turned and faced Peg and Heather. "I gotta take care of something," she said, then walked off.

THE END

About Intelligent Allah

Intelligent Allah's full name is Intelligent Tarref Allah, but he is affectionately known by family and friends as Intell. Born and raised on the turbulent streets of Brownsville and East New York, Brooklyn, he was a poet and aspiring rapper prior to becoming incarcerated in 1994.

Intelligent is a graduate of the Writer's Digest School's Novel Writing Workshop. He has also completed writing courses sponsored by Rising Hope, Inc., Shawangunk Valley School as well as writing and grammar courses at Bard College, where he is enrolled and pursuing his Associate in Liberal Arts. He is author of the *Don Diva* magazine #1 Bestselling n o v e l *Lickin' License* (Wahida Clark Presents Publishing). His essays and articles have been published in books like *Classroom Calypso* (Peter Lang Publishing) and on theurbanbooksource.com.

He has written editorials and personal essays for publications like *The Five Percenter* newspaper and *American Vegan* magazine. He has been contracted as an editor and copywriter for companies such as Cinobe Publishing and Green and Company. He is a contributing editor to numerous novels, including Wahida Clark's

New York Times bestseller *Justify My Thug* (Cash Money Content). Additionally, he has served on the editorial boards of prison newsletters *The Lifers' Call* and *Ujima.* An excerpt of one of his articles was published in *The New York Amsterdam News.* Intelligent is certified by the Department of Labor as a counseling aide. He has completed numerous courses offered by Binghamton University, Bard College, The Osborne Association, Exodus, AIDS-Related Community Services and the New York Department of Correctional Services. Intelligent is a member of the Harvest Moon Poetry Collective, Rehabilitation through the Arts, The Nation of Gods and Earths, People for the Ethical Treatment of Animals, the American Vegan Society, Vegetarian Resource Group and other progressive groups.

WAHIDA CLARK
PRESENTS
BEST SELLING TITLES

Trust No Man
Trust No Man II
Thirsty
Cheetah
Karma With A Vengeance
The Ultimate Sacrifice
The Game of Deception
Karma 2: For The Love of Money
Thirsty *2*
Lickin' License
Feenin'
Bonded by Blood
Uncle Yah Yah: 21st Century Man of Wisdom
The Ultimate Sacrifice II
Under Pressure (YA)
The Boy Is Mines! (YA)
A Life For A Life
The Pussy Trap
99 Problems (YA)
Country Boys

UNCLE YAH YAH

21ST. Century Man of Wisdom

VOL 2

COMING SOON!

AL DICKENS

CASH MONEY CONTENT
PRESENTS

Justify my THUG

New York Times Bestselling Author of *Payback With Ya Life*

WAHIDA CLARK

WWW.WCLARKPUBLISHING.COM

WAHIDA CLARK PRESENTS

NUDE
Awakening
A NOVEL

VICTOR L. MARTIN

CPSIA inform
Printed in the
LVOW04s13

439048I